For Charles, Henry and George.

1

From a Jack to a King

He'd gone to bed a nobody and woken up a somebody. Matt Millz's appearance on *The T Factor* had been the most exciting night of his life. It was etched into his brain in sharp, bright focus and it fizzed and crackled every time he delved back into it, which he had done many, many times since.

The smell of the crowd as he'd arrived, the jangling of his nerves when he walked on to the stage of the Hammersmith Apollo in front of all those people, the surreal experience of meeting the judges – people he'd only seen in photographs or on TV – and then the mind-blowing thrill of those laughs.

Stand-up comics had various words for it – he'd smashed it, he'd killed it, he'd stormed it, he'd ridden the gig home. All those people laughing had made him feel powerful, in control of his world for the first time in his young life.

Then had come the crashing disappointment as his real age – just twelve – had been revealed and he'd been disqualified. Followed by the rebound high as he realised it didn't diminish what he'd done in the minds of the audience in the theatre and the twelve million people watching at home on their TV sets and laptops. It enhanced it. Twelve million people! A third of the population! No, wait, that wasn't a third it was – um . . . hang on . . . twelves into sixty-five goes . . . four um . . . a quarter . . . no . . . wait . . . hang on . . . four twelves were . . .

Maths had never been his strong point. Which was a little unfortunate as at that particular moment Matt Millz happened to be sitting in a double maths lesson at Anglebrook School.

'Perhaps Master Mills could explain what a square root is?'

'Huh?' said Matt snapping out of his daydream and staring at Anglebrook's least popular teacher – Miss Stark (universally referred to as 'Mistake').

'My apologies, it's not Mills is it? It's Millzzzzzz,' she said sarcastically elongating the Z of his stage name. 'I hope I'm not keeping you from some television appearance?'

Matt rolled his eyes and inwardly groaned – he'd had to get used to a lot of that over the last couple of weeks. It seemed that the whole world had an opinion on his career.

'You know what I'd do in your position?' the postman had suggested. 'I'd do that jungle show where you have to eat bugs and stuff. I've heard you get paid half a million quid for that.'

'You should be playing big places like the O2,' said a kid in Asda.

'Ever considered panto?' said an elderly lady on the bus.

It was either career advice or suggestions for material:

'Here's one for you …' they'd say, which would then be followed by some offensive joke.

'Here's one for you …' Matt wanted to say. 'How about "go away!"' But he didn't. His manager, eleven-year-old Kitty Hope had said over and over again, 'You must never be rude to the general public – after all, they're the ones who put you where you are today.'

Unfortunately today he was in Mistake's double maths lesson.

'Well?' said Mistake, testily drumming her fingers theatrically on the desk, milking every moment of her power over him. 'I'm waiting …'

'Hmm, a square root?' said Matt furrowing his brow in mock thought. 'I guess that would be a parsnip that doesn't go out much!'

The class let out a big laugh. Matt smiled – he loved that sound.

'Sorry, no,' he said correcting himself. 'My mistake – I mean Miss Stark!'

Another, even bigger laugh filled the room, piggybacking the first. Matt turned and looked at his best mate Rob Brown six rows behind him and grinned. Rob flashed him a surreptitious thumbs up. Matt's smile didn't last long though.

'Go and stand outside!' bellowed the maths teacher, her face red and her eyes nearly popping out off her head, like she was choking on a gobstopper.

'Yes, miss,' said Matt gathering up his exercise book and pencil case, and stuffing them into his sports bag.

'See you in first break,' he whispered to Rob as he passed him on his way to the door.

'What's this all about?' Matt said to himself as he stood outside the classroom peering in through the window in the door, watching the lesson continue without him. 'They want you to learn, but if you're not up to speed they send you out of the room so you can't learn anything! Where's the sense in that? I'm standing here, I can see what she's saying but I can't hear it! It's like being taught in semaphore!'

Hey! That was an idea for a joke. He reached into his blazer pocket for his little black book and sat down on the floor and scribbled 'Stupid punishments'. He was off again to the world he loved – comedy – and he cast his mind back to the aftermath of his night of fame on *The T Factor*.

STUPID PUNISHMENTS

Learning times tables in semaphore. (This could be visually v. funny.)

Sweeping up leaves and then gluing them back on the trees.

Eating school dinners standing on your head.

Singing hymns in assembly backwards. (This would be tough to learn but really funny!!)

Going for a date with Miss Stark!!!

2

Return to Bathurst Street

He'd travelled back that night from the Hammersmith Apollo with his mum and stepdad Ian, and during the hour and a half it took to get home things had almost returned to normal. His mum had regaled him with tales of the exploits of her troupe of dachshunds – The Dachshund Five – at the dog show, Crufts.

'This year I had five dogs dancing to Justin Timblerlake's "Magic", finishing in a dachshund pyramid! Yes, one on top of the other – well, it brought the house down!'

Ian – an estate agent by trade – was beside himself,

having made contact with *T Factor* judge Simon Bewell. He had started to get really carried away with thoughts of reforming his teenage punk band. 'Now we've got a contact with Simon, Dead Toys could really go places,' he gushed.

Matt felt the crumpled business card in his pocket. It was true, he did have Simon Bewell's mobile phone number, as well as that of his hero Eddie Odillo, host of the top comedy show on TV – *Stand-up at the Apollo*, but he just couldn't imagine ever being able to call either of them out of the blue.

'Hi, Eddie, it's Matt here. Fancy going down Nando's?'

'Hi, Simon. Listen, I've got two tickets to the school play and wondered whether you are busy tomorrow night?'

It just wasn't going to happen. Maybe his moment in the sun had already been and gone? After all he hadn't actually won his heat – he'd been disqualified for being underage – and now he was heading back *from* London, not *coming to* it.

The answer to that question became all too apparent as Ian steered the family's Vauxhall Astra into their road. Number 77 Bathurst Street was bathed in a stark white light which shone from lamps perched high on poles erected in the front garden, and arrayed around them was a huge crowd of people consisting largely of teenage girls and a whole horde of photographers.

Parked in the street were two large vans with satellite dishes on their roofs, which appeared to be linked to a couple of TV crews. The sight took the whole family completely by surprise.

'Blimey!' said Ian. 'There must have been a burglary! You did put the alarm on before we left didn't you, Jenny?'

Before Matt's mum could answer, a cry came up from the crowd.

'There he is!' The throng turned as one and as it spotted Matt peering through the car window, it let out a huge cheer, then stampeded towards him.

'Stone me!' said Ian. 'There's no burglary, it's you

they're here for, Matt!'

'Yes, and they've got their hands all over your paintwork,' chipped in Matt's mum.

She was right, and it wasn't just hands – young faces were pushed up against the windows. A girl screamed his name: 'Matt, we love yooooou!' Grubby fingers tried to get the car doors open, blinding flashes zapped at Matt's face as fat camera lenses probed the windows, shutters whirred and clicked, trying to capture a little bit of him because, suddenly, a little bit of Matt Millz was worth something!

'What in the name of heck is going on?' said Matt, trying to keep a lid on his rapidly rising feeling of panic.

Ian was out first and trying to shoo them away, but without much luck. 'Come on, guys, it's late, well past his bedtime and he's had a long night.'

'That's his fault for being famous,' came the gruff response from the paparazzi, along with various insults too rude to print here.

'Famous?' thought Matt. 'Me? But I've only been on TV once!'

The car started rocking as the photographers and journalists started to get impatient. Then it happened – one of the photographers stepped back into one of Matt's mum's prize rose bushes and with a shriek she was out of the door and addressing the crowd.

'HOW DARE YOU TRESPASS ON OUR LAND!' she screamed in a low baritone. Suddenly everyone stopped what they were doing and turned to stare at this vision in a fur coat. 'Get away from

my front door or I'll set these on you!' she bellowed, producing five miniature dachshunds from deep inside her coat. On cue the little dogs bared their teeth and snarled at the motley bunch of assorted lunatics in front of them.

This prompted ninety per cent of the crowd to disperse back out into the night, but the core of the professional photographers – the paparazzi and the film crews – weren't budging.

'Just give us a couple of snaps of the kid then we'll sling our hook,' said one, lowering his lens like a big-game hunter stowing his rifle.

A woman in a business suit stepped forward clutching a microphone and took Matt's mum to one side.

'A word of advice,' she said. 'This bunch won't take no for an answer. If you don't give them what they want they'll be camped out on your doorstep all night. They'll grab what they can by any means available – even if that means shinning up a drainpipe and poking a camera through your bathroom window. If you're not careful you'll be looking at yourself in tomorrow's paper in your underwear – or worse.'

'Eugh! What a disgusting thought!' said Matt's mum, turning her nose up and curling her lip, but she could see the sense in what the woman was saying.'Very well!' she said forcefully. 'My son will be available for photographs for just five minutes. Matt! Get out here, darling.'

Matt tentatively emerged from the back seat of the car, looking nervously around for any crazed girls who mistakenly thought they were fans.

There was a series of blinding flashes as the hunters got their quarry.

'Over here, son!' shouted one.

'To me, Matt!'

'Straight down the lens, mate!'

'How 'bout a smile?'

After the initial shock, Matt started to kind of enjoy it. Every different face he pulled stimulated another round of clicks and flashes. He started almost playing the photographers like they were an audience.

But the fun was short-lived. He started to feel a bit like one of his mum's performing dachshunds.

'That's enough now. That's your five minutes,' snapped his mum, standing between Matt and the paps. 'He needs a bath!'

'Mum,' moaned an embarrassed Matt. The photographers all drifted off to their various vehicles with mumbled 'Cheers, luv!' and 'Comin' down the pub?'

'A quick quote for us?' It was the woman reporter in the suit again.

'Very well,' said Matt's mum. 'But then that's it! Finito!'

The two camera crews lined up their lights and microphones.

'How do you feel, Matt?' asked the woman reporter.

'Um ... a bit confused,' said Matt blinking into the lights. 'I mean, I'm nothing special, just a schoolboy!'

'Not any more!' she said. 'How does it feel being the youngest stand-up comic to raise the roof at the Apollo?'

'Er ... pretty fantastic!' said Matt with a grin, remembering why there was this sudden interest in him.

'You must have been gutted when Simon disqualified you though ...?'

'Um ... yes, well, for a bit, but my manager Kitty says it did the job so ...'

'What's the plan?'

'Not sure. I guess I'll have to wait to see what she recommends.'

'That was great,' said the reporter lowering her microphone. 'Good luck, Matt, it's a brilliant story. Just be careful over the next few days – there are some in this business who will try to trip you up.' The lights snapped off and the camera operators loaded their equipment into their vans and departed.

Suddenly Matt, his mum and Ian were standing alone in the dark and their street took back its usual tranquil atmosphere. Now the only light was from a street lamp, the only sound from a distant owl.

'Blimey! That was pretty mad,' said Ian closing the front door behind them.

'You can say that again,' said Matt.

'Yes, Ian, and I'm not sure we've heard the last of them,' replied his mum with a sigh.

3

Matt Millz Mania

It was half past five the next morning when the doorbell rang first. It was the paperboy clutching a copy of the *Daily Mail* and a marker pen.

'Is Matt Millz there?' he said to a rather groggy Ian standing in just his vest and pants.

'Er ... you know he is, Josh,' said Ian to the boy. 'You go to the same school, remember?'

'Hmm,' said the boy proffering the pen and paper. 'Any chance of an autograph?'

Ian unfolded the paper and glanced at the front page. There, looking back at him, was his stepson under the headline 'MATT MILLZ MANIA'.

'It's a Sunday, Josh! I only get one lie-in a week! Did you have to?' he said, scratching his head.

'Please?' said Josh pulling his most appealing, puppy-like face.

'Leave it with me.'

Ten minutes later the doorbell rang again. This time it was a workman in a fluorescent jacket.

'Oh, hello,' he said. 'We're working on the gas main down the road. Any chance of an autograph for me daughter? She's such a fan of the boy!'

'Leave it with me,' said Ian.

Another ten minutes passed and the doorbell rang again. This time it was a bloke in an anorak with a face full of bum fluff who looked like he hadn't washed for a week.

'My name's Gary,' he gushed. 'Is Matt there? I'd like a selfie please and can you get him to sign these cards?'

'Leave them with me, Gary,' said Ian, a little testily this time.

Ten minutes later the doorbell rang again.

'GO AWAY!' shouted Ian through the letter box, then noticed what looked like a policeman's uniform.

'Oh,' he said apologetically, opening the door to a policeman and a policewoman. 'Sorry, officer, I didn't realise it was ... um ... that is I thought ... can I help you?'

'Well, that remains to be seen, Mr Mills,' said the policewoman, 'but I thought you should know that it looks very much like your car's been broken into!'

Ian looked past the policeman and could see the Astra parked outside the house. The driver's window had been smashed.

'So you think the only thing missing is young Matt's coat?' said the policewoman, having finished her report.

'There was such a commotion when we got back, I left it in the car by accident,' said Matt.

'Hang on,' said Ian looking at the front door. 'Where's the door knocker gone?'

'It's on the front of the door where it's always been

isn't it?' said Matt's mum, bringing in a tray of teas for the group. But Ian was right – where the door knocker usually resided there were just two small holes for the screws that held it on.

'That's why I used the bell,' said the policewoman.

'Don't tell me someone's nicked that as well!' said Ian.

'Souvenir hunters, Mr Mills. Your young boy here is something of a celebrity now and, well, young girls and some young men no doubt will stop at nothing to get some part of his life, something he's touched – if not an autograph or a self-portrait photograph ...'

'That's a selfie, Sarge,' chipped in the policeman.

'Eh?'

'Selfies, they call them selfies for short ...'

'Ahem, indeed, well, I'm afraid they've had your door knocker away and I doubt very much whether you will see it again.'

'Aren't you going to do a house-to-house search?' said Matt taking a slurp of hot tea.

'A what?'

'A house-to-house search?' repeated Matt, feigning a look of concern.

'Sadly we don't have the resources. Not for something as minor as a door knocker,' said the sergeant.

'The only reason we came round,' continued the policeman, 'was on the off chance that you were in . . . ouch!' The sarge gave her sidekick a sharp kick to the shins.

'I don't think we need to go into that. Ahem,' she interrupted. 'No the knocker is of no consequence . . .'

'No consequence?' said Matt, sensing some mischief to be had. 'What if someone sticks it on their own front door?'

'Your point being . . .?' said the sergeant, a puzzled look on her face.

'Well,' said Matt, 'someone knocking on another door with our knocker would mean that technically they were looking for us . . .'

'Um . . . not sure I follow you . . .'

'Well if, say, a parcel was delivered to a different

house, only the postman knocked on the door using our knocker, then technically that parcel would be for us would it not?'

'Er ... yes ... I suppose, in a kind of way ...'

'Therefore anyone taking in that parcel would technically be a thief and liable to prosecution ...'

'I suppose, yes ... I ...'

'And the postman would be an accessory to that theft.'

'Er ... yes ... I ...'

'Well, we've only got one postman in Staplefirst. If you have to lock him up no one's ever going to get any letters!'

'Well, technically, I suppose ...'

'No letters getting through means no one would get parking fines or speeding fines or notifications to appear in court ... It would be ...'

'Utter chaos!' said the sergeant looking like she'd been struck by a thunderbolt of lightning. 'Right, Paulie, we'd better get going!'

'Where to?' said her hapless sidekick.

'House-to-house search! We need to find that door knocker before Staplefirst descends into anarchy!'

She drained the last drops of her tea, stood up, plonked her cap on her head, thanked Matt's mum and the two of them beat a hasty retreat. A few moments later there was a dull knocking on the front frame. Matt opened the door. It was the sergeant.

'Sorry,' she said, 'I forgot to mention, I have a twelve year old niece . . . any chance of a selfie?'

After Matt had finished his breakfast his phone buzzed into life – it was a text from eleven-year-old Kitty Hope, his manager. 'Lot of interest!!!!' it said. 'We need to talk ASAP. You around?' followed by a smiley-face emoji.

'Sure. Where and when?' he texted back. He'd meant to sign off with a smiley face too, but his thumb had accidentally pressed the emoji of a chicken drumstick, which made him laugh so he sent it anyway.

Kitty texted back: 'The DMC 30 mins,' adding an emoji of a pineapple as a joke. Suddenly Matt had an idea. What if people added emojis to the end of their sentences when they spoke?

'Hi, how you doing – smiley face!'

'Not too good – sad face!'

'Wanna meet for lunch – knife and fork! Pizza! Fries! Smiley face?!'

'No thanks already eaten – bowl of noodles! Chocolate-chip cookie! Spoon!'

He reached into the top pocket of his pyjamas for his little black book and hastily scribbled the idea down. Yeah, that felt like a sure-fire routine, and maybe once he'd set it up he could pepper emojis

throughout his act, make it a running gag. 'Yes!' said Matt punching the air. It was the first joke he'd written since being on *The T Factor*!

He nipped upstairs to his bedroom and got dressed. Out of his bedroom window he could see Gary in his anorak, a few of the girls from the night before and four or five photographers milling around on the pavement outside, smoking, drinking from thermos flasks and chatting.

'They're going to slow me down,' thought Matt. Then he had an idea. He went downstairs to his mum in the kitchen. 'Got any paper bags?' he asked.

She had a root around in one of the drawers – there's always one drawer stuffed full of carrier bags. 'There might be a gag in that,' he thought and scribbled it quickly into his notebook.

'Any good?' said his mum holding up a large plain brown paper bag, the sort you might get from a fancy bread shop.

'Great!' said Matt. He cut two holes in the bag roughly where his eyes were and wrote 'THIS IS

NOT MATT MILLZ' in large letters with a marker pen. Then he put his second best coat on, placed the bag over his head and walked out of the front door as bold as brass. As he came up level with Gary and the fans they looked at him quizzically. One of them raised her camera to take a photo then lowered it, unsure how to react – it worked! The paps were a bit smarter and snapped a couple of pics as he walked briskly past, but the whole thing had been much quicker than he'd feared.

Once he got round the corner he took the bag off his head and chuckled to himself. 'Result! the perfect disguise,' he thought. Maybe he should try to take it on *Dragons' Den*? 'Yes, Deborah, I want ten pounds to buy the bags and a marker pen in exchange for ten per cent of the business!' In his mind's eye he imagined all five 'dragons' sitting in their chairs with paper bags on their heads. He reached once again into his pocket and jotted it down – the ideas were certainly coming thick and fast!

He folded the bag up and put it into his

pocket – The Matt Millz Patent Anti-fame Mask was going to come in handy.

4

Meet Team Millz

As it was a Sunday, the school was deserted so the DMC (or Disused Mobile Classroom) was the perfect place to meet up, and although the school gate was locked there was a very convenient hole in the fence towards the back of the playing field which afforded access to the school grounds.

As Matt pushed open the door to the dilapidated building a loud cheer went up.

'All hail the conquering hero!' cried a voice which he immediately recognised as belonging to his best mate Rob Brown. Matt had thought he'd only be meeting Kitty but as he stepped inside the room he saw the whole gang – next to Rob was Rob's girlfriend Magda Avery, next to her their friend and self-styled tech wizard Ahmed Chalabi, and sitting cross-legged on the floor in front of them was ten-year-old body-popping champ, Neil Trottman.

'What are you all doing here?' said Matt a little perplexed.

'Meet Team Millz!' said Kitty stepping forward with a huge grin. 'We're going to need posters and publicity material so I've put Rob in charge of graphics and illustration.'

'Don't think he needs much publicity at the moment, judging by this morning's papers,' chuckled Rob holding up a dog-eared copy of the *Daily Mirror* featuring a massive photo of Matt onstage at the Apollo.

'Wow!' said Matt taking the paper from Rob and flicking through it. There was a full double-page spread about 'Britain's Youngest Comedian' by someone called Sally Vincenzo. As well as photos from *The T Factor*, there were also photos of Matt outside his house last night, photos of his mum and Ian, of the dachshunds, and even one of Matt and Rob onstage at their first gig at the school talent show – 'Anglebrook's Got Talent'.

'I've never even met this Sally woman!' exclaimed Matt. 'How have they got all this information?' He turned the page and there was a quarter-page photograph of none other than their headmaster Meredith Pavey under the banner 'I always knew he was destined for greatness! By the headmaster who trained him to be a superstar'.

'Holy moly!' exclaimed Matt, his eyes all but popping out of his head.

'Yeah, crazy isn't it? Pavey didn't waste any time getting in on the act,' said Rob laughing.

'Trained me?' exclaimed Matt.

'It's like he's making out that Anglebrook's some kind of fame academy, like that one that Adele went to,' said Ahmed, 'rather than what it is – a second-rate dump in the middle of nowhere!'

As Matt started skimming through the article, it was snatched from his hands by Kitty.

'Ahem! You can look at that later,' she said sternly. 'Although my advice is to keep well away from reading any of that tripe. You'll be getting a lot of stuff printed about you in the next few days, Matt, and most of it will have nothing to do with the truth and will just wind you and your family up. Now, I was in the middle of introducing Team Millz, remember?'

'Yes, sir!' said Matt, bringing his hand up in mock salute and shooting Rob a sly wink. 'Sorry, Kitty. Please carry on!'

'Yes, so Ahmed – with his knowledge of computers and IT – is heading up Facebook, Twitter and all your social media.'

'Yay!' said Ahmed high-fiving Matt. 'I'm gonna be a tech giant! I'm the next Steve Jobs!'

Matt smiled.

'Magda here is in charge of hair and make-up of course.'

'Ooh!' jeered Rob. Magda gave her boyfriend a playful slap and waved at Matt.

'My mum says we can use her salon any time, so it's pretty cool,' she said.

'Thanks, Magda,' said Matt.

'You know Neil Trottman of course – he's going to be your support act once I get some gigs booked in, for the time being anyway.'

'Until I get too big and everyone starts coming to see me, not you,' joked Neil.

'I'm sure that won't be long!' said Matt.

'And ... there's one more who's not here yet,' continued Kitty looking at her watch.

At that, the door opened and in walked a middle-aged Afro-Carribean lady carrying a couple of huge bags. 'And this is of course—' said Kitty.

'—Neil's mum!' interjected Matt, recognising the lady straight away. 'Hi, Mrs T, how you doing?'

'Mustn't grumble!' she said. 'But not as good as you're doing! Me and Mr T saw you on the telly last night. Lawd you were so funny! You should have won by rights ...'

'That's what they're saying,' joked Matt. 'It was sooo much fun and I can't wait to do it again.'

'Mrs T is going to help you with styling.'

'That's right, and I've got some great new shirts and jackets from the market for you to have a look at,' said Mrs T.

'Listen, everyone, thanks for helping me out, I really appreciate it,' said Matt. He was genuinely overcome at how this ragbag bunch of people were all pulling together on his behalf. 'I honestly couldn't have done whatever it was I did without you lot, so . . .'

The group broke into a spontaneous round of applause.

'I'd like to thank the academy, my manager, and everyone who knows me . . .' continued Matt, grabbing an empty water bottle off the floor and holding it up like it was an Oscar – he just couldn't help playing to an audience. 'I'd like to use this time to highlight the plight of orphaned sausage rolls. Yes, every year hundreds of sausage rolls are plucked from their mummies and sold in Greggs . . .'

Rob and Ahmed laughed, Mrs T threw her head back in a cackle, Magda however looked concerned.

'Oh, that's terrible,' she whimpered.

'I agree it's not a great joke,' said Matt with a smile.

'Eh?' said Magda.

'It was a joke – you didn't really think those sausage rolls are orphaned did you?'

'No! No!' said Magda, looking round awkwardly.

'No,' continued Matt, his face suddenly serious, 'most of them get adopted by Scotch eggs!'

'You!' said Magda with a frown and gave Matt a shove that sent him backwards on to Mrs T's lap.

The room erupted in laughter and Matt nodded.

'OK, you won that one, Mrs T!'

Kitty clapped her hands to grab their attention.

MUMMY!

ORPHANED
SAUSAGE ROLLS

(ADOPTED BY
SCOTCH EGGS)

'What's the plan, Kit?' asked Matt.

'Well, like I said in my text, there's a heck of a lot of interest in you!'

Matt raised a quizzical eyebrow. 'What sort of interest? Come on, Kit, spill the beans!'

'I've had enquiries from various shows wanting you to go on and talk about your *T Factor* experience, which I think is fine – it's good to get your face out there, capitalise on all the attention, strike while the iron's hot and all that . . .'

'Bring it on,' said Matt. This was sounding really exciting.

'Yes, but they're not gigs as such, so we need to limit the amount you do . . .'

'What do you mean?'

'Well . . .' said Kitty pushing one side of her bob behind her ear and looking at him over the top of her glasses. 'We want people to see you doing what you do so well – your act, being funny. We don't want them to just think of you as some sort of freak, as the kid that got rejected by *The T Factor.*'

'But can't I be funny on these shows …?' said Matt.

'Yes, of course, you can *try* to be funny but they won't want you to do your act. We'll have no control over it – they'll have their agenda and it won't necessarily match ours. Look, it's fine,' she said brightly. 'I think you should spend a day or so doing them. We've just got to be careful not to over expose you at this stage, that's all. We need to hit them when the time is right!'

'Yeah! Hit them when the time is right!' echoed Ahmed, nodding.

Matt took a moment to let Kitty's plan sink in. On balance it seemed to make a lot of sense. 'Can't argue with that,' he said. 'So when do I start?'

'Tonight, on *Sunday at Six*,' said Kitty handing Matt an itinerary.

Ahmed whistled. 'Wow!' he said. '*Sunday at Six*. That's with Amelia Wong – she's pretty hot!'

Rob and Ahmed nodded to each other.

'Don't be so sexist,' snapped Magda giving Rob

another one of her shoves. 'She's in that job because she's a good interviewer.'

Kitty quickly took back control. 'So someone will be calling you shortly for a research chat.'

'Research chat? What's that?' said Matt.

'They'll ask you about your experience on *The T Factor*, plus some background stuff which they'll then feed back to Amelia and Mark to work into the interview.'

Matt raised his eyebrows and nodded.

'It's OK. I'll be listening in just in case they start probing too deeply,' she said.

'Not sure Matt will mind being probed very deeply by Amelia Wong!' sniggered Rob, nudging Ahmed in the ribs.

Kitty ignored them and carried on with her brief. 'Then tomorrow you're on *Breakfast With Tubbs*.'

'He's great! Love him!' said Mrs Trottman.

'He's creepy,' mumbled Neil.

'He gets over six million viewers,' said Kitty, 'so it's massive exposure.'

'But haven't I got school tomorrow?' asked Matt.

'I've talked to the head and he's given you the day off.'

'Nice one!' whooped Ahmed.

'Not you,' said Kitty. 'Just Matt and me. He's being really supportive actually – he sees it as a really good thing for the school.'

'Yeah, and his career,' said Ahmed sarcastically.

'Again, you'll have a research chat for that after the *Sunday at Six* one. Then . . .' She took a deep breath. Just explaining the schedule to Matt was tiring let alone doing it. 'Then,' she continued, 'if you want to do it, *Late Lunch With Phillip Scruffold and Haley Wallaby* have been in touch.'

'Oh my days! I love that show!' cried Mrs Trottman. 'Phillip Scruffold is so hunky!'

'Mum!' said Neil, miming putting two fingers down his throat as if the idea made him sick.

'What?!' protested Mrs T. 'Ahmed said the same about Amelia Wong. So what's the difference?'

'S'pose . . .' said Neil meekly.

Kitty tried her best to ignore the interruptions and pressed on with her schedule.

'They get nearly eight million viewers so it's worth doing for sure . . . but that's a lot to get through in one day, and you'll have school on Tuesday . . . so it's up to you,' she said.

'I'm up for it if you are!' said Matt jumping to his feet. 'I mean all I've got to do is talk about myself, right? How hard can it be?'

'Yeah you're already an expert in that,' said Ahmed rolling his eyes.

The distant strains of 'There's No Business Like Show Business' rose up from Kitty's satchel. They all recognised it as the ringtone from her phone. She took the call then put it on speakerphone as she passed the handset to Matt.

'It's Mo from *Sunday at Six*.'

'Hello?' said Matt tentatively.

'Hi, Matt! We're really looking forward to you coming on the show – we're all big fans!' and with those words Matt relaxed and spent the next twenty minutes telling the researcher all about himself, his family, his love of comedy, how he'd started and of course took Mo step by step through his experience on *The T Factor* with Simon Bewell and the team.

In the meantime, with half an ear on the conversation, Kitty quietly went through her plans with the rest of Team Millz. She explained to Rob what was needed for a couple of local gigs she had planned for Matt. She went through hair, make-up and costume with Magda and Mrs T. Then she turned to Ahmed who showed her his plans for Facebook, Twitter and Instagram.

'That's really great, Ahmed,' she said approvingly, having watched several short clips of Matt on *The T Factor* that he'd uploaded to Matt's new Facebook page. 'We do need to keep an eye on tone though.'

'Tone?' said Ahmed. 'How do you mean?'

'Well, remember Matt's only twelve, so we don't want anything rude or offensive, because it'll be picked up by the press and the whole thing will get blown out of all proportion.'

'What are you saying?' said Ahmed in mock shock.

Kitty smiled. She may have been younger than the boys, but she wasn't stupid. 'You know exactly what I mean, Ahmed Chalabi!'

'I hear you,' said Ahmed closing his laptop and stowing it in his backpack.

Matt was just finishing up on the phone with Mo.

'Yes, great talking to you too . . .' he said. 'I'll see you tonight!' He handed the phone back to Kitty. 'Phew! I never knew talking about yourself could be so tiring.'

'Now you know how your friends feel!' laughed Rob.

Kitty's phone buzzed again and she handed it to Matt. 'It's Sally from *Breakfast With Tubbs*.' she whispered.

'Listen, I can see you're busy. If that's everything, Kit, I'll catch up with you later yeah?' said Rob getting up to leave.

'Yeah, I've got plenty of stuff I need to do too,' said Ahmed following suit.

Kitty nodded. Meanwhile Matt was deep in conversation with the *Breakfast With Tubbs* researcher.

'Elevenses at Greggs?' whispered Rob, sidling up to him.

'I'll be there,' nodded Matt, waving at Rob, Ahmed and the others as they started towards the classroom door, then he turned back to the job in hand – the job of selling himself. 'That's right, Sally, I could see Simon and David laughing as soon as I did my first joke . . .' Kitty noticed that his confidence had almost doubled since the first call.

An hour later, he was just finishing up with someone whose name he couldn't even remember but who worked on *Late Lunch* with Phillip and Haley. That hesitant first exchange he'd had with Mo had now become a slick series of anecdotes with its own pace, gags and rhythm.

'Yeah, see you tomorrow . . .' said Matt, signing off and handing the phone back to Kitty for the last time. 'Phew!' he said, slumping back into one of the old school chairs exhausted.

'See?' said Kitty after she'd finalised the details with the production company and hung up. 'You may just be talking on the phone or in a studio, but you're expending a lot of nervous energy, and energy's energy after all.'

'I know just the antidote for low energy,' said Matt looking at his watch.

'What's that?'

'A jam doughnut! If you need me I'll be in Greggs!' he said heading towards the door.

'Hang on,' said Kitty. 'Remember you've got *Sunday at Six* later!'

'Text me, yeah?' said Matt then added, 'Smiley face, pineapple, knife and fork! Bowl of noodles! Doughnut!' Before Kitty could reply he was through the door and running across the playing field towards the hole in the fence.

5

A Mysterious Stranger

Greggs was a nightmare. From the moment he walked in he became the centre of attention. In other words, constant interruptions from people asking for autographs or selfies, usually both.

'Would you sign my hand, Matt?'

'Would you sign my leg, Matt?'

'Would you sign my bum?'

It was plain crazy. It felt like every single mobile phone in the place was pointed at Matt Millz.

'Sorry, Matt, I can see you're on your private time but can I get a selfie?'

'Can I get one too, darlin'?'

'My turn now please. Oh no, hang on . . . I can't get the thing to work . . .'

'Give it here,' said Rob testily, trying to rescue Matt for the umpteenth time. He snatched the phone from the middle-aged lady's hand and snapped a photo of her and Matt together.

'Technically that's not a selfie,' said Matt.

'What are you talking about?' said the middle-aged lady.

'Well, you didn't actually take it yourself did you? So it's not a selfie, so strictly speaking it's not valid,' explained Matt, enjoying winding the lady up.

'Oh!' she said looking a little flummoxed. 'Can I get another one then? Coz that don't count?'

'Hurry up, luv, there's a few of us waiting!' said a gruff bloke behind her in a fluorescent jacket and a hard hat.

'I'll take as long I need to, thank you very much!' said the lady turning angrily to confront the man.

'Just get a move on,' the man snapped. The woman gave him a shove and he fell back, tripped over a chair and tumbled to the floor. Another so-called fan went to help him up, but the man pushed him aside into the middle-aged woman, who pushed him back, and before they knew it there was a full-scale brawl going down. Matt looked at Rob and nodded.

'I think this is where we escape,' he said and the pair made a beeline for the door. Unfortunately, by now word had got out that Matt was in the shop and there was a huge bottleneck of people cramming in at the door.

The boys looked around for an escape route and saw Doris behind the counter, beckoning to them.

'This way!' she said urgently.

'Come on,' said Rob and they headed towards her. As they got close she lifted a section of the counter top up allowing them into the kitchen, then slammed it back down hard to stop anyone else from following.

'Follow me!' she said leading them through the kitchen, past the various ovens and fryers, and finally to a door that opened to the road behind the shop.

'Cor! You're a lifesaver, Doris! Thanks so much!' gushed Matt.

'No problem,' said Doris, reaching into the pocket of her overalls, 'but you do understand don't you?' she said, holding up her smartphone.

'Of course,' said Matt, putting his arm round her as she snapped a selfie.

'Thanks, darlin',' said a very happy Doris. 'Now scarper before that lot cotton on!'

The two friends didn't stop running until they were a safe distance from the high street and wandering through the sleepy suburban roads that made up the majority of the town.

'This is crazy, Matt!' said Rob leaning up against a lamp post and catching his breath.

'Yeah, you're right,' said Matt. 'I've only been famous for about twelve hours and already it's starting to wind me up! But it can't last . . .'

'Oi! Come back 'ere!' came a voice. They both looked behind them to see, in the distance, the man in the hard hat and fluorescent jacket from Greggs and a whole bunch of selfie-seekers running towards them.

'What do we do now?' cried Rob.

'Search me!' said Matt. He couldn't keep this up all day.

As he spoke there was a squeal of tyres and a huge black stretch limousine pulled up next to them.

The door swung open with a silent smoothness that spoke of luxury and a voice from the dark interior called out to them.

'Jump in!'

Matt looked at Rob.

'We're not supposed to accept lifts from strangers! What do you think?'

'Quick! Jump in!' came the voice again.

Rob looked down the road at the approaching mob and shrugged. 'What choice have we got?' he said and they both dived into the limo. The door closed behind them and the huge car quietly glided off down the road.

It took a while for Matt's eyes to grow accustomed to the dark interior of the luxury vehicle. There was a strong smell of leather and some sort of pine aftershave. There was a line of LEDs that followed the shape of the seats and trim, creating a soft glow. After a few moments he could make out the rough figure of a man sitting at the far end, with his back to the driver. He was holding a cut-glass tumbler of what looked like whisky and ice.

'Hi, Matt,' said the man reaching forward and shaking Matt by the hand, the ice clinking gently in his glass. 'My name is Richard Hart, although most people call me Dickie and I run the Excalibur Management Group.'

Matt studied the man's face. His skin was pale, like he hadn't seen daylight for years. There were a number of small scars on his cheeks and a dimple on his chin. He had a couple of deep furrows etched into his forehead which held his face in a sort of scowl. The whole picture was framed by a jet-black quiff and sideburns that had obviously been dyed. He looked to Matt a bit like a crow had crash-landed on a snowman. He wore a long black leather coat over a light grey three-piece suit and snakeskin cowboy boots.

'Thanks for the lift, Mr Hart,' said Rob. 'Cool car!'

'Yeah, got a few of these,' said Mr Hart, scratching his chin. 'I thought you might need some help. That's the business I'm in really, helping young talented people like yourself, Matt. Chewing gum?' he added, offering him an open packet of Wrigley's.

'Thanks,' said Matt taking one and popping it into

his mouth.

Matt was sure he'd heard of Excalibur Management, but couldn't quite remember how or where he'd seen the name.

'I look after a couple of people you might have heard of, like Russel Perkins . . .' Mr Hart continued.

Suddenly the penny dropped – that was it! Russel Perkins – a young comic in his mid twenties – who was already selling out arenas with his combination of boyish good looks and observational humour. It wasn't to Matt or Rob's taste – they considered it a little too mainstream, too broad, kind of derivative, lacking the edge of, say, their comedy hero Eddie Odillo, but there was no doubt he was a big star. Russel had a late-night TV show on Channel 4 called *Scoff at the Week*, billed in the papers as a 'sideways look at the week's news'. How would you look sideways at the news? Matt wondered. Surely it would just make it much more difficult to read? He'd seen the name Excalibur at the end of the show, credited as the production company.

'You make *Scoff at the Week*, right?' asked Matt.

Dickie Hart nodded. 'Yes we do. We take care of all aspects of Russel's career – promoting his tours, doing press and marketing. We make all his TV shows exclusively in all territories throughout the universe . . .'

'Hmm, throughout the universe!' said Rob. 'What are the ratings like for *Scoff at the Week* on Mars?' he joked. Mr Hart ignored him and pressed on with his sales pitch.

'We even arrange his haircuts . . . and it's a service

I think you could really benefit from, Matt ...'

'Oh, I quite like the quiff!' said Matt, putting a hand up to his hair as if checking it was still there.

'Not the hair so much, my agency. I've got to be frank with you, Matt – I thought you were fantastic on *The T Factor*. I think in the right hands you've got a bright future ahead of you in this business.'

'Well, that's very kind of you, Mr Hart ...'

'Please, call me Dickie,' said the agent, leaning forward with a smile that revealed a small piece of spinach stuck to one of his front teeth.

'Er ... OK ... er, Dickie ... it's a kind offer but I've already got a manager so ...' Mr Hart leant even further forward, right up to Matt's face and cut him off mid sentence.

'Yes, Kitty ... er ...' he said struggling to remember Kitty's name.

'Hope!' interjected Rob. 'Kitty Hope. She's amazing!'

'Yes, she's eleven years old as I understand it?' said Dickie.

Matt nodded. 'You're right, she's young but like Rob says, she really knows what she's talking about you see . . .'

'Hmm, has she got any other acts on her books?'

'Oh yes!' said Matt brightly. 'She looks after Neil Trottman . . .'

'Who is . . .?' asked Dickie raising an eyebrow.

'Oh . . . um . . . well, he's a body-popper, he's ten . . .'

'So she's got you and a ten-year-old body-popper?' said Dickie nodding his head.

'Yes, well she hasn't been going long . . .' said Matt defensively.

'It's entirely up to you of course, Matt. I'm sure this Kitty will become a very successful agent one day. I'm only thinking of your best interests. I know I can get you the best deals, the best offers, the best exposure and, with a bit of luck, propel your career into the stratosphere!' he said reaching into the side pocket of the limo door and handing Matt a glossy brochure. Matt took it and read aloud the legend embossed on the front: 'Excalibur Management

EXCALIBUR™
MANAGEMENT GROUP

"PULLING THE SWORD OF TALENT FROM THE ROCK OF INEPTITUDE!"

Group . . .' he said. 'Pulling the sword of talent from the rock of ineptitude!'

'Yeah that's our slogan,' said Mr Hart. 'I was quite pleased with it . . . we offer a one-size-fits-all service that is guaranteed to get results . . .'

Matt flicked through the brochure which showed full-colour photos of Russel Perkins and others on stage and in various TV shows, then closed it and handed it back to Dickie Hart.

'Well, it's very kind of you to think of me but I'm with Kitty Hope and she knows me pretty well, so she can fit stuff in that suits me best . . .'

'Sorry, did I say one size fits all?' said Mr Hart, backtracking. 'I meant bespoke. Yeah, we offer a bespoke service, tailor-made to fit the specific individual needs of our clients . . .'

'That's very impressive I'm sure,' continued Matt, determined to change the subject, 'but as I say, I'm very happy with the . . .'

'That's fine . . .' said the stranger in the leather coat. 'I just know how fragile fame can be if you don't play it right. I've seen so many start well with a big fanfare, then poof! It's all over in the blink of an eye. Remember Frank Took?'

Matt shook his head.

'Exactly! Five-minute wonder. What about Jenny Cake?'

'Hang on!' said Matt – he'd heard of Jenny. There'd been a lot of fuss about her a few years ago, then nothing. 'You managed Jenny didn't you?'

'Yes I did and she didn't take my advice. Now where is she? Up Nowhere Creek without a paddle.

Russel Perkins on the other hand is following my advice well – and just look at him! One of the top TV acts in the country! He's playing the O2 Arena for two whole weeks starting Tuesday night.'

'That's very impressive, I'm sure,' said Matt, 'but it doesn't change the fact that—'

'I can get you and your mates tickets if you'd like?' said Mr Hart, raising a sly eyebrow.

'That would be great!' interjected Rob. Although Matt and Rob weren't particular fans of Russel's work, free tickets to an arena show ...? It was a no-brainer!

'Er ... Yes! I guess, um ... Yeah we'd love to come,' agreed Matt.

'No problem. I'll put four tickets in your name at the box office and just to be sure you get there on time, I'll send a car for you.'

'Result!' said Rob.

'Wow! Thanks,' said Matt, feeling slightly uneasy about taking something for nothing. 'But, just to be clear, I'm very happy with my manager so . . .'

'No need to make a decision now,' said Dickie Hart firmly but gently. 'I understand your loyalty to this . . . girl . . . it's highly commendable – in fact we value loyalty extremely highly at Excalibur. All I'm saying is keep me in mind, that's all.'

The limo slowed to a halt and Mr Hart pointed out of the window.

'This is your place I believe,' he said. 'Nice talking to you, Matt.'

Matt squinted out of the window. Sure enough, the limo had pulled up outside his house.

'That's right! But how did you know where I live?' he spluttered, confused.

'Oh, I know everything,' said Dickie Hart

handing Matt his business card. 'Give me a bell if you need to talk.'

'Thanks, Mr Hart, much appreciated,' said Matt.

Dickie Hart nodded and pressed a button in the armrest of his seat. There was a clunk and the door swung open. Matt and Rob scrambled across the leather seats and out on to the pavement and the door swung shut behind them.

'Be seeing you,' said the mysterious Mr Hart, pressing another button. The window rose silently shut until Matt was left standing staring at his own reflection in the tinted glass. Then the limo purred quietly off down the road. Matt and Rob followed it with their eyes and then turned to one another.

'Now that's what I call persistent,' said Rob. 'But you know, maybe he's right, maybe you should think about new management? I mean, Kitty's great but . . . Russel Perkins is massive!'

'Yeah he is, Rob, but you're forgetting one thing . . .' said Matt.

'What's that?' said Rob.

'He's not very funny, is he?'

Rob laughed. 'You're right! Ha ha! Come on, I'm gasping for a cup of tea!'

'Oh, hang on a sec,' said Matt reaching into his pocket and retrieving his brown paper bag.

'What the . . .?' asked Rob watching wide-eyed as Matt carefully slipped it over his head.

'Don't ask,' replied Matt and the two lads headed past the paps, Gary and the other autograph hunters, up the garden path to the house.

6

Sunday at Six

'A very nice man from Guinevere Management came round earlier ...' said Matt's mum, plonking down two big mugs of tea and a slice of carrot cake each in front of Matt and Rob.

'Excalibur!' said Ian, poking his head round the door. 'He was most impressive wasn't he, Jenny?'

'He had a very expensive coat on, I noticed that, and a limo! He was asking me all about the Dachshund Five – said he might be interested in taking them to the next level ... Not sure they'd take kindly to a new face though. The last time I took them to that new grooming parlour on Stonebridge

High Street, Mr Topps La-La Fitzpatrick bit the girl on the till! They don't like change,' added Matt's mum.

'Yeah, but he's obviously doing very well judging by the brochure,' said Ian, producing a copy of the same booklet that Dickie had handed Matt. 'I mean, look at the quality of the paper it's printed on! Must have cost a fortune! Yes, he's obviously loaded and he seemed ...'

'A tad creepy?' suggested Matt.

Rob laughed. 'Ha! Yeah he was a bit!'

'Well, yes, maybe a bit creepy,' said Ian, 'but very keen to get involved – he was even interested in managing my old punk band ...'

'Your old punk band?' said Matt a little gobsmacked.

'I don't think that's worth resurrecting!' said Matt's mum rolling her eyes to the heavens as she opened a tin of dog food.

'But you said you hadn't seen any of the old band since you were eighteen,' said Matt.

'Yeah, well they got in touch!' said Ian excitedly.

'Got in touch? All of them? When?' asked Matt.

'This morning after you'd left! They'd seen my picture with you in the paper and tracked me down via Facebook. You're not gonna believe this, Matt, but Dead Toys might be getting back together! We've got a rehearsal round at the drummer's house tomorrow night!'

'Midlife crisis,' muttered Matt's mum under her breath, rattling a spoon in a ceramic dog bowl.

'Yeah, he's a quantity surveyor now,' said Ian showing Matt a picture of a portly middle-aged man in a hard hat.

Matt could hear the dog flap whirring as seven dachshunds came running into the kitchen from the garden for their tea.

'Here, Matt?' said Rob, interrupting this picture of domestic bliss. 'Have you seen what time it is?' He tapped his phone. Matt squinted over – it was half past two. 'They'll be picking you up for *Sunday at Six* soon!'

'Oh, I love that show,' said Matt's mum. 'I never miss a single episode do I, Ian?'

Ian shook his head. 'Oh I don't believe it!' he said holding his phone up to the group. It showed a page from the *Daily Mail* and at its centre was a photograph of him in his vest and underpants on the front step of their house talking to the postman. 'I'll never live this down!' he groaned.

'You're right, Rob,' said Matt with a chuckle, suddenly full of energy. 'I'd better go and get myself together. See you in a bit!'

7

Six O'Clock Show Time

A sleek silver Mercedes S-Class pulled up outside Matt's house and the horde of paps and selfie-seekers crowded round it. There was a groan of disappointment as the door opened and the diminutive figure of Kitty Hope got out and walked up the path to Matt's house. 'Where's your door knocker?' she said as Matt opened the door to a flurry of camera flashes.

'Stolen!' said Matt looking at her more closely. She'd done something with her hair and was wearing a really smart little outfit.

'Yes, it was nicked by the phantom door-knocker

stealer of Old Staplefirst. Local legend states that whosoever has their door knocker stolen will end up on *Sunday at Six*,' he said, looking past her at the silver Merc.

'That's the second nice car I'll have been in today!'

'The second? How come?'

'Nothing for you to worry about,' he said pulling her into the house and closing the door.

'We should have got the train, it would have been a lot cheaper.'

'No, Matt, can you imagine the fuss if you tried to take a train up to London? You'd be mobbed! Don't worry about the cost – *Sunday at Six* are paying. There's no fee for doing these sorts of shows but they do pay transport. You all set?' she said.

Matt took one last look in the hall mirror and ran his hand through his freshly combed quiff.

'Yup let's get to work!' he said, opening the front door.

There was a flurry of activity as the paps swung into action, but it had almost become like water off a duck's back for Matt now.

'Good afternoon, Matt!' said the chauffeur. 'Big fan! I've got the rest of your team on board already!' He opened the door to reveal Rob, Magda and Mrs T stuffed on to the back seat like sardines. 'Blimey!' said Matt 'This is going to be a bit of a squash. Perhaps I should sit in the front?'

'Sorry, bruv, already taken!' Ahmed's face appeared from around the front passenger seat.

'You?' said Matt.

'I'm your tech guy,' giggled Ahmed. 'Plus, am I going to miss a chance to meet the one and only Amelia Wong? No way José!'

Matt shook his head and climbed into the back next to Mrs Trottman, followed by Kitty. He spent most of the journey with his face squashed up against Mrs T's hair. At one point he wondered whether it was possible to survive for an hour and a half only breathing pure hairspray. 'Actually,' he thought, 'there's an idea for a gag.' He tried to reach for his little black book but he was jammed in so tightly he couldn't reach it.

'I need to see you after school on Tuesday to go through the schedule,' said Kitty. 'I'm looking at a few options for gigs. You'll need to work on some new material before you can go on stage again.'

'Really?' said Matt. 'What's wrong with the stuff I've got?'

'You did ninety per cent of your act on *The T Factor* audition so I'm afraid that stuff is pretty much dead and buried. That's the problem with doing your act on TV – once those jokes are out there you've got to write new ones. It's all about turnover I'm afraid! Like I say, we need to start small, do a few low-profile gigs to work up some new stuff and fill up the tank again.'

The idea that his act was over as soon as he'd got the hang of it hadn't even occurred to Matt, but he knew from seeing comics on TV doing stuff more than once that it was diminishing returns – gags just didn't fly if the audience already knew the punchline. The surprise was gone and one thing he had learnt was that a punchline was pretty much just a very big surprise – that's what made people laugh. Remove the surprise and you removed the laugh too.

Kitty continued. 'No, the secret to being a successful TV comic is either turning over a lot of material – like say Jimmy Carr, but he's unusual – or to come up with a TV format where you can be funny and use your stand-up skills without having to do your act. That's why so many comics do panel shows and chat shows.'

JIMMY CARR FACTS

Deadpan comic and TV host (8 Out of 10 Cats) – shows little emotion, hardly moves from behind the microphone.
Style – decidedly dark humour, mainly one-liners.
Gags – I had a survey done on my house. 8 Out of 10 people said they really rather liked it.

I worry about my nan. If she's alone and she falls, does she make a noise? I'm joking, she's dead.

When you eat spicy food, you can lose your taste. When I was in India last summer, I was listening to a lot of Michael Bolton.

'How do you know all this stuff?' asked Rob, a perplexed look on his face.

'My dad told me and his dad told him,' explained Kitty.

'The great Sir Bernie Hopestein,' said Matt, tapping the name into his smartphone then passing it to Rob.

'Oh, I've been meaning to tell you, my great-uncle Buddy's coming over from the States,' Kitty said excitedly.

'Wait a minute? Great-uncle ... You mean ...?'

'Yes, my grandad Bernie's younger brother. I say younger but he's in his nineties now, and still going strong. He used to work with Bernie but they went their separate ways back in the sixties. Bernie stayed over here and ran his show-business empire—'

'Including the Apollo . . .' said Matt.

'Including the Apollo,' agreed Kitty. 'And Buddy moved to the States. He runs one of the largest TV production channels in New York. He's a force of nature, he really is – he still turns up for work every day.'

'Who could be bothered, with all that money?' said Magda.

'You should meet him,' said Kitty.

'I'd love to!' said Matt.

'Who's Bernie Hopestein when he's at home?' asked Ahmed from the front seat.

'You're having me on?' said Mrs Trottman shifting in her seat and suddenly allowing Matt to take a couple of lungfuls of hairspray-free air. 'Everyone knows Bernie Hopestein!' she exclaimed. 'He used to be at all those royal variety shows back in the day!'

Kitty nodded. 'He owned the theatres—' she said.

'Including the Apollo!' chipped in Matt, basking in the reflected glory of being associated with the great man's granddaughter.

'You mean he was your grandpa?' said Mrs T in wonder. Kitty nodded again.

'Why didn't you tell us sooner? If that was me, I'd be telling everyone as soon as I met them. I'd even have a T-shirt printed with his face on!'

'It just muddies the waters, Mrs Trottman,' said Kitty. 'This way I can't be accused of trading on his name.'

'Oh! *That* Bernie Hopestein!' said Rob, reading through the old impresario's Wikipedia page. 'Looks like he pretty much ran show business in the fifties and sixties.'

'That's because he did!' said Matt.

'He was very, very successful,' said Kitty.

'Amazing!' said Mrs T.

'So anyway, I've got some ideas for gigs, Matt,

and I just need to go through them with you – when you haven't something else on your mind like TV appearances. So late Tuesday afternoon would be great.'

'Ah, there's a problem with that,' said Matt. 'See, I've got a gig.'

'A gig?' said Kitty suddenly stiffening in the seat next to him. 'I thought we'd agreed you'd only do gigs that we'd worked on together? I mean I don't mind in principle but I would prefer it if I was kept in the loop – this is a very crucial time for you ...'

'No, silly!' said Matt cutting her off before she got too carried away. 'I'm not *doing* a gig, I'm going to one! Me, Rob, Ahmed and Mags here have been offered free tickets to Russel Perkins' gig at the O2!'

'Wow! Those tickets are like fifty pounds each!' said Kitty.

'I know,' grinned Matt, 'and they're sending a cab to pick us up!'

'They?' said Kitty looking a little confused. 'Who are "they" exactly?'

'Er . . . some bloke from a management company,' offered Rob. 'Dickie somebody . . .'

'Hart,' Kitty said tersely. 'Dickie Hart, one of the most unscrupulous operators in the business.'

'Yeah?' said Matt with a grin. He loved it when she got wound up. 'Free tickets for the O2? What's not to like? It's not costing us a penny!'

'Hmm, there's no such thing as a free lunch,' said Kitty ruefully as the car slowed to a halt.

'He didn't mention lunch . . .' joked Matt.

'I've got Matt Millz in the back for *Sunday at Six*?' said the driver, pulling up at the barrier outside the TV studio.

The gatekeeper, in an official-looking peeked cap peered through the window. As he saw Matt he smiled and gave him the thumbs up. 'Big fan!' he said. Matt smiled back, the man raised the barrier and waved them through.

As the driver opened the back passenger door they literally fell out on to the pavement. One of Matt's legs was numb. He staggered slightly and gulped in the cool, early evening air. Team Millz arranged themselves on the pavement. Matt took a look at them and felt a lump in his throat. It was amazing how these people were giving up their time just for him.

They were met by a young man in a headset and carrying a clipboard.

'Hi, Matt, I'm Mo, we talked earlier on the phone? How was your trip down?'

'Great. Not only was it a very nice car but we also broke the Guinness World Record for the number of people you can fit in an S-Class Mercedes!' said Matt.

Mo looked blankly at him and continued, 'So you've got about an hour before the show starts. Let me take you to your dressing room. Are these people . . .?'

'Yes, we're with him!' said Kitty.

'I'm his tech giant,' said Ahmed playfully.

'Is that so?' said Mo. 'Maybe I could wangle you a visit to the gallery, if that is of interest?'

'Er . . . Rob's the one who's interested in art, bruv,' said Ahmed.

'Ah, not that sort of gallery,' explained Mo. 'The gallery in a TV studio is where all the tech people hang out.'

'In that case count me in,' said Ahmed looking really excited at the prospect.

Team Millz followed Mo through some double doors, up a couple of floors in a lift, down another corridor and up some stairs, then along another corridor.

'This place is enormous!' said Rob.

'Yeah, takes a while to get used to,' said Mo. Eventually they came to a corridor with a series of doors off it. One of the doors opened as they passed it and a small guy in little round black-rimmed glasses and a trilby hat peered out.

'OMG! It's will.i.am!' said Magda.

'Hi,' said Will. Then he clocked Matt and a big smile lit up his face. 'Hey! You're that kid off the show! Man you were funny!' He took Matt's hand and attempted a complicated handshake, which sadly Matt wasn't able to reciprocate. 'Best thing on that show! Shoulda won! And who's this lovely lady . . .?' he said indicating Mrs T, who started to shriek with nervous laughter.

'Hope you don't mind, Will, can we get a selfie?' said Magda, producing her phone from her pocket.

'Sure,' said Will. 'On one condition, that I get one with my man here!' He pointed to Matt. Matt couldn't believe it, this felt like proper showbiz!

'Here we are, star dressing room number three,'

said Mo moments later, dialling in a code and opening the door.

'Hear that?' said Ahmed. 'You're a star apparently, bruv.'

'Can I get anyone a cup of tea or coffee?' asked Mo.

Mrs T looked like she was going to have kittens at the prospect – she was even more excited at the idea of a cup of tea than meeting will.i.am.

'So I'll be back in about twenty minutes to take you down to make-up. In the meantime, just relax and help yourself to snacks and drinks.' Mo hurried out, leaving them to it.

Before the door had even clicked shut Rob and Ahmed were up and exploring the room.

'Woah! There's a minibar!' Rob said opening the door to a little fridge under a worktop that was loaded with bottles of water, juice and Cokes.

'And look! Chocolate!' said Ahmed moving over to a coffee table with a basket on it loaded with mini versions of chocolate bars. Rob immediately took a couple of handfuls and stuffed them into his pockets.

As he reached to take another his hand took a hefty slap.

'Ow!' he exclaimed.

It was Mrs T. 'Behave, you two!' she barked.

Before they knew it, Mo was back and leading them all down the corridor the way they had come. Mo introduced Ahmed to another runner who took him off to have a look round the studio gallery. He then dropped Mrs T and Rob in the green room before taking Matt, Magda and Kitty to a narrow room lined with mirrors – the make-up room.

'Hello, Matt! Take a seat,' said a blonde lady who was wearing a lot of make-up. 'She obviously practises on herself,' thought Matt.

'Is this your girlfriend?' she said looking at Kitty.

'Er no . . .' said Kitty, uncharacteristically flustered.

'Not yet anyway!' said the make-up lady.

'Kitty's my manager,' said Matt firmly, taking a seat in front of her and looking in the mirror facing him.

'Good, well, I'm Vanessa. Now, before I start, are you allergic to anything?'

'Penicillin!' said Matt.

Vanessa the make-up lady laughed. 'No, I mean make-up wise?'

'How would I know?' shrugged Matt. 'I'm a twelve-year-old boy! I've never worn any make-up!'

'Fair point,' she said. 'Well, I think you'd better get used to it judging by your performance on *The T Factor*!'

Matt was amazed at just how many people had caught his short set. It had only been five minutes long but it seemed to have had a huge impact.

'You've got good skin so I'll put as little as possible on you – we don't want you coming out in spots in a few days time, do we?' said Vanessa.

'What's that you're using to put it on with?' asked Magda, taking a step forward.

'Oh, it's a kind of diffuser, like an airbrush,' said Vanessa. 'You fill the little bowl at the end with foundation and turn it on, and it turns it into a fine spray. A lot of the girls use a brush but I prefer this as it ensures an even coat. We can't have him looking patchy can we?'

'Magda here's interested in doing what you do,' said Matt as Vanessa set to, spraying him with make-up.

'Yeah?' said Vanessa. 'Well, you're welcome to hang out back here with me and see what it involves.'

'Oh, that would be soooo cool!' swooned Magda.

Once Vanessa was happy with his make-up, Matt and Kitty were taken down a corridor and shown through a door into a fairly plain-looking room with a couple of sofas and a small bar area. Sat on the sofa watching a large monitor were Team Millz.

'Looking good, boyfriend!' joked Rob.

'Yeah, but steady, Matt – remember Amelia is the one for me,' laughed Ahmed, helping himself to a handful of cheese Wotsits from a bowl on a coffee table in front of him. The monitor was showing a live feed from the studio before the show started.

On another sofa was an older man with a pigeon in a cage, and an actor who Matt thought he vaguely recognised, plus various others.

Matt didn't have long to wait till Mo wandered back in to get him.

'Matt?' he said. 'Can I take you through to the studio now please?'

'Ten seconds, people!' announced the floor manager as Mo led Matt on to the studio floor.

'It looks—' started Matt.

'I know,' said Mo, 'it looks much bigger on TV.'

The floor manager started to count down backwards from ten on his fingers as Matt watched the announcer on the studio monitor.

'And now on BBC 1 we join Amelia Wong and Mark Butcher for *Sunday at Six*!' said the announcer.

'Roll titles,' said the floor manager.

'Wow! There they are!' said Matt in wonderment as he spotted the two hosts through the forest of cameras. Matt couldn't believe he was actually standing less than six metres from the hosts of one of his mum's favourite TV shows.

'They're—' started Matt.

'I know, much smaller in real life,' said Mo

somewhat wearily. 'So the running order, just so's you know: you're on last and before you we've got an item on a one-legged pigeon called Nelson, then we've got that bloke from the sci-fi thing – you know *Chair of Swords* or whatever it's called – talking about the new series, then we've got a rather sad item about homelessness, and then it's Matt Millz time! You'll stay on after your bit as we go to an item on international sausage day. Are you OK to try a sausage?'

'Yes! Of course, ha ha!' Matt laughed. The line-up was a real hotchpotch of serious, sad, funny and quirky items plus a bit of food-tasting – in other words, a classic *Sunday at Six*.

The title sequence finished and Mark and Amelia started their introduction, headlining what was coming up. Matt grinned like a Cheshire cat as he heard his name being mentioned. 'But first our reporter Rod Hall this week caught up with Nelson, a disabled pigeon . . .'

GLOSSARY OF TV TERMS

VT - Videotape. Usually a pre-recorded item sometimes referred to as an 'insert'. Although most of these items are in digital formats and no longer on tape.

FLOOR MANAGER - The person responsible for moving the show along. For coordinating all the various personnel - make-up, props, costume, etc. The secret of a good floor manager is someone who is firm, calm in a crisis but not so bossy that he or she upsets people.

PRODUCTION COMPANY - The company that is paid by the broadcaster to make the show.

PRODUCTION MANAGER - The person mainly responsible for the

show's budget and how the money given by the broadcaster to make the show is spent. The production manager is usually the person on the team who looks the most worried!

PRODUCER - The producer literally produces the show, coordinating all those people who work behind the scenes on a show and who are very rarely seen. The producer is like a manager, and much of his or her time is spent in the office, on the phone or in meetings coordinating the team. It's the producer's job to advise the writers and adapt the programme to the budget and to be the main point of contact with the people who run the production company.

VISION MIXER - Controls which shots appear on the main studio monitors. In a live broadcast these are the shots that the audience at home see too, but in a pre-recorded programme the final pictures can be changed in the edit.

EXECUTIVE PRODUCER - (often shortened to 'exec') - Usually runs the production company and is the person or people (there are often more than one) who liaise with the broadcaster.

THE DIRECTOR - Controls the camera operators and decides what shots to take to best tell the story - close-ups, mid shots, wide shots, etc. In TV dramas and sitcoms they'll also have an opinion on the actor's performance, like a theatre director.

GREEN ROOM – The chill out zone where performers, interviewees, their managers, friends and family and others wait while the show is being recorded or broadcast. They're not usually green and no one really knows why they are referred to as such.

THE GALLERY – The place where the director, producer, lighting designer and other production staff sit and control the production during the show. There's a bank of monitors showing all the different camera shots, which the vision mixer uses to choose his or her shots.

Matt heard a voice in the floor manager's ear that barked 'Roll VT!' and as the filmed item on Nelson the one-legged pigeon appeared on the monitors there was a flurry of activity. Vanessa from make-up rushed in and started powdering Amelia's face. The lady from wardrobe appeared with a clothes brush and started picking lint off Mark's jacket. The floor manager darted in with a couple of bottles of water for them both and talked them through the next item. At the same time they were responding to comments from the director in the gallery through their earpieces.

Matt was impressed at how calm everyone was. He watched as the floor manager showed the two presenters something on his clipboard then looked over and pointed at Matt.

'OMG! Matt Millz!' said Amelia Wong looking genuinely pleased to see him. She beckoned him over. Matt looked briefly around to check she wasn't talking to someone else, then stepped forward through the ring of cameras to say hi. Both Amelia and Mark were on their feet and quick to shake his hand.

'You were brilliant on *The T Factor*!' raved Amelia. 'Oh my god, you totally owned Simon!'

'You did really well, Matt,' said Mark. 'Where are you playing next?'

'Well, my agent has got a couple of options she's looking at,' said Matt. 'I don't know whether you know the Anglebrook region of Kent at all?'

They looked blankly at him, then the floor manager intervened. 'Can I ask you just to step aside for a moment, Matt, the guys need to concentrate on the next item.'

'The one-legged pigeon?' said Amelia.

'That's right, Napoleon!' said Mark.

'No, Mark – Nelson, remember?' said Amelia.

'Mo will take you to the green room, Matt . . .' said the floor manager, waving to Mo who was a couple of steps behind him.

Mo guided Matt round the back of the studio over the various cables and back to the green room.

'Everything OK?' said Kitty.

'Yeah, I guess,' said Matt, still a little dazed from his first glimpse of a live studio show. 'When you watch it on TV it just looks like two people having a chat but it's as busy as anything out there! And they're all so calm!'

'Well, we do this a lot,' chipped in Mo. 'Every Sunday in fact, so . . .'

They sat watching the show on the monitor as it unfolded – Nelson the one-legged pigeon was quite a character. Half way through the interview with his owner he decided to fly up to the studio ceiling, found a perch on the lighting rig and refused to come down – even when Mark offered him a piece of bread.

The young actor from *Chair of Swords* was pretty relaxed and had a couple of well rehearsed anecdotes about his time on the show. As the item on homelessness started, Mo stuck his head round the green-room door.

'OK, Matt, you're on!'

'Wish me luck, guys!' said Matt turning to Team Millz.

'Good luck, Matt!' they all replied in unison.

'Hey! Remember to give Amelia my mobile number!' said Ahmed with a wink.

Matt took one last swig from his bottle of water and followed Mo to the studio floor. A sound man in headphones came and clipped a tiny microphone to the lapel of Matt's jacket, placed the battery pack in his inside pocket, then listened intently in his headphones. 'Yup, you're good to go,' he said.

'Roll VT,' came the tiny voice in the floor manager's ear and once again there was a whir of activity on the set as Matt was whisked in to sit opposite Amelia and Mark on the sofa.

'OK, Matt?' said Amelia, shuffling through some notes. 'Just relax, this should be fun!'

Matt nodded.

'Back to the studio in five ... four ... three ... two ... one ...'

The video about homelessness came to an end

and the two presenters shifted abruptly into performance-mode.

'A very sad story there and we wish them well,' said Amelia sombrely.

'Right!' said Mark, picking up the pace. 'Well, for any fans of *The T Factor* watching, you'll know that on Saturday's show a twelve-year-old boy was disqualified for being too young to enter the competition, but not before he'd brought the house down at the Hammersmith Apollo, no less. Let's take a look.'

'Roll VT,' squeaked the tiny voice.

Suddenly the monitors were showing Matt live on stage at *The T Factor* – and it dawned on Matt that it was the first time he'd seen it. As he watched the tiny version of himself on the screen it all came flooding back and amazingly he found himself laughing – laughing at his own jokes!

'Simon Bewell, ladies and gentleman, the only person in show business who has his hair dry-cleaned! I know a lot of you are looking at me thinking, blimey he's young! It's true – I'm so young that if I'm having a drink I still like to have a rusk with it!'

The VT played for about twenty seconds then the cameras picked up Amelia back in the studio laughing.

'Very funny,' she chuckled. 'And Matt joins us now.'

Matt was now staring at himself on the monitor, sat on the *Sunday at Six* sofa.

'You certainly had some funny lines about poor old Simon's hair there, Matt . . .'

'Thanks!' said Matt. Amelia looked at him and waited for him to say something further, but Matt just stared back at her smiling.

'Good,' said Mark with a slight laugh in his voice. 'It must have been pretty nerve-racking going up there for the first time?'

'Yeah, it really was!' said Matt, nodding his head, smiling and looking round at the cameras. Again, there was a pause as the presenters waited for a little bit more from Matt but nothing was forthcoming.

Amelia shuffled quickly through her notes and Mark put a finger to his ear as if he was listening to an instruction from the director.

'How have your friends reacted to your new-found fame, Matt?' asked Mark.

'Great!' said Matt, nodding his head and twiddling his thumbs. Then something really weird happened. Nelson the pigeon decided to find a new perch. He swooped down, and landed right on top of Matt's head!

'Aargh!' cried Matt waving his hands about, completely startling the pigeon. Unfortunately Nelson did what birds do when they're startled. He pooped on Matt's head. A thin streak of white doo-doo trickled down Matt's forehead. Mark burst out laughing. Amelia just about managed to hold herself together.

Matt looked up and quipped, 'I guess I now know how Nelson's statue feels!' Even the camera operators were laughing. Amelia thanked Matt for coming

along to the studio and started to announce the next item – National Sausage Day – but the absurdity of the situation suddenly made her dissolve into uncontrollable laughter.

'Cue the sausages,' squeaked the voice in the floor manager's ear and seven adults dressed as sausages ran on to the set and started dancing to a disco track. Matt, Amelia and Mark were in hysterics.

'Ha ha! Well, that's all we've got time for. Ha ha!' said Mark, with tears streaming down his cheeks. 'That's all from *Sunday at Six*, have a good week!'

'Roll credits,' squeaked the voice, the lights came up and the show was done.

The sound man came in and unclipped Matt's microphone from his jacket.

'Well done!' he said cheerily. 'Your first time on a chat show was it?'

'Er . . . yes, yes. Did it show?' said Matt.

'Just a little bit, but don't worry, you'll get used to it – these guys have been doing it for years.'

'Oh, that was so funny, Matt!' said Amelia as someone raced over to wipe Matt's forehead with a wet wipe.

'Well, it was nothing I did,' laughed Matt. 'It's Nelson you need to thank!'

'Yeah, thank god for Nelson!' said Amelia. 'Because up until that point it was a bit of a struggle, wasn't it?'

'A struggle?' asked Matt.

'He's only young, Amy! Give him a break!' said Mark.

'The interview, you weren't saying much were you?' said Amelia.

'Well, I was just answering your questions,' said Matt oblivious of any problem.

'Ah,' continued Amelia. 'OK, so a word of advice. When interviewers ask you questions, they don't necessarily want to know the actual answers.'

'Huh? What do you mean?' said Matt.

'Well, it's an entertainment show. Yes, it's pretty far down the show-business food chain but people tune in to be entertained – so in an ideal world you should be entertaining.'

'What? You mean, make up an answer?' said Matt. It suddenly dawned on him what she was getting at.

'Well, embellish it. Take the kid from *The Chair of Swords*: those stories he told weren't necessarily true, but were loosely based on something that happened – and he had them ready to go when we asked him. You've seen how busy the show is – you don't get long to make an impression! So my advice to you, starting out, is when you do a show like this – and I'm guessing you've got a few lined up . . .'

'I'm doing *Breakfast With Tubbs* and *Late Lunch* tomorrow,' said Matt.

'There you go then. So between now and tomorrow morning just jot down a few stock answers. You see there's no time on a show like this for waffle. Anyway, you got your laugh on the clip and the pigeon was priceless. Maybe you should make Nelson's owner an offer!'

'Thanks, Amelia,' said Matt, and he meant it. 'I really appreciate your advice. I'll do that tonight when I get home.'

Amelia smiled and patted him on the shoulder. 'Good luck, you deserve to do well with that attitude.'

'Oh, Amelia,' said Matt, rushing to catch up with her in the corridor a few moments later.

'Everything OK?' she said.

'Yes, yes. Are you by any chance going to the green room?' he asked.

'I usually pop in and say a few thank yous, why?'

'Well, I wondered whether you'd do me a favour . . .?'

'Well done, Matt!' said Kitty as he walked into the green room.

'Felt a bit weird,' said Matt sheepishly. 'I mean I hardly said a word! How did it look?'

'It just about did the job,' she said handing him a glass of water.

'Ah! Were you nervous, babe?' asked Magda with a look of concern.

'What was it with the long silences?' said Ahmed, characteristically cutting through the others' politeness. Kitty shot him a frosty look.

'Just a teething problem!' she said breezily.

'Don't worry, Kit. I know what I need to do before the next one,' said Matt.

'The good news is I got the pigeon doin' its business on my phone. I uploaded it to Facebook and you've already had half a million hits!' said Ahmed proudly.

'I'll ignore that,' said the producer, popping in to thank Matt for doing the show.

'Didn't Amelia look gorgeous in that frock though?' said Neil's mum.

'You're telling me, Mrs T!' said Ahmed suddenly perking up. 'Gorgeous is the wo— woh— woh . . .!' Ahmed's words dried in his mouth as Amelia Wong walked into the green room.

'Hi, Matt!' said Amelia walking over to join them. Ahmed jumped to his feet and stared with his mouth open in wonder.

Amelia winked at Matt then turned to Ahmed.

'Aren't you going to introduce me to this gorgeous hunk?' she said raising one eyebrow.

'Er, that's . . . I mean . . . I'm Mr Chalabi— I mean Ahmed. Who are you? I mean how do you do?' said Ahmed sticking out his hand to shake hers.

Amelia ignored the handshake and went in for a hug, lifting the boy clean off his feet.

'Mmmm. Strong too,' she said with a seductive smile. Ahmed's face was bright red as he landed back

on solid ground.

Amelia leant in and whispered in his ear, 'Call me, yeah?' She then handed him a piece of paper. 'OK, well, nice to meet you, Matt, and good luck with Mr Tubbs! See you again soon I hope, Ahmed,' she added winking, and with that she sailed out of the room.

'Did that really happen?' said Rob in wonder.

Matt watched Ahmed unfold the piece of paper and start to read it.

'What's it say, Ahmed?' said Rob excitedly.

'Yeah, what's it say?' said Matt, hardly able to control his giggles.

'Er, it says ... um ... "This was a set up from your mate ... Matt Millz. Kiss ... kiss, kiss!"' read Ahmed.

'Priceless!' cried Rob. 'Nice one, Matt. You were well and truly pranked there, Ahmed!'

'Ha ha! You should have seen your face when she went in for that hug!' laughed Matt.

'She really swept you off your feet!' chuckled Magda, laughing along.

'YOU!' said Ahmed jabbing Matt with his finger. 'I'll get you back for this!' He grabbed Matt round the waist, pushed him on to the sofa and started hitting him with one of the cushions.

'Everything OK?' came a voice from behind them. Ahmed stopped mid-whack and spun round. It was Amelia again.

'Sorry, Ahmed, that was my fault really. Shall we get our selfie?'

*

'Did all that really happen?' said Matt on the way home.

'Apparently,' said Ahmed, holding up his phone and scrolling through his photos so Matt could see. There was a photo of Matt with his arm round will.i.am, a screen shot of Matt with a pigeon on his head and one of Amelia with her arm round Ahmed.

'That's not all,' said Ahmed, flicking to Instagram.

'will.i.iam's put his selfie of you and him up on Instagram and it's had three million likes!'

As the car pulled up outside Matt's house the posse of about ten fans surged around him for selfies, then, once satisfied, they left him alone. Kitty walked with him to his front door. As he turned to say goodbye he noticed she had a worried look on her face.

'What's up, Kit?' he said placing his hand on her shoulder.

'What you said earlier about that Dickie Hart trying to poach you,' she said crossly. 'You don't understand, Matt. Those guys at Excalibur

Management are ruthless. They chew talent up and spit it out – it's all "stack-it-high-and-sell-it-cheap" with them, exploit one comic and then when he's left floundering and in debt, move on to the next one.'

'Debt?' said Matt. 'What do you mean, debt?'

'Dickie Hart's got a very dodgy way of doing business. He may have a glossy brochure, a big car and swanky offices in London but he doesn't operate within the usual rules of the industry – though he's not stupid, he does operate within the law – so there's no way anyone can pin anything on him. It's a morality thing rather than a legal thing.'

'Well, Russell Perkins seems to be doing OK. I've never heard anyone complaining?' said Matt. 'And there's not a single interview with a comedian in the last couple of years that I haven't read.'

'That's just it. Dickie gets them to sign NDAs,' she said.

'NDAs? What's that?'

'Non disclosure agreements – he gets his acts to promise, basically, that they won't bad-mouth the company, which really means they can't go to the press with the truth!'

'Hmm, sounds like someone's a bit jealous,' said Matt, giving her a nudge. 'Worried that your top act is going to get poached by a bigger player? That the shark is going to snap up the minnow?'

Kitty turned to face him. 'I'm not at all worried that my top act is going to leave me – I have every faith in Neil Trottman!'

'Ouch,' said Matt with a mock grimace. 'That hurts!'

'Believe me, Matt, they're a bad bunch. I mean I know I'm basically just a schoolgirl, and my office is nothing more than a shabby old mobile classroom but I really believe in you, Matt. I hope you know that. Promise me you'll keep Dickie Hart at arm's length.'

'Yeah, well, I'm only going to a gig – I'm not getting married to him,' said Matt.

'Right, well I'd better get back. I said I'd call Mick at the Rose and Crown in Sossinghurst after last orders – he's interested in running a regular comedy night. It would be a great place to work up some new material.'

'There you go again,' chuckled Matt. 'Always with the new material!'

'Jokes are the fuel of any act, Matt,' Kitty said, turning serious again. 'And you need to keep topping up the tank.' Gathering herself up to her full height of three feet six inches, she headed back to the waiting car.

Matt watched her as she strode purposefully up the front path and remembered Simon Bewell's words after his big night on *The T Factor*. 'You've got yourself a good manager there,' he'd said. Matt had no intention of jumping ship.

8

He Who Laughs Last

'They're still out there!' said Ian, peeking through the curtains at the front garden. 'I mean when do they go to the loo?'

'*Where* do they go to the loo, more importantly!' said Matt tucking into a full English breakfast.

He was due on *Breakfast With Tubbs* in a couple of hours but despite it being half past five in the morning, his mum had got up and very kindly cooked him a fry-up.

'Ha! Nice one, Matt!' said Ian, walking in from the hallway in his dressing gown holding up the cover of the *Daily Mirror*.

'*T Factor* Boy In Cunning Disguise! See if you can guess who it is.' It was a picture of Matt with the paper bag on his head. 'Turn to page 3 to find out.'

Ian flicked to page three and there – under the headline 'The Jokes Keep Coming!' – were a series of photos taken with a telephoto lens of Matt at the front door of 77 Bathurst Street taking the bag off his head and entering the house.

'Yes it's twelve-year-old surprise star of *The T Factor*, Matt Millz!' read Ian. Matt jammed the last piece of sausage into his mouth, jumped up and grabbed the paper off him. There was also a photo of Matt with the pigeon on his head on *Sunday at Six* and Amelia and Mark doubled up with laughter. Both were satisfyingly credited 'Copyright Ahmed Chalabi'. This was great publicity. Just then the doorbell went.

'You'd better answer that, Matt,' said Ian. 'I don't want to be in the papers in my pyjamas as well as my pants . . .'

Matt dashed into the hall and opened the door. It was Kitty. 'Ready for another round of questions?' she said with a smile. 'Great bit in the *Mirror* today!' She handed Matt another copy of the paper. 'Ahmed's doing a really good job!'

'Yeah! I've seen it,' said Matt. 'Hang on a sec and I'll get my coat.' He said his goodbyes, grabbed his coat and followed her down the front path, through the cold, crisp morning air to the waiting car.

'Can I have a selfie, Matt, please?' said the bloke in the anorak. He was about twenty-five Matt reckoned, had thinning sandy hair, a rather bad rash on his chin and looked a little bit like he needed a bath.

'It's Gary isn't it?'

'That's right,' said the man, holding his disposable camera up and pulling Matt in for a selfie. Matt caught a sharp whiff of rather pungent BO.

'I'm your number one fan, Matt,' said Gary with a grin.

'Great!' said Matt, forcing a smile for the camera.

Then Matt and Kitty got in the Mercedes and pulled away from the crowd at the gate.

'Do you watch *Breakfast With Tubbs*?' asked Kitty as they headed down the M20 to London for the third time in three days.

'Not really my cup of tea,' said Matt. 'My mum likes it though – not sure why.'

'Yes, I know what you mean – it's a bit dry isn't it? Not like *Sunday at Six*. Tubbs won't be as much fun as Amelia and Mark.'

'Well, I went through my stuff last night and I've got a few funny answers sorted out, so hopefully I won't end up looking like a complete lemon like yesterday,' said Matt.

'You didn't look like a lemon,' said Kitty with a mock frown.

'Oh yes I did! I watched it back when I got home. I was just sitting there giving one word answers!'

'Well, you looked like what you are – inexperienced,' said Kitty

'OK, I looked like an inexperienced lemon!'

INEXPERIENCED LEMON

'That's not how it looks in the *Daily Mirror*! I'm glad you watched it back though,' said Kitty. 'It's the only way you'll learn to improve how you come across.'

The pre-rush-hour traffic was light and they made it to the BBC Studios in Portland Place in double-quick time. They were met by a production runner and led through a very similar routine to the day before – first they were shown to a dressing room, then to make-up, then mic'd up by a sound man, then shown to the green room where, instead of Wotsits and cans of Coke, there was a tea urn, a flask of coffee and a tray of croissants.

Just as Matt was about to tuck in to his second breakfast of the day, the floor manager grabbed him and whisked him off to the studio. Before he knew it, he was sitting on the sofa opposite the great (-ish!) man himself.

Quentin Tubbs was a portly man in his late fifties. He'd started his TV career reading the news then, realising he was a safe pair of hands on live TV, the bigwigs at the BBC moved him sideways to breakfast television. To say he wasn't known for his sense of humour would be something of an understatement – in fact he wasn't really known for any particular personality traits. He was just a very straightforward sort of character who played it very, very safe.

To give you some idea of how straightforward he was, he owned one of Europe's largest collections of historical cardigans. He'd been doing breakfast television for nearly twenty-five years and, if truth be known, he was very, very bored with his job. Every morning he had to be up at half past three to get the car to the studio, ready to start work at half past five.

He was completely unflappable. Over the years he'd seen everything that could possibly go wrong in a TV studio and had interviewed virtually everybody who was anybody, plus a vast number of nobodies too. Sadly the early starts had taken their toll on his face. His eyes were permanently bloodshot and he had the air of someone who had just woken up. He looked, thought Matt, like he was dog-tired – and

BLOODHOUND IN A WIND TUNNEL!

the dog in question was a bloodhound. He looked like a bloodhound in a wind tunnel that hadn't slept for twenty-five years.

'Now here's Joanne with the news at eight thirty,' droned Tubbs.

As the newsreader started to read out the morning's headlines, the floor manager introduced him to Matt.

'Morning, Mr Tubbs!' said Matt brightly.

'Hello,' said Mr Tubbs ponderously, not looking up from his printed schedule.

Matt then shifted awkwardly on the sofa, not quite knowing what to do or where to look.

'Right, nearly there,' said Tubbs looking at his watch as the newsreader handed over to the weatherman. 'Let's get this over with, then we can all go home.'

There was a short trailer after the weather advertising a new crime drama that was coming up later on BBC1. Then came the *Breakfast With Tubbs* ident and Matt and Tubbs were live on air.

'My next guest may be familiar to some of you . . .' intoned Tubbs, reading the autocue, his face a picture of indifference. 'He is the youngest stand-up comedian to raise the roof at London's prestigious Hammersmith Apollo. He is Matt Millz.' Tubbs turned mechanically to look at Matt for the first time since he'd joined him on the sofa. 'Welcome to *Breakfast With Tubbs*. Tell us a little bit about how that happened,' he said robotically.

'Thanks, it's great to be here. My mum is such a fan of the show,' said Matt trying to pick up the pace. 'Yes, she's not the smartest person – she went to a mind reader and he only charged her half price!'

Tubbs looked at Matt as if he was completely mad. 'Pardon?' he said.

'Um ... I was just saying about my mum, that she's not that clever. The other day she asked me to give her a hand with a jigsaw puzzle of a chicken – it was a box of cornflakes!'

At this point there was a loud laugh from the three camera operators but the look on Tubbs' face was one of complete and utter confusion. Matt suddenly realised what the nation had already worked out – that Quentin Tubbs had absolutely no sense of humour whatsoever.

'Anyway,' said Matt, changing the subject, 'to answer your question, I was a contestant on *The T Factor*!'

'Oh ... er ... um ...' said Tubbs. The look in his eye had changed to one of panic. Matt wasn't quite sure why at first, then he looked across at Tubbs' autocue and realised that it had gone blank. Somehow it had malfunctioned and without it the veteran presenter, having never encountered *The*

T Factor or pretty much any show on rival channel ITV, had absolutely no idea what to say.

'Er, *The T Factor* ... um ...?' What's that?' spluttered Tubbs.

'It's a talent show on ITV?' ventured Matt, watching as behind the camera, two men with screwdrivers were fiddling frantically trying to get the autocue to work. '... The winner gets to perform at the Royal Variety Show in front of the Queen. Yeah, it's given the world such stars as Martin and his Performing Cats? Although that year the Queen brought along one of her corgis and when it saw the cats, it jumped out of the royal box and tried to attack them.'

'Really,' said Tubbs.

'Of course not,' said Matt with a chuckle. 'I'm kidding! No, that would be a helluva jump for a corgi – they've only got short legs! It didn't make it to the stage – it landed on the grand piano in the orchestra pit!'

'Good heavens!' said Tubbs with a look of

amazement, suddenly engaged.

'Yes, it was running up and down the keys for twenty minutes trying to avoid being caught. They grabbed it eventually but not before it had picked out Chopin's Third Piano Concerto in D Minor with its little tiny feet!'

'That's amazing!' said Tubbs.

'Not really,' said Matt. 'It was a joke!' This was weird. Here was a man who believed every word he told him because he didn't understand what a joke was!

'Would I be right in thinking that you're not really a fan of jokes, Mr Tubbs?' said Matt. He'd almost forgotten that the two of them were being beamed live into people's homes.

'Jokes?' repeated Tubbs. 'No, you're right, I've never been one for jokes. Even as a child I never really understood what people were laughing at.'

'Is it right that you're more interested in ... cardigans?' said Matt raising his eyebrows provocatively. Suddenly Quentin Tubbs sat up and for the first time that morning, and in fact for a very long time, looked truly awake.

'Oh yes!' he said his eyes losing their dull look in exchange for something approaching a sparkle. 'I love cardigans! Red cardigans, blue cardigans, chunky cardigans, fine-knit, lambswool, cashmere. I've even got a cardigan knitted from the wool of a yak! Did you know that the cardigan was named after the seventh Earl of Cardigan who led the Charge of the Light Brigade at the Battle of Balaclava?'

'Balaclava? You mean there was a battle between the cardigans and the balaclavas?' said Matt. 'Was that the Great Knitwear Wars of 1825?'

CARDIGANS vs BALACLAVAS!

Tubbs looked at Matt with a stunned look, then something very odd happened. He started to laugh. Just a little chuckle at first, which grew into a titter then became a full-blown guffaw. And once he'd started, he couldn't stop. It was like fifty years of bottled-up laughter was finally being allowed to escape!

'Ha! Ha! Ha! Ha! Ha! Ha ha! Hee Heee! He! Ho! Ha! Knitwear Wars! Ha ha!' howled the hapless breakfast-TV presenter, tears running down his face. 'Aho hoo hoo! Hee! Balaclava fighting a cardigan! Ha ha! That's the funniest thing I've ever heard!'

There is something irresistible about another person laughing, so Matt really had no option – he started laughing too, as did the cameramen, the floor manager, the runner, the newsreader, the weatherman and, in the gallery, the entire production team. The cameras shook as Quentin Tubbs, convulsed with laughter, slipped off his famous sofa and rolled around on the floor clutching his cardigan-clad stomach. Anyone tuning in at that point would have thought that the whole world had gone completely mad. In the green room Kitty Hope's face broke into a broad grin and she nodded to herself. This was dynamite!

The production team had to cut to a taped item about a sewage farm to buy themselves a little time to regain their composure, but the presenter was still chuckling right until the credits rolled.

'Thank you so much for coming on the show,' said a newly invigorated Quentin Tubbs as they stopped filming. This had been an edition of *Breakfast With Tubbs* unlike any other.

'Oh well,' laughed Matt, his sides actually hurting from laughing. 'I'm not really sure what happened there. It wasn't really anything I did . . .'

'Oh yes, you did!' beamed Tubbs, putting a thankful arm round Matt's shoulders. 'You've helped me more than you can ever know!'

'Holy cow, what a funny show!' said the producer, joining them on the set. 'What happened, Quentin? I've never seen you like that!'

'I'm not sure I've ever been like that before, but I've realised something today . . .'

'Oh yes? What's that?' asked the producer, intrigued.

'I've realised I've had enough of getting up at half past three in the morning,' he said with a look of total joy on his face. 'You're going to have to come up with a new name for the show!'

'Huh? Why's that?' asked the producer.

'Because I've decided I'm not going to do it any more! Tomorrow morning I'm going to have a lie-in and when I finally do get out of bed I'm going to have some fun! Ha ha!' And with that he skipped off the set and out of the studio for the very last time.

Matt and Kitty arrived back at Bathurst Street after the morning's exertions at about half past three that afternoon. They'd gone on from *Breakfast With Tubbs* to *Late Lunch With Phillip Scruffold and Haley Wallaby*, which was a lot more like Matt's experience at *Sunday at Six*. Phillip and Haley were fans of *The T Factor* and seemed genuinely interested to learn of his experience on the show, asking for all the backstage gossip, and it gave Matt a chance to trot out some of the slightly exaggerated anecdotes he'd rehearsed the night before. After a quick couple of selfies and autographs with fans at the studio door, he and Kitty had got another car home.

Once again the gaggle of fans and photographers at the front gate surged around him as he got out of the car.

'Is it true you got Quentin Tubbs the sack?' asked a reporter shoving a microphone into his face.

'No! NO! That's not what happened!' said Matt.

'Matt needs to get some rest now,' snapped Kitty, giving him a shove in the lower back to get him through the gate and down the path to the front door. 'He's had a very early start!'

'Right,' she said once they'd reached the safety of the kitchen, 'I've still got a few details to sort out for the gigs I've got planned. Maybe we could catch up at the DMC in first break tomorrow?'

'That would be great,' said Matt, suddenly remembering that his little run as a TV celebrity was coming to an end and tomorrow he'd be back at school like any other twelve-year-old.

'You did really well today,' said Kitty. 'Just be careful with the press though, they'll be out to trip you up.'

'That's a bit of an odd thing to say,' said Matt. So far all the press coverage he'd received had been really supportive.

'Maybe, but they're an odd bunch – they build people up but they can knock you back down if they choose to, so it's as well to be wary. I'm sure you'll be fine. See you tomorrow.'

TIPS ON DOING CHAT SHOWS

Plan what you might say. Know the areas they're going to ask you about and have a couple of anecdotes prepared just in case.

Research the other guests – find out who else is on the sofa and have a think about any gags you can chip in. If it's an actor plugging their TV show, make sure you've seen at least one episode so you know what they're talking about.

Run through your set list – You never know when you might be able to slip a gag in here and there.

Be polite — although it's important to make an impression, keep quiet when it's not your turn — no one likes pushy!

9

No Ordinary Schoolboy

'I've found your coat by the way,' said Ian that evening after he got back from his stint at the estate agent's.

'No? Really? Where?' asked Matt.

'Here! Take a look at this . . .' he said and turned his laptop to face Matt. It was logged on to eBay and there, for sale, listed under 'Genuine Matt Millz Memorabilia' was Matt's coat.

'Holy moly!' exclaimed Matt. 'That's outrageous!'

'Yeah, and look at the price,' said Ian. 'Sixty quid!'

'That coat only cost twenty new!' said his mum wandering in from the kitchen.

'They'll never sell it ...!' said Matt just as a bid went in for the asking price.

'Are you thinking what I'm thinking?' said Matt. Ian nodded. They spent the next hour sorting through and photographing Matt's old clothes and loading them up on to eBay. By eleven o'clock they'd uploaded over twenty items of clothing, including an old pair of his socks and a string vest.

'How are the prices doing?' said Matt as Ian logged in to check.

'Hmm, not great,' said Ian. 'I think we might have flooded the market!'

'Good to see you, Matt!' said the bus driver as Matt hauled his sports bag on to the bus. 'I thought you was well funny the other night on *The T Factor* – although the wife didn't care for it much, but then a sense of humour is a very personal thing. It's probably why we haven't seen eye to eye for fifteen years, but never mind – fight the good fight, eh?'

Matt nodded, smiled and turned to head down the bus to find a seat.

'I thought maybe you wouldn't be on the bus from now on,' continued the bus driver turning his head and calling after him, 'on account of all the fame and fortune that's come your way. I thought maybe you'd be travelling in a bit more style, you know a Roller or some such. To be honest I did wonder if you'd even be coming back to school. I said to the wife, if I was him I wouldn't bother. I'd be well shot of it. I mean what's the point of school when you've got all that celebrity and money sloshing about? No, if I had your dosh I'd be living it large, up the West End . . . How much they pay you for last night? Half a million? I hope you don't mind me asking. I said probably more but the wife said she read in the *Daily Mail* that they were cutting back, anyway—'

'Hang on a sec,' said Matt, striding back to confront the bus driver and stopping him mid sentence. 'I've been taking this bus for the last three years and this is the first time you've so much as spoken to me! You've never even said hello before!'

'Well, you know, I'd been meaning to say hello all those years. I was just waiting for the right moment,' replied the bus driver sheepishly.

'And that just happened to coincide with my appearance on national TV did it?' demanded Matt.

'Alan,' said the bus driver thrusting his hand out. 'My name's Alan, and I'm a bus driver and I'm very pleased to meet you,' he said.

'Get a move on!' bellowed a voice from the back of the bus.

'Don't take any notice of him,' said Alan. 'Ignore 'em, all of 'em, flaming passengers! That's what I do – it's the only way I can get through the day!'

'I'm Matt,' said Matt sarcastically, shaking the bus driver's hand, 'and I'm a passenger.'

Matt made his way up the bus to find a seat and as he went virtually everyone had something to say to him. Most of them pulled out their smartphones and snapped him as he walked past, others dived in for a selfie, and that was pretty much how it went for the rest of the day.

People stopped him at the school gates, then they stopped him as he walked into the playground. Kids came running at him from all angles, shouting his name, pulling at him, grabbing photos. Then two girls from the year above got rather agitated.

'Oi! I was here first!' snapped one, pushing the other.

'No you weren't, I was!' spat the other. Before Matt could intervene, a fight had broken out, fists and feet were flying, hair was being pulled and clothes were being ripped. Matt waded in to try and break it up but somehow managed to end up on his back on the floor.

'That's enough,' came a voice from above and everyone froze. The crowd of kids parted and the familiar face of Mr Archer the PE teacher (and coincidentally Magda's dad) loomed over their heads and into view.

'She started it!' said one of the girls.

'No I didn't, she did!' said the other, then they

lunged at each other again. Mr Archer grabbed the two girls firmly by their collars and held them apart like a couple of pit bull terriers.

'You two had better see me for some extra training after school – and I don't mean boxing,' he snapped. 'Now get to assembly!' and he gave them a shove towards the school hall.

As the other kids dispersed, Mr Archer leant in and helped Matt up. 'I see you've finally got all the girls fighting over you then, Matt!' he said with a wry smile.

'It's crazy, sir! I'm the same person I was a couple of days ago!'

'Hmm, not in their eyes. I watched the show the other night – you did a great job and Magda and her mum were thrilled, so thank you for that. Let me know if you get any more bother from those two!' he said nodding towards the girls who were now arm in arm, skipping to assembly. 'You'd better get a move on and join them. I hear Mr P is planning a bit of a speech ...'

'Thanks, sir!' said Matt and jogged after them, maintaining a safe distance.

'Good morning, school!' said Mr Pavey brightly from behind the lectern.

'Good morning, Mr Pavey,' droned the whole school back at him.

'Mr Pavey can't hear you!' said Mr Pavey, punching the air with his fist. 'I want to hear you make some noise!'

Matt, Ahmed and Rob looked at each other and burst out laughing, closely followed by the entire school. Including the teachers.

'What is he on?' whispered Ahmed.

'Er ...' said Mr Pavey, suddenly flustered and looking at his notes. 'Not that sort of noise!'

The whole school then immediately started talking to each other.

'Not that sort of noise either!' bellowed Mr P, his face red and his composure all but gone. This was the Pavey the kids were used to, the red-faced, shouty one. The school, as one, returned to obedient silence.

'Thank you,' said the headmaster with a sigh, taking a moment to pull himself together.

'Now, many of you will have seen a certain television programme the other night ...'

There were a couple of cheers from the back of the hall. Matt turned round to see if he could see who was responsible and realised the entire school was looking at him.

'... and I don't mean the *Ten O'Clock News*!

Ha ha!' continued Mr P, but he was the only person laughing. 'Oh,' he said, shuffling his papers. 'I thought that would go for more. Ahem! No, of course I'm talking about *The T Factor* and our own pupil, Matt Millz.'

There was a spontaneous round of applause and cheering that seemed to Matt to go on forever.

'I'm sure you'd like to congratulate Matt on a job very well done. I think you'll all agree, as you younger generation say, he smashed it!'

Another round of applause started up even louder than the first.

Matt jumped to his feet and took a bow, which sent the kids into a frenzy – they started stamping their feet and chanting his name. For the first time since *The T Factor* Matt took a moment to bask in his new-found glory. 'Could things get any better than this?' he wondered.

'I thought I'd find you in here,' said Matt's English teacher Mr Gillingham, bursting into the DMC at first break as Matt, Ahmed and Rob waited for Kitty to turn up to reveal her masterplan. Mr G had been a big supporter of Matt's right from his and Rob's attempt at a double act in the school talent show – 'Anglebrook's Got Talent' – just a few weeks earlier.

'You're a rather difficult boy to track down, Matt,' he puffed.

'We're hiding, sir!' said Ahmed.

'Hiding?' said Mr G.

'Yeah, if I go out into the playground I either get mobbed or threatened with physical violence,' said Matt.

'Ah, the price of fame,' said Mr G wistfully. 'Celebrity is a mask that eats into the face. Who said that?'

'You did, sir,' said Matt.

'No, I mean who said it originally?'

'Lady Gaga?' ventured Ahmed.

'John Updike – an author I'd strongly recommend, but I'm guessing you've got other stuff on your mind right now. I thought you were great on *The T Factor*, by the way, really self-assured – but don't forget while all this attention is swirling around you that you have an exam at the end of term. You're good at English, Matt – you've got a great way with words and I'd like to see that reflected in your grade.'

'What about my way with words, sir?' chipped in Rob.

'I think we'd both agree you're better with a paintbrush than a pen, Rob.'

'Don't worry, sir, I promise my studies won't suffer,' said Matt with a grin.

'Good, and I do expect another strong issue of "Pavey's Punchlines" for the school magazine this week, too.'

'We're on it, sir!' said Rob.

'Was that all you came to tell me, sir?' asked Matt, swinging his legs absent-mindedly. 'It's just when you walked in it seemed like there was something urgent . . .'

'Good point, I almost forgot,' he said. 'The head wants to see you!'

'Pavey wants to see me?' said Matt sitting up with a start.

'*Mister* Pavey, yes he does . . .'

'What have I done this time?' said Matt exchanging a worried glance with Rob.

'I've no idea, but you'd better get over to his office pronto. Lessons start in ten minutes.'

As Matt walked up the corridor past the staff room to Mr Pavey's office, he racked his brains as to what minor infringement of school rules he may have committed. He checked his tie – yup, top button done up. He checked his lapels – no unauthorised badges. He checked his shoes – hmm, they hadn't seen any polish for a while, so he stopped for a moment to buff each one up in turn on the back of his trouser legs.

As he approached the head's office he read the brass plaque on the door: Meredith Pavey (NPQH).

'What do those letters stand for?' wondered Matt. 'Not Pretty, Quite Hairless? Um . . .'

He reached into his pocket for his little black book

and scribbled 'What initials really stand for'. Yes, people were always using abbreviations but what if they stood for something else? That might be a nice little routine.

As Matt scribbled the ideas in his little black book

ABBREVIATIONS TABLE (TBA)

Abbreviation	Real Meaning	Matt's meaning
LOL	Laugh Out Loud	Lick of Lolly
BTW	By The Way	Big Time Wimp
NASA	North American Space Agency	Not A Sign Of Aliens

NATO	North Atlantic Treaty Organisation	Never Accept Terrible Offers
BA	British Airways	Bad Acne

TBA	To Be Agreed	Terribly Bad Acne

OMG	Oh My God	Odd Message Generator
DIY	Do It Yourself	Did It Yesterday

AKA	Also Known As	Alternative Koala Accumulator
GSOH	Great Sense Of Humour	Giant Slice Of Ham
IMHO	In My Humble Opinion	I Made Hot Onions
TGIF	Thank God It's Friday	Thank Greggs It's Fried
WLTM	Would Like To Meet	Wouldn't Like To Marry

the door to Mr Pavey's office swung open. Matt looked up and to his surprise out walked Kitty Hope.

'Hi, Kit! What are you doing here?'

'I've just had a really weird meeting with Mr Pavey,' she hissed, a slightly perplexed look on her face.

'Weird? In what way?' said Matt.

'Well . . .' she hesitated, looking genuinely puzzled, then she leant up and whispered in Matt's ear. 'He asked me to represent him!'

'What?' exclaimed Matt, his eyebrows shooting skywards hitting his fringe and then bouncing back down to form a frown.

'Yes, he wants me to look after him for all his "media work"!'

'Media work?' said Matt. 'What media work?'

She shrugged. 'He seems to be under the impression he's got a big future on TV! He also said he was going to try and work more comedy into his assemblies . . .'

'More comedy?' said Matt with a smirk. 'You're right, that is weird.'

'And he wants me to organise a big gig at the school for Children in Need.'

'Well, that's not a bad idea,' said Matt. 'It's a great cause.'

Just then the door to Mr Pavey's office opened and the man himself appeared, his bald head catching the bright sunlight that was streaming from behind him through his office window and reflecting it directly into Matt's eyes. 'Jeez,' thought Matt, 'that head's so shiny you could send signals with it!' but before he could jot it into his little book, Mr P had grabbed his hand and started shaking it vigorously.

'Ah, Matt! Good to see you!' beamed Mr Pavey, looking very pleased with himself. 'Thank you, Kitty, it was very helpful talking to you. Do let me know your decision and rates. This is the start of a whole new era for Anglebrook! Now, Matt, you'd better come on in. We have much to discuss!' He gave Matt's hand a yank and pulled him into the fusty wood-panelled office.

Matt felt a sense of déjà vu as he sat down in the battered old red-leather chair opposite Mr P's desk – he'd been here many times before, usually when he was in trouble. Mr P reached into his desk drawer, produced a dusty old tin, leant across the desk and offered it to Matt.

'Would you like a toffee?' he said.

Matt had been caught out by those toffees before – it seemed that Mr P wasn't aware of things like sell-by dates.

'No thank you, sir, I've already eaten.'

'Yes well, good,' said Mr P taking a toffee from the tin, popping it into his mouth, giving it a quick chew then discreetly spitting it out into the palm of his hand and dropping it into the bin. 'I'll get straight to the point. We were all terribly impressed with how you conducted yourself the other night on *The F Factor*—'

'*T Factor*, sir,' interjected Matt.

'What?' said Mr P.

'It's a T, not an F.'

'A cup of tea?' said Mr P. 'Certainly, forgive me! Thirsty work!' he leant forward and picked up the handset of the phone on his desk and pressed a button. 'Steven, could you bring a cup of tea in for my guest please? Thank you. Milk and sugar?' he said to Matt, putting his hand over the receiver.

'Er . . . just milk thanks . . .' said Matt, more than a little baffled at how the meeting was progressing.

'Just milk, Steven, please! What? Steven's asking if you'd like a biscuit?'

'Really, I'm fine, sir, thank you!' said Matt, figuring that if the toffees were anything to go by it was probably best to steer clear of the biscuits too.

'Good . . .' said Mr Pavey hanging up the phone, leaning back in his chair and cracking his knuckles. 'Now where was I?'

'Um, you were talking about *The P Factor*, I mean *The T Factor*.'

'Exactly,' said Mr P sitting forward again. 'Yes, as I was saying, we all thought you were marvellous on *The F Tractor*, I mean *The T Factor*. This could be very good for the school, Matt! We at Anglebrook want to attract the very finest pupils, and the sort of shop window that all this media attention your performance has garnered us could work wonders for the calibre of children applying, and therefore our exam results and our OFSTED report. What's good for the school of course is good for the head teacher of that school – in other words, ahem, me. You're sure you don't want a toffee?' he said proffering the tin again.

'I'm fine thanks, sir.'

'Save one for later,' said Mr P, taking a moist-looking toffee out of the tin and placing it on the desk in front of Matt. He then licked his fingers and pulled a face like a dog that's just chewed a stinging nettle.

'Plenty more where that came from if you play your cards right, Matt,' continued Mr P, turning to admire his own reflection in the glass bookcase to his right. He licked his index finger and ran it coquettishly over his left eyebrow, leaving behind a small deposit of toffee and spit.

'Thank you, sir,' said Matt, watching as a large bluebottle landed on the toffee on the desk in front of him. 'I appreciate the compliment, but I'm not sure what you want me to do.'

The bluebottle took one sniff of the toffee and decided it didn't fancy it either. Unfortunately its feet were firmly embedded in the ancient sticky sweet and it was stuck fast.

'Your future is our future, Matt! If you continue to er . . . smash it . . .? Is that the correct term?'

'Um, yes, smash it, or storm it, sir.'

'Yes, I really must learn some of these terms. Perhaps you could write me a list of useful stand-up-related phrases?'

'Yes, yes, I can do that, sir,' said Matt, even more perplexed now.

'Naturally as headmaster of Anglebrook, there's been a lot of interest in my input into your success. How I shaped and moulded you, how I recognised this raw, untamed talent and shaped it into the highly entertaining young comedian that you have become . . .'

'Is that before or after you gave me a detention for my effort in the school talent show?' chirped up Matt. He wasn't going to let Pavey get away with that! The idea that Mr P had created his success really irked him. He'd done well on *The T Factor* for one reason and one reason only – because he'd spent every spare moment of his free time with Kitty in the DMC working on his routine.

'Eh?' said Mr P, pausing for a moment. 'Oh! Well, yes, a slight misunderstanding on my part! I don't think we need to dwell on that! I mean it was early days, but even then I noticed something in you, this tiny little burning ember of talent that I fanned and nurtured. I gave it oxygen so that it might grow into the raging inferno that it has become.'

As Mr P continued bigging himself up, Matt noticed that the bluebottle was flapping its wings furiously in an attempt to free its feet from the toffee. Matt snuck a look at his watch – nearly the end of break time! He felt a bit like that fly.

'Sorry, sir, but lessons are about to start,' he said looking back up at Mr P, '... and I don't want to be late. I mean it's really important for Anglebrook that I get good grades isn't it, sir?'

'Oh! Yes of course,' said Mr P. 'Quite so, yes, the world is watching, Matt! I suppose all I'm saying really is keep me abreast of developments. Let me know if there's anything you need me to do, you know, if you want me to come along to any of these TV appearances and chip in and so forth ... keep me in the loop, so to speak!'

'Will do, sir,' said Matt, getting to his feet.

'Oh, and Matt ...?'

'Yes, sir?'

Mr P hesitated and fiddled with his tie awkwardly.

'Would you put in a good word for me with Kitty Hope regarding representation? She didn't seem at all sure ...'

'Well ...' said Matt, but before he could answer, the bluebottle finally managed to become airborne – unfortunately its feet were still attached to the toffee. It rose up from the desk on its toffee hoverboard, lurching first to the left, then to the right, then up towards the ceiling, bounced off the light shade and came to rest on top of Mr Pavey's bald head and stuck fast.

'I'd save that for later, sir!' quipped Matt, quick as a flash. The door opened and in walked Steven with a cup of tea. Seeing the fly, he let out a scream and sent the tea flying. Matt seized the opportunity and headed for the open door.

As he skipped down the corridor he couldn't wait to tell Rob and Ahmed what had happened.

STAND-UP COMEDY TERMS

Smashed it, stormed it, killed it, raised the roof – the audience loved it.

Bombed, died a death, tanked – the audience didn't like it at all.

10

O2 What Can the Matter Be?

'Rob! Where have you been? We're going to be late!'

It was ten minutes before the cab was due to pick them up and Rob had only just turned up on Matt's doorstep. Ahmed had arrived a good forty minutes early but here was Rob looking flushed, breathless and slightly dishevelled and, more importantly, on his own.

'Where's Magda?' said Matt.

'That's why I'm late,' panted Rob. 'She twisted her ankle playing netball. I've just left her at A & E – she's not coming.'

'That is so lame,' said Ahmed.

'Er ... yeah, by definition if she can't walk on one leg then yes, she is lame – what's your point?' said Rob testily – he was clearly under a lot of pressure.

'Just sayin' there's a fifty-quid ticket wasted, bruv. If I'd known, I could have asked Jasmine.'

'Yeah, you could have asked her and looked like a right idiot when she turned you down,' shot back Rob. He was starting to get angry.

'Yeah well—' continued Ahmed, but Matt stepped in.

'Listen, never mind all the backchat, you're here now. Ahmed's right though, we've got a spare ticket.'

Just then the doorbell went.

Matt looked at his watch. 'That'll be the minicab,' he said and went off to answer it. When Matt opened the door, standing before him was an older gentleman in a grey three-piece suit, peaked cap and driving gloves.

'Master Millz?'

'That's right,' said Matt.

'My name's Alf. I'm your chauffeur for the night,

sir. Your chariot awaits. Do you have any luggage, sir?'

Matt looked past the gent and standing in the road in front of the house was a shiny black Rolls Royce Phantom.

'Er . . . you sure you've got the right address?' said Matt.

'Oh, very definitely, sir. Mr Hart sent me, to take you and your colleagues to the O2.'

'Woah! Look at that!' said Ahmed, mouth agape, peering round the door. 'Is Justin Bieber in town?'

'He says it's for us,' said Matt.

'That is some minicab, bruv,' chortled Ahmed. 'Rob! take a look at this!'

Rob joined them. 'You never stop amazing me, Matt,' said Rob, joining the other two at the door, equally astounded.

'Ahem!' said the old gent. 'I hate to chivvy things along but we really must be going if we are to make the start of the show. Particularly if you have any pre-show refreshments in mind.'

'Come on,' said Ahmed, hurtling up the garden path towards the Roller. Rob chased after him and Matt grabbed his jacket and followed suit.

'Wow! there's a fridge!' said Rob nestling into the plush leather seats and pulling open all the little drawers and cupboards.

'Help yourself to drinks and snacks,' said Alf from the driver's seat.

'Woah! And a TV!' said Ahmed, pulling open a flap to reveal a TV that was bigger than the one he had in his front room at home.

'Just the three of you, sir?' said the chauffeur pulling away from the house and down the steep incline of Bathurst Street.

'Yeah, the three musketeers,' said Ahmed.

'Oh I understood there were four of you?' said Alf. 'That leaves one ticket unused. Such a shame as I understand the show is sold out.'

Suddenly Matt had an idea. 'Alf?'

'Yes, sir?'

'Do we have time for a small detour?'

'A very small one, yes, sir!'

A few minutes later the limo pulled up outside a large red-brick detached house in a rather leafier lane than any of the three boys lived in.

'Won't be a sec,' said Matt, hopping out and hightailing it up to the entryphone on the gate.

'Hello?' came a familiar female voice.

'Kitty? It's Matt. What are you up to?'

'Um, I've just come off the phone to Mick at the Rose and Crown – he's thinking about the gig, which is good news, and now I think I'd better do my geography homework. Anyway, what are you doing here? I thought you were going to see Russel Perkins at the O2 . . .?'

'Magda couldn't make it – I've got a spare ticket.'

'You mean . . .?' asked Kitty

'Yes, the geography homework will have to wait – you're coming with us!'

'What?'

'I've got a car outside, courtesy of Excalibur Management, and a ticket with your name on it!'

There was a click as she hung up.

'Wow!' thought Matt. 'She really has got it in for Dickie Hart if she's happy to pass up a free night out at the O2!' Then he heard the front door of the house open and the clitter-clatter of a girl's shoes on the garden path. He looked up and sure enough pulling on her coat and attempting to brush her hair at the same time was Kitty Hope.

'Keep your friends close, and your enemies closer still,' she said cryptically as she passed him and clambered into the car.

There were a few disgruntled snorts from Ahmed and Rob as Kitty made herself comfortable in the back of the Roller. They'd never fully accepted Kitty into their circle of friends – she was a year younger after all – but she was perfectly capable of holding her own and pretty soon the four started to relax and enjoy the trip.

They loved the looks they got as they pulled up at traffic lights. You could see the other drivers craning their necks to see who was in the back of the luxury vehicle, but of course they couldn't see through the smoked-glass windows. A couple of times Matt had slowly lowered one of the windows to reveal just the top of his head as a tease. Another time the three boys had all hung out of the window pulling faces – until Kitty had told them to behave themselves.

After a while they settled down and Matt asked Kitty how she was getting on booking him some gigs.

'Don't worry, Matt, I'm working on it. I'm just finalising the last few details. I thought maybe I could meet you in the DMC tomorrow after school to run you through it,' she said.

'That's great news!' said Matt, eager to get back on stage.

The traffic got heavier as they hit the outskirts of London and the car slowed down to a snail's pace, but before too long they were pulling up outside the giant dome of the O2.

'It's massive!' said Ahmed.

'Twenty thousand seats to be exact,' said Kitty.

'Imagine one person and a microphone selling that number of tickets!' exclaimed Matt.

'Yeah, but he's doing two weeks,' said Ahmed. 'He must be minted!'

'One day, Matt,' smiled Rob, putting his arm round him and giving him a squeeze. 'And you won't forget your old friends when it comes to spreading the money about will you?'

'Come on, lads. Keep up!' barked Kitty who was already striding towards the huge glass doors.

Matt thanked Alf the driver as the boys piled out of the car and ran to catch her up.

'Shall we go and look at the merchandise?' said Kitty. 'It's always interesting to look at subsidiary revenue streams.'

'She swallowed a dictionary, or what?' Rob laughed.

'She knows what she's talking about,' said Matt.

'And she can't half run fast for a shorty!' said Ahmed, struggling to keep up.

Once they got to the 'merch stand' and had seen

all the different variations of T-shirts, badges, bags, DVDs and souvenir programmes, they realised they couldn't actually afford to buy any of it.

'Look at the prices, Kit,' said Matt, wide-eyed.

'Yes, someone's making a lot of money. Look at the queues!' she said, aghast at the huge number of people lined up patiently to buy a souvenir of Russel Perkins.

'I wouldn't mind, but he's not even very good,' muttered Rob.

'Yeah,' said Ahmed. 'You'd have to *pay* me to wear a Russel Perkins T-shirt!'

'Shh!' hissed Matt. 'Someone might hear you. We're his guests don't forget.'

They put what little money they did have together and had enough to buy two portions of chips and a bottle of water between them.

'Why would anyone pay for water when it's free out of the tap?' mused Matt. 'I mean, you don't pay for bottled air!'

'Is that a gag?' said Rob.

'It is now,' said Matt reaching for his little black book.

Bottled Air... walk around with a tank on your back and a mask.

Air from fancy places – Swiss Alps more expensive.

Cheaper air from places like Bromley/Birmingham.

Fizzy air?

Gluten-free air?

ARTISAN AIR! ™

(BREATHED BY YAKS IN BORNEO)

An announcement came over the tannoy asking the audience to take their seats.

As they walked up to the ticket check and security, Rob pointed to one of the queues with a sign over it saying 'VIPs only', which was pretty much empty.

'What's a VIP?' he said.

'That, my friend, is what we are,' said Matt. 'Come on!'

As they approached the desk a girl appeared with a clipboard.

'Hi,' she said brightly. 'You're Matt aren't you?'

Rob nudged him and whispered, 'You're in there, mate!'

'I'm Claire,' she continued, 'and Mr Hart has asked me to look after you tonight. Here's a few little things that he wanted you all to have.'

She handed them each a carrier bag. Matt peered into his – there was a Russel Perkins tour T-shirt, an 'I Love Russ!' badge, a souvenir programme and a copy of his latest DVD.

'eBay,' whispered Rob under his breath.

'Great! Thanks, Claire!' said Matt, digging Rob sharply in the ribs.

'That's my pleasure,' said Claire. 'Now, if you'd like to walk this way I'll show you to your seats.'

As they followed her through the doors into the auditorium Matt started moving in a very odd way, like he was holding a pencil between his bum cheeks.

'What *are* you doing, Matt?' said Kitty.

'You heard her, I'm walking that way!' he laughed, pointing to Claire as she clattered along in her mini skirt and high-heeled shoes. Rob and Ahmed laughed along and started imitating her too.

All four of them gasped as they entered the auditorium.

'It's enormous!' said Rob.

'If you wait in your seats at the end of the show, I'll come and take you to the after-show!' chimed Claire.

'Great seats,' said Rob as they sat down. He was right – they were only three rows from the front. Matt looked around at the other people in their block, and spotted a few faces he recognised off the

TV. There was the Radio One breakfast-show host Nick Arbuckle, the TV presenter Liam O'Deary, a few of the girls from *The Only Way Is Kent*, and then he spotted him.

'I don't believe it! Look, Rob! There's Eddie!'

'Where?' said Rob, craning his neck round to see where Matt was pointing. He was right! About siz metres away was Matt's all-time comic hero, Nigerian-born stand-up and host of *Stand-Up at the Apollo* – Eddie Odillo.

'Look, Matt! He's waving at you!' said Rob. Matt looked round to see if there was someone standing behind him but there wasn't – Rob was right, Eddie was actually waving and smiling at him. So Matt tentatively waved back. Surely he didn't remember him from when they'd met backstage after his *T Factor* audition? Eddie raised his hand in a thumbs up. Then went back to chatting with his mates.

'OMG,' said Rob. 'He remembers you!'

Matt just laughed. This was turning into quite a night. Just then the lights dimmed, the music got louder and a voice came over the PA.

'Ladies and gentlemen, please welcome Russel Perkins!'

The crowd erupted in cheers and applause as the young comic ambled on in just a pair of jeans and one of his own tour T-shirts.

'Good evening, London!' he bellowed into the mic. 'Let's hear you make some noise!'

'Sounds like he's taken a page out of Pavey's book! What sort of noise does he mean?' Matt whispered to Rob.

'Yeah, bit corny,' said Rob.

'I mean, I could do my impression of a chicken! Cluck-cluck-cluck!'

'I don't think he means that sort of noise,' said Rob.

'Or my elephant caught in a lift! Phwwwweeeeeeeeep!' joked Matt with a grin. 'All I'm saying is he needs to be more specific about the sort of noise he wants us to make, that's all!' As he was saying this he was reaching for his little black book again. He found a blank page and scribbled in it 'Make some noise/opener'.

Make some noise!

ELEPHANT
CAUGHT IN A LIFT

LIFT

Elephant in a lift.
Heron in a shopping trolley.
A baby with a full nappy.
A dog that realises his ball is just out of reach.

Your mum when one red sock in the washing machine has made all her white clothes pink.

The noise your dad makes when someone cuts him up in their car at the traffic lights.

The noise bubble wrap makes when it's being popped.

Polishing a bald head (Pavey's!)

Russel Perkins was usually described in the papers and online as 'young, fresh-faced' and 'boy next-door type', and his humour reflected that. It was broadly observational humour on the kind of subjects that affected twenty-something people and in particular blokes. So stuff about relationships, stuff about texting, stuff about getting drunk – that sort of thing. Not the sort of stuff that particularly excited Matt and his friends, but Matt had to admit that he seemed to know what he was doing.

'Where have you come down from?' he asked a girl in the front row.

'Essex!' she squealed back at him.

'I'm sorry?' he said.

'Essex!' she squealed even louder.

'No, I heard you the first time, luv, I'm just sorry!' he said, then moved on to another victim. It went really well for about the first ten minutes – big laughs, one rolling into the next – then it started to slow up. He wasn't being helped by the acoustics.

'It's weird,' whispered Matt to Kitty, sitting next to him. 'There's like a delayed reaction.'

He was right. As Russel delivered a gag, it hit the front few rows first and then took maybe a couple of seconds to hit the back of the arena, where the audience were pretty much just watching him on the giant video screens. So there was a strange effect of the two halves of the audience laughing at different times, which seemed to really upset Russel's comic timing.

'He's struggling,' whispered Kitty. 'The venue's just too big.'

'If you're sitting up the back, you might as well be

watching the DVD,' chipped in Rob.

After twenty minutes, the audience response had all but creaked to a halt – after forty they started to get restless. An hour in and Russel's set was punctuated by the sound of seats flipping up as people walked down the rows to the toilets or to get a drink. He just about managed to pull it round at the end, and the audience gave him a good applause. He bounded back on a bit too quickly for his encore and then he was off and the lights were up. The whole show had lasted an hour and a half.

'Not great value if you were paying top price,' said Kitty, shaking her head.

'It was pretty slow, wasn't it, Matt?' said Rob to his old mate.

'Everyone has tough gigs I guess,' said Matt, a fact he knew only too well from bitter experience.

'You're being too generous,' said Kitty. 'There were great long pauses! He just didn't have the charisma to fill that stage – not yet anyway. If he'd been playing a smaller place maybe it would have taken off, but here? In this barn? Big mistake.'

Ahmed was the least enamoured.

'It was SOOOOOO lame,' he said.

'Stand-up wasn't designed for these sort of places,' said Kitty.

'That's not always true, Kit,' said Matt and pointed out he'd seen Lee Evans and Michael McIntyre really kill on the same stage in their live DVDs.

'True,' said Kitty. 'But imagine what those shows would have been like if they'd been at the Apollo!'

'Still, think of the money,' said Rob.

11

Backstage at the Dome

As they stood up, Claire appeared.

'Mr Hart asked me to come and find you to take you backstage to meet Russel,' she said brightly.

'No, you're all right,' muttered Ahmed with a snicker. Rob stamped on his foot causing him to let out a yelp.

The girl seemed surprised that the group didn't look more excited at the invitation. In fact Rob, Ahmed and Matt had all simultaneously looked at their shoes.

'That's if you want to?' continued the girl, a little embarrassed.

'That would be great,' cut in Kitty.

'Right then, follow me,' Claire said and led them through a doorway to the side of the stage and down a corridor.

'That was the best acting I've seen all night, Kitty,' whispered Rob as they fell in behind Claire and made their way backstage.

They followed her down a long corridor, then down another at right angles to the first, down some steps, along another corridor and through a door marked 'GREEN ROOM'.

'More like the red room than the green room,' whispered Rob as they walked in. And he was right! The whole room was suffused with a murky red light and was packed to the rafters with people. People of all different shapes and sizes, and it seemed that every last one was shouting at the top of their voice to the person next to them. There was a dull, distant throb coming from some speakers and through the crowd Matt could see the dim figure of a DJ.

'This way,' said the girl as they snaked through the

vast throng until suddenly, as if they were walking through a forest, they came to a people-free clearing. There in the centre of it was the blond-haired, snaggle-toothed star of the show, Russel Perkins. For someone who'd just finished playing to 20,000 people he didn't look particularly happy.

'Russ, this is Matt Millz and his friends,' said Claire, '. . . sorry, I didn't catch your names.'

Matt held out his hand to shake the older comic's hand, but Russel didn't take him up on the offer – he just stood staring into the middle distance like he'd lost something.

'Eh? Oh, hi?' said the comedy superstar, snapping out of whatever it was that was bothering him. 'Did you enjoy the show?'

'Er . . . yes! Yes!' said Matt. 'Yes it was great! How about you?'

'Bit slow wasn't it?' said Russel, his eyes roving round the room as if he was looking for someone in particular. 'Have you seen Dickie?' he said to the girl.

'I'll see if I can find him,' she said and delved back

into the forest of people.

The four youngsters stood awkwardly staring at Russel and Russel just looked back at them and then at the half empty glass of something, which he swirled around in his hand. It was Kitty who broke the silence.

'How did you find the room?' she said.

'Er ... bad, right? I mean it's like playing an aircraft hangar,' said Russel.

'It's not exactly built for comedy, that's for sure,' said Kitty.

'That's what I said to him,' said Russel, suddenly engaged and animated. 'I told Dickie – I said I'd much rather do somewhere smaller for more nights, but they weren't having any of it ...'

'It would have been great at the Apollo – I mean it was good, don't get me wrong, but at the Apollo, although it's over three thousand people, everyone's got a good view, and they can hear every word you say ...' said Kitty.

'At the same time as each other!' chipped in Matt.

'Exactly!' said Russel, suddenly interested in these kids. 'You are spot on – sorry I didn't catch your names?'

'Oh! Sorry, yes. Kitty Hope!'

'Matt Mills, hi! Kitty's my manager,' said Matt as Kitty stuffed one of her business cards into Russel's hand.

'Manager?' said Russel studying the card. Then the penny dropped. 'Oh, I've got it! You're the kid off *The T Factor*? The one that got disqualified for being too young – that Matt Millz!'

'Yes, that's right. Mr Hart invited us along.'

Russel rolled his eyes at the mention of that name. 'Huh! Did he, yeah ... every free ticket he gives out costs me two-thirds of the ticket price.'

'That can't be right,' said Kitty. 'Surely it should come out of the promoter's allocation?'

'You'd think, right?' said Russel, intrigued by her apparent knowledge. 'Anyway, it's not that, I mean ... I don't begrudge ... I'm glad you could make it. So you're the youngest comic to raise the roof at the Apollo?' said Russel. 'What's that like?'

'I can't explain,' said Matt. 'Just very, very, very exciting.' He'd long given up trying to communicate the thrill of that special night. 'But surely you must have played it?'

'Sadly not,' said Russel. 'Dickie fell out with the management.'

'Ah,' said Kitty.

''Ello, 'ello, is someone taking my name in vain?' came a voice from behind them and a hand grabbed Russel's neck, then worked its way round to his shoulder. There was a strong whiff of pine aftershave.

'Nice one, Russ!' said Dickie Hart puffing on an e-cig. 'Started good anyway. Lost 'em a bit in the second half. Sorry about that heckler but I sorted him out.'

'Sorted him out?' said Russel.

'Had him thrown out – can't have my boy being made a fool of on his big night can we?'

'I think he was just trying to tell you to turn the sound up,' said Kitty.

Dickie peered down at her and gave her a withering look.

'Yeah well, any form of shouting is not to be encouraged.' Then he noticed Matt and the others.

'Matt! Glad you could make it. Car turn up OK?'

'Yes thanks, Mr Hart, that's some car!' said Matt, a little more star-struck at Dickie Hart than at Russel Perkins.

'Well, I thought you deserved a taste of what could be to come. This kid could have a big future, Russ, if only he could get himself some decent management.' He shot another even meaner look at Kitty, who shot a similarly aggressive one back. Then he let out a big guffaw. 'Only joking! You all right for a drink? Here, darlin'!' he called to a passing waitress. 'Get these young men a lager!'

'Aren't they a bit young?' said the waitress.

'We're fine for drinks thanks, Mr Hart,' chirped up Matt. 'We need to be getting back soon anyway, school tomorrow and all that. Thanks for the tickets and laying on the car.'

'Which part of the car did you lay on?' chipped in Rob. 'The roof or the bonnet?'

'Eh?' said Dickie. 'What's he talking about?'

'He's just very excited,' said Matt. 'We all are. Oh, I should introduce you to . . .'

'I know who this is,' said Dickie Hart with a self-satisfied grin. 'Your eleven-year-old manager.'

'That's right, I am his manager, Mr Hart,' piped

up Kitty, standing her ground.

'What work have you got in the pipeline for Matt then?' he said.

'Er ... well ... there's a possible regular gig in a pub in Sossinghurst which would be great for ...' Kitty tailed off, realising, standing as they were in the O2, how small-time it sounded.

Dickie Hart gave a dismissive snorted. 'Hmm, well, good luck,' he said. Then he leant in close again, only this time not even bothering to whisper.

'You know we'd love to look after you at Excalibur Management, Matt. We could make you a big star, just like Russel here. We have our own production company, Excalibur TV, our own publicity company, Excalibur Promotions, a film company, Excalibur Motion Pictures ... What's your friend here got apart from a laptop and an iPhone?'

'Low overheads,' said Kitty stepping between them. She couldn't believe this man was trying to poach Matt right from under her nose. Well, she wasn't standing for that.

'All your companies are taking a percentage off the top,' she continued.

'Really?' said Russel looking more than a little startled.

'Matt has representation, Mr Hart! Yes, he's had a bit of attention, lots of shows would like him on the bill, but there's no such thing as an overnight success. He needs to grow his act organically. It's a marathon – not a sprint.'

'She's got a point,' said Russel.

'Who asked you?' snapped Dickie. A spec of saliva landed on Matt's glasses.

'Sorry, Mr Hart,' said Russel, looking wounded.

'I suggest you go and sign some autographs. Do some networking.'

'Yes, yes, good idea . . .' said Russel and dived into the throng of people.

'Well, I'm on the end of a phone day or night, Matt. Call me when – I mean if – you change your mind. But don't leave it too long. Once your moment's gone, that's it. You only get one chance in this business.

Right, well, I've got some important people to meet. Glad you could make it. *Au revoir.*' With that he turned on his cuban heel and pushed through the crowd of people towards some men in suits.

'Bye!' said Matt sheepishly.

'*Auf wiedersehen,*' said Rob once he was out of earshot.

'What a prat!' said Ahmed, shaking his head in disbelief. 'Did you see the way he treated Russel? I mean, I'm no Anthony Joshua, bruv, but he needs to stand up to him.'

'He's scared,' said Kitty with a frown.

'Scared?' said Matt.

'Yes, he thinks he owes all his success to Dickie Hart and Excalibur Management, but it's the other way round.'

'Weird how no one was talking to Russ much, even though he was the whole reason they were all there . . .' said Rob.

'Yeah,' said Matt. 'It was like he was a guest at his own party!'

As they walked across the O2 forecourt to Alf and the waiting Rolls Royce, Matt reflected on the whole experience. All in all, it had been a very weird night.

12

Kitty's Master Plan

The next day after school, it was just Kitty who greeted Matt in the DMC. She was sitting at one of the old discarded desks with some A4 sheets and a calendar.

'Hi, Matt,' she said.

'Hi, Kit. Can't wait to hear the plan,' said Matt, noticing that her teeth were black from sucking the wrong end of a marker pen.

'OK,' began Kitty, with a slightly wary look in her eye. 'The first thing you should know is that *Stand-up at the Apollo* have been in touch and they want you to appear on the show.'

'YEEEESSSSSS!' cried Matt, punching the air with his fist. 'YES! Get in! Nice one!' He then sprinted round the room and slid towards Kitty on his knees coming to rest at her feet.

'*But*,' said Kitty sternly, '... I don't think you should do it!'

'WHAT?!' screamed Matt. 'What do you mean you don't think I should do it? I love that show! It's the best stand-up show on TV! I haven't missed a single episode! It's the chance of a lifetime! I must do that show!'

It was true, Matt had been an avid fan of the stand-up show since it had started three years previously, and it had not only entertained him, it had educated him too. Virtually anybody who was anybody in the world of stand-up comedy had appeared on it – from Al Murray's Pub Landlord, to Joe Lycett, Sara Pascoe and beyond. It wasn't that Matt loved every act that appeared on it – far from it. Often there were whole episodes where he felt like shouting 'Get Off!' at the TV screen – indeed sometimes he did exactly that. He almost enjoyed the acts he didn't like as much as the acts that he did. He was constantly surprised at how some acts who he'd seen on TV panel shows and hadn't been particularly impressed with were unexpectedly hilarious doing straight stand-up, while others just couldn't cut the mustard when put under the spotlight of a twenty-minute set.

He kept a list in the back of his little black book of the names of the acts he'd liked and examples of some of their best gags. By watching the show he'd started to get an idea of the sort of jokes and humour he liked and inevitably what sort of comic he hoped to become.

LIST OF COMICS AND EXAMPLES OF THEIR BEST GAGS

Tim Vine: One-armed butlers – they can take it but they can't dish it out.

Michael McIntyre: Posh hotels have a turn-down service. I had never heard of this and there was a knock at the door and a woman said 'I've come to turn down your bed' To which I said 'Well many women have in the past, why should you be any different?'

Sean Lock: I like the pope. You know that white thing on his head? If you push that down and twist it, he's full of sweets.

Jo Brand: I was not a particularly small child. I was the one who always got picked to play Bethlehem in the school nativity.

Bill Bailey: Toughest job I ever had, selling doors door-to-door.

Ricky Gervais: Where there's a will there's a relative.

Nick Helm: I needed a password eight characters long so I picked Snow White and the seven Dwarves.

Aisling Bea: What's Postman Pat called on his holidays? Pat!

Jack Dee: A sewage farm — in what way is it a farm? Is there a farm shop?

Ross Noble: How come Miss Universe is only won by people from Earth?

Josie Long: When I was a kid I asked my mum what a couple was and she said, 'Oh, two or three! And she wonders why her marriage didn't work out.

Sara Pascoe: If Adam and Eve can't make it work in Paradise, how am I gonna make it work in Lewisham?

'I know you love that show,' said Kitty, 'and listen, I want you to be on it just as much as you do, but hear me out. When you do it, and you will, we need to make sure that you are absolutely brilliant! My worry is that you're not ready for it yet.'

'But you saw them the other night – they lapped it up. And that was at the Apollo!'

'Yes, but you tailored that for *The T Factor* audience. The crowd for the *Stand-up* show are very different, less forgiving, and there'll be an expectation of you now . . .'

'But . . .!'

'AND you need to get some new gags don't you?'

'I've got loads of ideas!' said Matt.

'Ideas are not the same as tightly crafted routines and one-liners,' said Kitty. 'We need to get you match fit for that big gig and my plan, if you agree, will deliver that. My granddad Bernie—'

'Ah the great Bernie Hopestein! I wondered how long it would be before you brought him up . . .' said Matt testily, a sign of his mounting frustration.

'Bernie used to say that a career in show business is a marathon, not a sprint,' continued Kitty.

'Yes well, it seems to me like you're running in the opposite direction to the one I want to go in,' said Matt.

'Matt, just calm down for a sec and think this through properly. I'm not saying no to the Apollo, I'm saying we just put them off for the time being.'

'My nan always said "Strike while the iron is hot!" and "Make hay while the sun shines!" What if they go cold on us?'

'That's a risk we have to take. What I do know is if you do that show and bomb then it will be very hard to recover.'

Matt slumped down in one of the many old school chairs scattered throughout the dilapidated classroom and let what Kitty had said sink in. The idea of doing the Apollo show was utterly thrilling to him but he couldn't argue with her logic.

'So what you're saying is, we won't be saying no to *Stand-up at the Apollo*, just delaying it?'

'Exactly,' said Kitty.

'OK, I'm cool with that,' he said.

'Great. I'm sure you won't regret that decision . . .'

'I certainly hope not,' said Matt.

'Good, I'm glad I've got that out of the way – I've been worrying about how you'd react. So, I know you're anxious to get some more gigs booked in but I don't want you to do just any old stuff. I think it's important we have a clear aim and something to work towards. Yes?'

'Great, yes, Kit, I'm all ears,' said Matt and as he said it an image flashed into his mind – a big ear with tiny legs and hands – All Ears. He filed it away and

ALL EARS!

promised himself he'd stick it in his notebook later.

'OK, so ...' said Kitty handing Matt a clear plastic folder containing two A4 sheets held together by a paper clip. 'So what's our aim?' she said standing and pacing up and down.

'Um ... fame fortune and everything I ever dreamed of?' smiled Matt with a twinkle.

Kitty rolled her eyes. Sometimes Matt wondered if she actually had a sense of humour.

'To make you a better comedian,' said Kitty. 'Yes?'

'Yes, ma'am,' said Matt standing to attention and saluting. Kitty ignored him and pressed on with her presentation.

'So how best do we do that, given the amount of press attention you've been getting?'

'National tour of arenas finishing with two nights at Wembley Stadium?' said Matt, the more Kitty resisted his gags the more he loved bowling them back at her.

'No.'

'I was joking . . .'

'I realise that, Matt.'

'Well, try telling your face!'

Kitty ignored him and pressed on.

'Broadly the thing to avoid at this stage is overexposure . . .'

'Bit late for that isn't it? I'm everywhere!' said Matt.

'Ah yes, that's true. You've had a lot of coverage for what you did on *The T Factor*, there's interest in you, but there's a huge amount of interest in what you'll do next and believe me the knives will be out. There are certain sectors of the press that will be willing you to fail. For them it's about selling papers. They build you up just to knock you down. So we need to make sure that when you do the next big, high-profile gig, it goes as well as if not better than *The T Factor* show.'

Matt half closed his eyes and tried to imagine a gig going better than that night at the Apollo.

'Impossible ...' he said with a distant look in his eye.

'I know it seems like that now, but anyone can be brilliant on one night – the hard thing is to be consistently good, which means practice and new material.'

Matt nodded. Suddenly her seriousness was starting to make him nervous. He knew that the only reason he'd done so well on that fateful night was because of all the hard work he and Kitty had put in beforehand.

'So?'

'So ... what I'm planning is small gigs, scattered

over a number of weeks to help you build up some new gags and routines . . .'

'Small?'

'Yes. I've persuaded Mick, the landlord of the Rose and Crown in Sossinghurst, to let you do every other Monday.'

'Hmm. Not exactly Wembley Stadium . . .' mused Matt.

'No, but it's a start. Plus I've agreed to Mr P's idea to organise a gig at the school, for Children In Need.'

'Great,' said Matt nodding.

'And . . .' Kitty hesitated.

'And what?' said Matt suspiciously.

'. . . we're going back to the Cavendish Hotel in Frittledean!'

'Woah!' said Matt, remembering the night before *The T Factor*, when he'd played there and died on his elbow – he'd been pretty much booed off.

'That hasn't exactly been lucky for me. It's a graveyard,' he complained.

'That was then,' said Kitty, taking control. 'The

fact is it's well set up as a venue, Barry the manager is keen to make it work and he's said he'll make sure there are no stag or hen parties this time.' Matt nodded. He couldn't really argue with that.

'For both gigs I'll put a bill together of some of my other acts.'

'Neil?'

'Yes, Neil will be one of them – he's working on a new routine and wants to branch out into rap . . .'

Matt raised an eyebrow. He was curious to see how a rap routine would go down in rural Frittledean. What would he be rapping about, he wondered. How busy the post office is on a Tuesday because it's pension day? This time he couldn't resist it – he reached for his notebook and jotted the idea down as Kitty continued to outline the shape of these new gigs.

'I've got another couple of acts I'm looking at too – an older comic called Bobby Bath—'

'Bobby? No, I don't think I've heard of him,' said Matt shaking his head. 'Was he on one of the DVDs you sent me?'

'Bobby was big back in the seventies but not for long. It's an odd one really because I think he's still really funny.'

'That's good enough for me,' said Matt.

'I've also discovered a new impressionist . . .'

'Love impressionists!' said Matt. 'What's his name?'

'*Her* name is Alex. She's in year nine at St Winifred's.'

St Winifred's was the private school up the road. Matt had seen the kids about in their purple blazers.

'A girl, eh?' he said.

'Yes – is that so strange?' said Kitty giving him a withering look. 'Some of the greatest comedians of all time have been women, thank you very much.'

'I stand corrected,' said Matt.

'Anyway,' said Kitty, 'I'm organising a get-together on Friday after school so you can all get to know each other. I hope you'll be able to make it,' she said.

Matt opened the envelope she handed him. It was an invitation.

INVITATION

'Great,' he said, tucking it into his blazer pocket.

'OK, any questions?' she said.

'Yeah, when's my first gig?!' said Matt impatiently.

'A week on Monday – can you wait twelve days?'

'Just about!' said Matt.

'Oh, and Matt?' said his eleven-year-old comedy manager.

'Yes?' said Matt.

'Thanks for trusting me.'

Matt shrugged. 'You'd better be right, Kit, cos' if you're not, with regret, you will be fired!'

*

That evening when Matt got home, Ian handed him a Jiffy bag with his name on it.

'Kitty Hope dropped this round for you,' he said. 'Looks like it might be some more DVDs.'

Matt tore open the Jiffy bag – Ian was right. Inside was a DVD with the words 'Some of the Greatest Comedians of All Time' written on it in marker pen in Kitty's handwriting.

'Shall we have a watch later on?' said Ian. 'Guess what I'm up to tomorrow night?'

'Showing someone round a one-bedroom flat and trying to convince them it's a castle?' ventured Matt.

'Ha, no. You'll never guess, so I'll tell you. I'm only getting the band back together!'

'You're kidding,' laughed Matt.

'No, the original line-up of Dead Toys – last gig 1978 – together at last! Jim the bass player's wife's left him so he's got the house to himself. He's only in Bromley. Can't wait!'

After the family had eaten, Matt and Ian sat down in front of the TV and Matt slipped the DVD into the player and loaded it up. It was divided into chapter headings each with the name of a different comedian. A different *female* comedian.

Jo Brand, Joan Rivers, French and Saunders, Victoria Wood, Sara Pascoe, Bridget Christie, Sarah Millican ... the list went on. Matt smiled to himself – they certainly broke the mould when they made his manager. He then spent the next hour and a half laughing his socks off. Kitty Hope had made her point in the best way she possibly could, through laughter.

JO BRAND FACT FILE

Ex-psychiatric nurse turned comic.

Style – Deadpan one-liners, often self-deprecatory.

Influences – Linda Smith, voted wittiest person on Radio 4 a few years ago. Victoria Wood. Sue Townsend, author The Secret Diary of Adrian Mole, Aged $13\frac{3}{4}$, The Queen and I (in which the Royals are relocated to a council estate).

Gag – I am the one in my family who does all the driving, because my husband never learnt to drive ... in my opinion.

Shows – Saturday Live, Jo Brand Through the Cake Hole, Have I Got News For You, The Great British Bake Off, An Extra Slice.

BRIDGET CHRISTIE FACT FILE

Winner Foster's Comedy Award, Edinburgh Festival 2013.

Style – Quirky, irreverent, ingenious political satire often featuring cleverly structured set pieces.

Influences – Laurel and Hardy, Jo Brand, Mark Thomas, Josie Long, Roseanne Barr, Lucille Ball.

Gag – I asked all my black and minority – ethnic friends if they thought I was racist or not, and they both said that I wasn't.

Show – Stand Up For Her (Live DVD, 2010).

SARA PASCOE FACT FILE

Style – Slightly surreal, often political.

Shows – TV: Mock The Week, LIVE: Animals; Lads, Lads, Lads.

Influences – Tina Fey, Noel Fielding, Josie Long, Bridget Christie.

Gag – You can't lose a homing pigeon; if your homing pigeon doesn't come back, then what you've lost is a pigeon.

VICTORIA WOOD FACT FILE
(1953 – 2016)

Style – Observational stand-up, quintessentially British. Also performed her own hilarious songs on the piano.

Influences – Morecambe and Wise (TV Double Act 1970s), Joyce Grenfell.

Shows – First Break was TV talent show New Faces 1974, Victoria Wood as seen on TV (sketch series with Julie Walters 1985-7), An Audience With Victoria Wood 1988.

Gag – When I told jokes about cystitis, people would write in and say, 'I've got cystitis and it isn't funny,' so I would reply, 'Well, send it back and ask for one that is.'

JOAN RIVERS FACT FILE
(1933-2014)

Style – Wisecracking outrageous one-liners, often autobiographical, usually near the knuckle.

Influences — Lenny Bruce, Phyllis Diller.

Gag — I've had so much plastic surgery, when I die they will donate my body to Tupperware.

Shows — DVD: Joan Rivers (Still A) Live. At The London Palladium Allegedly (15)

13

Bath from the Past

'Where's your plus-one, bruv?' said Ahmed as Matt arrived at the DMC for Kitty's party that Friday after school. She'd put some balloons up, pushed some desks together and covered them with throwaway paper tablecloths. There were slices of pizza, crisps, nuts, Wotsits, Hula Hoops, some sausage rolls – the usual party fare. Matt had racked his brains but hadn't managed to come up with a 'plus-one'. He looked across at Rob who of course was with Magda, who looked great, then back at Ahmed.

'Same place as yours I think, Ahmed,' he said.

'Ah well, that's where you're wrong,' said Ahmed

with a smile. 'I've asked Janine so ... she should be here any minute.'

A deep croaky voice came from somewhere above him. 'Hi, Matt,' it said. Matt turned to see Neil Trottman.

'Wow! Neil! How you doing?' Matt hadn't seen Neil for a week and was surprised at the change in him.

He had a couple of spots on his chin, a dark fuzz of hair on his top lip and he appeared to Matt to be a couple of inches taller.

'Pretty good, you know ...' croaked Neil.

'How are the routines coming along? What are you working on?' asked Matt.

'Neil's not doing the body popping so much now,' said Kitty, handing Matt a plastic tumbler of Coke and a paper plate with a slice of pizza on it.

'Kitty's right,' croaked Neil. 'I'm more interested in my music – well, rapping. My mum bought me some decks and I've been sampling stuff and mixing it down on my computer, so ...'

'Hmm, that's good to hear,' said Matt.

'Yes,' said Kitty. 'We always knew Neil wouldn't be able to do that same act once he got ... er ... a bit bigger ... It's just come along a little sooner than we thought.'

'It's really cool stuff,' came a girl's voice from behind him. The voice belonged to a very pretty girl with dark hair. She put her arm through Neil's and beamed up at him. Neil blushed a deep purple colour.

'Who's this then, Neil? Aren't you going to introduce us ...?' said Matt taking a closer look at the girl – she was really very pretty indeed.

'Oh, this is my girlfriend, Aiesha,' said Neil. Matt was stunned.

'Girlfriend?' he thought. 'Girlfriend?!' First Rob and now here was Neil, a good two years younger than him.

'Where's my girlfriend?' he thought to himself. 'I'm the one who's been on TV!'

Actually, he'd had quite a lot of interest from

girls since *The T Factor* – but he hadn't encouraged anything to develop because he was so wrapped up in his so-called comedy career.

'Great,' said Matt, limply shaking the girl's hand. 'Nice to meet you, Aiesha.'

'Is this it?' asked Aiesha grumpily. 'I mean is this everyone that's coming along?'

'Not quite …' said Kitty. 'Unfortunately Alex couldn't make it but there is one more person I'd like you all to meet. I don't know where he's got to – he should be here by now …'

Just then the door burst open and in came a man wearing a leather biker jacket and a motorcycle helmet that completely obscured his face.

'Sorry I'm late, Kit,' came a voice with a thick northern accent from inside the helmet. 'But I won the lottery this morning and had to spend the money before the wife found it. It's surprising how much ten quid will buy you in Marks and Spencer's isn't it? I got two whole sandwiches and a packet of crisps!'

The man put his hands up to the helmet and tried

to take it off his head but it wouldn't budge. 'Give us a hand getting this off will you, luv?'

He bent his head down and Kitty pulled at the motorcycle helmet but it appeared to be stuck fast.

'It's no use, it's stuck again,' she said

'You'd better see if you can get some butter,' said the man, his arms flailing about as if he was about to lose his balance.

'Here, let me try,' said Matt nudging Kitty out of the way. He gave the helmet an almighty wrench. Suddenly it released its grip on the man's head, causing Matt to stagger back with the helmet in his hands while the man went the other way, crashing into the desks laden with food and drink, knocking cups, snacks and paper plates flying and ending up sitting on the floor.

'For my next trick!' joked Rob.

'Sorry about that,' said the man straightening himself up. 'I wouldn't mind – but I haven't even got a motorbike! My bobble hat's in the wash!'

It was only now that Matt was able to get a good

look at the new arrival. He was an older man – old enough to be Matt's grandad – tall, skinny, with wispy grey hair framing big wet, slightly bloodshot eyes, and uncommonly big eyelashes, so he almost had the appearance of a doll. It struck Matt that there was something kind and well ... *funny* about him.

'Matt?' said Kitty. 'I'd like you to meet The Kitty Hope Comedy Agency's latest signing – Bobby Bath!'

'Hello, son! Love your work!' said Bobby, dusting himself off and shaking Matt by the hand.

'Bobby . . .?'

'Bath! Bath's the name, comedy's the game – or it was. What's the phrase all you kids use? "Back in the day?" Yes, that's it. Back in the day, although to be honest it was mainly nights. Back in the nights – no, doesn't quite work that, does it?' chortled Bobby.

Matt laughed. There was something *really* funny about this guy.

Matt wanted to say, 'What the heck is an old guy like you doing at a comedy agency being run by an eleven-year-old girl?' but he didn't want to sound rude. However his face must have said it for him.

'Now, I know what you're thinking . . .' grinned Bobby, helping himself to a slice of pizza. 'What's an old guy like me doing being looked after by a schoolgirl?'

'Ha! You're a mind reader as well as being a comic then?' said Matt.

'Ha ha! No, not quite. Believe me if I was able to see into the future I'd probably never have become a comedian in the first place. No, well, I'm here because – ha! If I'm honest this little wonder was the only one who was interested! Ha ha!' Bobby rolled those big eyes of his and laughed and Matt, Rob, Magda, Neil, Aiesha and Kitty couldn't help but laugh along with him. Kitty cut in to explain.

'Bobby's being modest, as usual. He was a huge star back in the seventies . . .'

'And now it's fizzled out!' laughed Bobby.

'What have I told you about being positive?' said Kitty with a frown.

'Ooops! pardon me!' said Bobby, putting on a mock serious face. 'No, my star hasn't fizzled out, it's crashed into my house and burnt it down!'

'Bobby, please!' snapped Kitty, before trying to continue filling Matt and the others in on the real facts.

'Bobby had a lot of success early on in his career but that sort of success is always very difficult to maintain ...'

'Particularly if your act stinks!' joked Bobby again, derailing Kitty's little speech. Unperturbed she pressed on.

'... so in recent years – how shall I put it ...'

'No one would touch me with a bargepole?' interjected Bobby. 'I'm about as popular as Jimmy Carr's tax bill. I'm as welcome as a cold sore at a singles night, as a fart in a lift. For me to get booked on a show all the other comedians in the world would have to die from a mystery virus that only killed funny comedians!'

They were all laughing helplessly again. 'This guy was really funny,' thought Matt.

'As I was trying to say ...' said Kitty, regaining her composure, 'Bobby's style of humour went out of fashion a bit ...'

'Yes, along with tuberculosis and smallpox!' joked Bobby.

'But I happen to think that you're either funny or you're not and as you can see Bobby Bath is still very funny!'

'I'll drink to that,' said Matt, taking a swig from his tumbler of Coke.

'Oh well, thanks, luv,' said Bobby dropping the gags for a moment. 'I try, you know, and you're right, it's been a chequered career at best – and it's not been easy, particularly since my Sarah died – but the fact is I do think I'm pretty good at what I do, and I love to make people laff so . . .' His voice tailed off. There was a moment of silence, not uncomfortable but sweet and affecting. Matt could feel a lump in his throat.

'Besides . . .' Bobby continued, 'I'm too old to try anything else now. What other job could I do with this face?' he said with a big grin. 'If you saw these eyes at the window at the drive-through McDonalds, you might think twice about having the Filet-O-Fish!'

They all laughed again.

'You should keep that in,' said Matt. 'That's really funny.'

'Thank you – I will! Cheers!'

'So how come you found out about Kitty?' said Rob.

'Oh! Well, my granddaughter's in her class. I'd seen Matt on the talent thingy and she told me about her, so I thought what have I got to lose? I'll try anything once, well twice if it's got chocolate on – sorry, I can't help it, I have to make a joke about everything. Annoys the hell out of my wife . . . Sorry . . . it did . . .' He tailed off again and looked at the floor. 'Eee, it's taking some getting used to . . .'

'When did your wife pass away, Bobby?' asked Magda taking his hand to comfort him.

'1974! Ha ha!' said Bobby with a grin. 'Ha! Yes, the same year as my tailor! I can't help myself, sorry! Everything's up for grabs! Eighty-two years old and still playing! Right, is there any more of that pizza? I'm starving!'

For the next hour or so the gang stood around

chatting, drinking and eating and catching up on the gossip as Kitty darted about refilling glasses and plates. Matt made a beeline straight for Bobby. He couldn't wait to hear his story.

'I was on *Op Knocks*!'

'Op what?' said Matt.

'*Opportunity Knocks* – it was a talent show back in the seventies. It was massive at the time, upwards of twenty million viewers – the equivalent of your *T Factor*, and I won. Yeah, on that show if you won you came back the following week. Well, I kept winning and went back thirteen weeks in a row, which was great for my profile. I couldn't go anywhere without someone shouting my name or bugging me for an autograph, but after thirteen weeks I'd pretty much used up all me material. Suddenly everybody wanted me. Clubs that in years past had not even returned my calls were phoning me up to book me. I had more work than I knew what to do with. In those days there were a lot of variety shows on TV where you could do five minutes and get a big cheque at the end of it. Well, I couldn't keep up with the demand – you know how difficult it is to come up with new jokes.'

Matt nodded.

'What I needed to do was work on new material but there just wasn't time. My agent was telling me I should make the most of my moment in the sun. Anyway, ITV offered me a twelve-week TV series and, well, I had two young kids and a wife to support so I agreed, of course I did – I signed straight on the dotted – but I had no idea what I were going to do, like.'

'So what happened?' said Matt.

'Well, they got writers in didn't they?'

'They?' queried Matt.

'The TV company, they got writers in but it was all stock gags . . .'

'Stock gags?'

'Yeah, you know, gags that any bloomin' comic could tell – you know "Man walks into a pub", that sorta thing. They were funny, but they didn't sound like ME! And it were me that the audience watching

Opportunity Knocks had voted for every week for thirteen weeks. So the show was mainly stock gags, and a few that I'd got round to writing, padded out with guest acts – you know, singers, dancers, a magician and sketches. Unfunny sketches! Then at the end I'd finish on a song. A song! Me! Ha! I mean I can hold a tune but it's not a pretty voice by any means – I'm no Val Doonican . . .'

'Who?'

'Val D . . . never mind! The show was cancelled after one series.'

'What did you do then?' asked Matt.

'What any comic does when he's run out of jokes – I did a game show! *Bobby Bath's Swing Time*,' said Bobby, shaking his head. 'Well, my heart just wasn't in it. It was a stupid idea – to start with no one played golf in those days. It was just posh people in fancy clubs. The ratings were terrible from the start and never picked up. The show was cancelled half way through the first series. As we both know, you're only as good as your last show. Pretty quickly after that the phone stopped ringing and it hasn't rung much since to be honest, ha ha! To add insult to injury, when I went back to the clubs, they'd all heard it before. It was a relief really, it meant I could go back to stand-up. I developed the act and it was going great guns – then the world changed. All you alternatives came in . . .'

'Alternatives?' said Matt.

'The alternative comics came in – lads like that Ben Elton and Rik Mayall, Dawn French and Jennifer Saunders. They came in and us lot looked like dinosaurs, ha ha!' He gave a wry chuckle. 'So now I do the odd club, an after-dinner speech here and there, benefit nights . . . Oh yes, I do my share of charity work – any excuse to get back on stage – because I still feel funny! I'm still that bloke who won *Opportunity Knocks* – well, inside anyway.'

'That's very honest, Bobby, I appreciate it,' said Matt.

'A warning from the past! Remember, it's a marathon not a sprint!' said Bobby.

'Well, it's really good to meet you,' said Matt.

'Likewise!' said Bobby. 'Can't wait to work with you.'

'You're funny – for a grandad!' said Ahmed, gatecrashing their chat.

'I'll take that as a compliment, my young friend.' said Bobby, forcing a laugh.

'No sign of Janine then?' said Matt returning the smug smile he'd got off Ahmed earlier.

'Nah. Just my luck. No sign of Amelia Wong either!'

That night after Kit's party, Matt sat squinting at his smartphone, watching a grainy image on YouTube. There was a brief title sequence – some cheesy music and then an equally cheesy voice.

'Ladies and gentlemen, it's *Bath Time*!' and suddenly there he was – it was Bobby! Oh sure, he looked different, younger – he must only have been in his forties but you couldn't mistake that face.

'All right everyone?' said Bobby to the audience with a grin.

'Bath?' they all shouted back.

'No thanks, I had one this morning!' said Bobby, and he was away, reeling off gags and pulling faces, falling over – it was hilarious and although it was over forty years ago, it still seemed really fresh to Matt. Matt clicked on another link – *Bobby Bath's Swing Time*! This time Bobby – a bit older now, some of his hair was going and he'd filled out in the face and round the middle – was hosting a weird quiz about golf, and it wasn't at all funny. In fact it was kind of cringey. Bobby's body language had changed – he was no longer bouncing about like a puppy. He looked, well, scared, and fear is never funny.

'It's a sprint, not a marathon,' he muttered to himself.

14

The Road to Sossinghusrt

'Blimey, some of these lanes are tiny,' said Ian, swerving to avoid a sheep that was crossing the road. 'You couldn't have booked a venue more off the beaten track, Kitty!' He looked in his rear-view mirror at Kitty sat on the back seat of the Astra next to Neil.

'The Apollo it ain't!' he added, nudging Matt to try and get a laugh out of him, but Matt was lost in his own world. In his mind he was already at the gig and having the night of his life, rolling out gags, making stuff up on the spot and doing twice as long as he was booked for because the laughs were lasting twice as long. Then there was the encore, then the second encore . . .

It had been over two weeks since he'd last been on stage and he'd spent that time jotting down ideas for gags and running them in front of Kitty in the DMC. He'd worked up a set list that consisted of some of this new stuff, but if he was honest he planned to rely a fair bit on the tried-and-tested bits he'd done on *The T Factor* to get the audience on his side.

SET LIST
Old.

Tongue out — looking young — Rusk/
bedtime
Voucher for Mothercare
Mention T Factor — Simon/
Amanda gags / fake backstory/
David Wallnuts / voting face
Nan mix-ups (hair in knitting!)

'BRAKE!' screamed Kitty from the back seat of the Astra. Ian slammed his foot down hard, the car swerved to the left slightly, then there was a high-pitched squeal as the wheels locked and the back end swung round, coming to a halt at right angles to the hedge, blocking the road, and five centimetres away from a policeman.

'You seem to be in a hurry, sir!' said the policeman 'Oh, it's you, Matt!'

'Is there some problem, officer?' said Ian. 'It's just that Matt here needs to get to the Rose and Crown for a gig!'

'I'm fully aware of Matt's engagement – that's what I'm doing here . . .' said the policeman.

'Glad to hear you're still a fan,' said Matt with a cheeky grin.

'If you take a look a little further down the road,' continued the policeman, ignoring Matt's interjection, 'you'll see that you are not the only ones heading for the venue.'

Matt, Ian and Kitty stuck their heads out of the windows and, sure enough, there was a huge queue of cars snaking ahead and disappearing round a bend in the road.

'That queue goes on for three miles,' said the copper. 'And it's presenting something of a hazard!'

'I thought this was supposed to be low-profile gig?' said Matt looking back at Kitty.

'I saw it in the *Daily Star* this morning!' piped up Neil.

'Indeed, and I saw it on the breakfast news with that new bloke who's taken over from Quentin Tubbs, whose name escapes me . . .'

'Ahem!' coughed Ian. 'So what's the plan, officer?' he said.

'Well, I'm afraid you'll just have to wait in line like everybody else. Unfortunately there's only one route to the pub and that happens to be the same route back. Their car park takes only fifteen cars, so we do have what could be described as a bit of a build-up!'

'It's gridlock!' said Matt, stepping out of the car and walking a couple of yards up the line. Just then there was another screech of tyres and an almighty bump as a car came flying round the corner and right into the back of Ian's precious Astra.

'Oi! Watch where you're going!' he said jumping out of the car and running round the back to inspect the damage.

'Sorry, mate, I didn't see you! Not sure about your road positioning either! Do you normally park across a country lane?' said the driver of the other car, a burly man in his mid fifties with a broken nose and hands like bunches of sausages.

'You were going far too fast, mate!' said Ian,

taking out his mobile phone and photographing the damage. 'That's gonna cost a fortune,' he said shaking his head.

'It's just a scratch!' said the other driver. 'A little bit of polish and it'll be right as rain!'

'No, mate,' said Ian, 'the Astra bumper comes as a single unit – they'll have to replace the whole lot . . .'

'Gentlemen, please, if you could just swap details, all this will be settled by your respective insurance companies. In the meantime we need to work out a way to get young Matt here to his engagement . . .' said the police officer.

'Eh? Hang on!' said the bloke squinting past Ian and clocking Matt for the first time. 'You mean . . . that's Matt Millz's car?'

Ian nodded.

'You mean, the actual car that Matt Millz is travelling in?'

'Yeah,' said Ian. 'I'm his stepdad.'

'I knew it! I've seen you in the paper!' the bloke exclaimed.

Ian nodded again – by now he was all too familiar with this routine.

Unfortunately the bloke had also clocked Matt. 'I don't believe it!'

'Uh-oh!' said Ian and gestured to Matt to get back in the car.

'Do your windows up and lock the doors,' said Ian quietly, getting back into the driver's seat.

'Girls! Girls!' the bloke shouted through the window of his car – it's him! It's Matt Millz!'

There came another squeal, and this time it wasn't tyres. The back doors of the other car were flung open and out got identical-twin girls who looked about eight or nine.

'MATT!' they screamed in unison. 'Matt Millz!'

Unfortunately, thanks to two of the loudest voices in Kent, their secret was out. There was a series of clicks and thuds as the message travelled up the line of cars and their occupants got out and ran towards the Astra.

'Ian?' said Kitty quietly from the back seat. 'Do

you think you'd be able to turn the car round?'

'Well, it'll be a job and a half . . .' said Ian.

The policeman tried to stop the approaching hordes from getting too close, but there was no reasoning with them. They were like a herd of wildebeest charging across the Serengeti. Pretty quickly the policeman found himself sitting in a ditch at the side of the road.

'Backup needed in Sossinghurst!' he barked into his radio.

'Sossinghurst? Where the 'eck's that?' crackled the radio in reply.

'Everyone get back in their cars please,' said the policeman, having extricated himself from the ditch. No one took any notice. They swarmed around the Astra like bees round a bag of wet Haribos, like Kim Kardashian round a Gucci handbag. Suddenly they were rocking the car back and forth.

'Yikes!' shouted Matt.

'This is going to do wonders for my suspension!' yelled Ian. Suddenly there was a thud from above.

'They're on the roof!' shouted Kitty.

'I'm frightened!' yelled Neil – for all his height he was just ten years old.

Then someone came sprawling across the bonnet, his face pressed against the windscreen and with a wild look in his eyes. A face that to Matt seemed vaguely familiar – bald with glasses but with a very broad flat nose. Then an arm hooked round the man's neck from behind. The man let out a gurgling noise and went cross-eyed. As the arm pulled him away from the glass, his nose sprung back into place and it became clear just who he was.

'Blimey, it's the head!' exclaimed Matt. 'It's Mr Pavey!'

'He's gone loco,' said Ian with a nervous chuckle.

Suddenly a high-pitched squeal cut through the air followed by the distorted voice of the policeman.

'Get back in your vehicles now!'

Matt looked out of the back window. The police officer was standing on the roof of the car behind with a megaphone raised to his lips.

'Anyone not in their cars after I count to five will be arrested,' he continued. 'One ... two ...'

There was a panicked scurry of feet and the clunks of doors being slammed shut, and by the time he had got to three the crowd were all back in their vehicles. The police officer let out a weary sigh as he climbed back on to the road.

'What happens now?' said Ian, winding his window down and poking his head out.

'Well, there's no way your concert—'

'Gig!' chipped in Matt.

'Gig . . . can go ahead. As you can see it's a health and safety nightmare.'

Matt, Kitty and Neil groaned in unison.

'But I've waited so long to do this,' pleaded Matt, knowing that he would have to wait almost another full week for his next chance to strut his stuff.

The policeman shrugged and once again brought the megaphone up to his lips.

'The gig has been cancelled!' he roared. A few of the cars started honking their horns. The policeman then walked back along the line of cars and started the slow process of backing them up.

'Sorry, Matt, this was my fault,' said Kitty as they reversed slowly back down the lane. 'I should have restricted the numbers, made sure that only a select few knew about it.'

Matt sighed, then he started laughing.

'What are you laughing at?' said Kitty grumpily.

'Ha ha! Look at the windscreen!' said Matt barely able to speak for laughing. They all looked, and there on the windscreen was a greasy imprint of Mr Pavey's face. The entire car erupted in laughter.

Matt felt a sharp buzz from inside his jacket which meant he'd got a text. He fished out his phone and checked the message.

'Gig cancelled? Someone messed up big time. Call me.' It was from Dickie Hart at Excalibur Management.

15

Return to Frittledean

Matt took the cancellation of the Sossinghurst gig pretty badly. He'd been looking forward to it with almost a hunger. Oh sure, he'd gone to school every day like any normal twelve-year-old, he'd sat in his lessons and some of the time he'd even looked like he was paying attention, but his mind was elsewhere.

Sometimes he'd be on stage at London's Comedy Store, rubbing shoulders with his heroes – bumping in to Eddie Odillo, comparing set lists with Michael McIntyre and John Bishop or just chatting about why a joke did or didn't work with the floppy-collared loon Harry Hill. Sometimes he'd be at the

Apollo or the Palladium, other times he'd imagine how the cancelled Sossinghurst gig might have gone.

Over the next week the crowd outside his house had gradually dwindled. There were still a couple of regulars but they lived two doors down, so it wasn't a huge journey for them, plus the ever-faithful Gary and his anorak, taking his nightly selfie. He'd almost become one of the family. A couple of times Matt's mum had taken him out a cup of tea, and once, when it had been raining he'd even come in for Sunday lunch. Apart from the odd selfie or autograph, Matt's day-to-day life had started to get pretty much back to normal. Although the paps and journalists had been a real pain when they'd first pitched up on his doorstep, Matt knew that they were an indicator of how popular he was. He started to worry that maybe his moment in the sun had been and gone.

'The Frittledean gig is going to be a real test,' he said to himself as he pulled on his stage suit and brushed that famous quiff.

*

They'd arranged to meet in the car park at the back of Greggs. As Matt rounded the corner he could see them all standing there – Neil with a wicked afro and Nike tracksuit, little Kitty in her black mac, and a new girl he hadn't met before – she was tall with dark hair, kind of kooky-looking. Her face lit up as Matt arrived.

'Hi, Matt,' said Kitty. 'This is Alex. She's on the bill!'

'Great!' said Matt, shaking Alex by the hand and looking her straight in the eye. 'Hi, I'm Matt. What do you do?' he said.

'I'm an impressionist,' she said with a nervous laugh.

'Oh, so *who* do you do would be a better question.'

'I guess,' replied Alex. 'You know, I do Taylor Swift, I do Miley Cyrus, um—'

'Alex does a great Theresa March!' chipped in Kitty.

'What we need is strong and stable government!' said Alex, suddenly adopting the voice and mannerisms of the prime minister.

'Wow!' said Matt. 'That's spooky!'

'She's good, isn't she?' said Bobby Bath wandering in to join them.

'Hi, Bobby!' said Matt, tearing himself away from Alex for a moment. 'I didn't know you were on the bill.'

'No, son, not this time. I'm a little rusty still and besides, it's not really my crowd. No, I like to see the room before I play a gig. I thought I'd sit this one out and case the joint, you know, see how it plays out. I'm looking forward to seeing your set though. Have you got much new stuff?'

Matt looked surprised – he hadn't expected that question.

'I've got a few bits I want to try, but I'm going to have to rely a fair bit on the tried-and-tested, play it safe,' he replied. Alex nodded in agreement, hanging on Matt's every word.

Bobby pulled a face.

'What's up?' asked Matt, a little puzzled.

'Oh, nothing,' said Bobby.

'Come on, Bobby, I saw that face ...'

'It's nothing, Matt. I've had a lot of trouble with my teeth – I've got a loose filling and it gives me a bit of jip. I don't know why the dentist gave me a filling there in the first place!' said Bobby.

'Why's that?' said Alex.

'I've got false teeth!' laughed Bobby.

'Is that a new gag?' chuckled Matt.

'It is now,' laughed Bobby.

'I'll write it down for you,' said Matt, reaching for his little book.

JOKES FOR BOBBY
Filling in my false teeth

'What's this, the Adams Family?' boomed a voice from across the road.

They all turned as one to see Mr Gillingham

leaning out of the window of his battered old Volkswagen Beetle.

Matt blinked and took a mental snapshot of the scene – there he was in his sharp suit, little Kitty with her big glasses, and then there was tall, bald pensioner Bobby, Neil with his afro, and the slightly kooky-looking Alex. Mr G was right – they did look a bit of a weird bunch!

With a clunk and a grinding of gears, Mr Gillingham steered the car into the car park.

'You'd better get in,' he said.

'Eh?' said Matt.

'Gillingham Cars at your service,' said the big man with a grin.

'I knew Mr Gillingham lived in Frittledean and so I asked him if he'd very kindly give us a lift,' said Kitty.

'What? All of us? In that thing?' said Matt.

Bobby laughed. 'He only rides in Mercs and limos now you know, Kit!'

'It'll be fine,' said Kitty. 'Now stop dawdling and get in the car!'

It was pretty cramped in the back of the VW. Bobby took the front seat but for the entire journey Matt had to put up with Neil Trottman on his lap and he was a lot bigger now – he seemed to be growing taller every day. Every time they went round a corner Matt's face got pushed up against the window, which was streaming with condensation. His right leg not only went to sleep, it started snoring.

When they arrived at the Cavendish, they were met by the owner Barry Wonsall and his wife Tanya.

'Pleased to have you back!' said Barry shaking Matt warmly by the hand.

'It's an honour,' said Tanya with a curtsey.

'Don't be daft, Tan, he's been on TV once. He's not royalty,' tutted Barry.

'Will you be singing for us tonight, Tanya?' said Matt, turning on the charm. Tanya shuddered and shook her head. The memory of the last time she'd taken the stage was still fresh in her mind. 'No,' she said. 'No, I've put all that behind me.'

'Same drill as last time,' said Barry. 'Only this time I've not allowed any stag dos in. You're quite a draw, Matt! We could have sold it out ten times over, so fingers crossed we're all in for a good night. Tanya will show you backstage. Do you fancy a drink?'

'I'll have a Coke please,' said Matt. How things had changed! Last time he'd been there he'd had to pay for his own drinks. 'And Alex and Neil will have . . .?' he continued.

'Oh! That's sweet. I'll have a Coke too please, Mr Wonsall,' said Alex.

'Just tap water for me,' said Neil. Barry nodded.

'This way then,' said Tanya leading them up the steps towards the venue.

As they entered the function room where the gig was actually being held, Matt flinched as he remembered what had gone on that fateful night just three weeks earlier. The crowd had been drunk and rowdy, he'd been unable to control them and his act had lasted no more than a couple of minutes.

That was of course before he'd done *The T Factor*, before he'd got a name for himself, and before he knew what he was doing. He wasn't an inexperienced hopeful any more – no, in his mind he was returning a conquering hero. 'Well, there's no way it could be as bad as last time,' he muttered to himself.

Neil was on first and really got the crowd going. He did the dance routine that had bought him the top prize in the school talent contest, and another one to a Michael Jackson number which softened the crowd up. Then he went into his new rap, all about being a kid and having to do what you're told. Not only was it a really good track, it was funny too.

NEIL'S RAP

Hey people there's something that I
    wanna say to you,
My parents always tellin' me just what I
    gotta do.
If you think I look weird from my head
    to my toes
That's because my mum chooses all of my
    clothes.
I got no money, too young for a job
'cept round the house when my dad calls
    me a slob.
Then I'm hanging with my mandem
    feeling fine
Which is cool but I gotta be in bed by
    nine.
If they really think that being in bed is so
    cool,

How come early next morning it's time
    for school?
I say 'Hey back off, and what's the fuss?'
Next thing I know I'm waiting for that
    bus.
Now don't get me wrong school ain't all
    bad
But it ain't the best time that I ever had.
The food for a start – dinner ladies don't
    get tips
'Specially since they started serving salad
    'stead of chips!

I get it that we got to learn to read and
    write
But so many of the lessons well, they give
    me a fright.
What's the point of maths? I hate to be a
    traitor
But I can do all that on my calculator!
French vocabulary really makes me

groan!

If I need to know a word there's an app
     on my phone!

And I really don't wish to sound like a
     jerk

But when we're workin' all day what's
     with the homework?

I'd really like to make a takeover bid

'Coz it ain't much fun just bein' a kid!

Then he went straight into another rap which didn't go so well. He wasn't quite as on top of the words as the first one – in fact at one point he seemed to forget them completely and went into a bit of the first dance routine to cover. He didn't quite finish on the high that he'd hoped for, but there was a really strong round of applause as he finished going into his trademark splits – then he jumped up and took a bow.

'Well done, Neil!' said Kitty handing him a tall glass of iced water and a towel to dry the sweat from his face. 'The new rap was brilliant!' She seemed almost as excited as he was.

'Yeah, I was really pleased with that. I completely lost it in the second one though,' he said laughing, then taking a long guzzle from his glass of tap water. Matt could tell he was buzzing with adrenaline and longed for that feeling himself.

'Yes but you kept going,' said Kitty reassuringly. 'That's the main thing . . .'

'She's right,' chipped in Matt, patting Neil on the back. 'I don't think the audience even noticed.'

'That's as maybe, but I did,' said Neil.

'Well, you won't forget it next time,' said Bobby joining the throng, clutching a pint of beer. 'Honestly, Neil, that were great. I don't know where you get the energy!'

'I'll have to show you sometime,' laughed Neil.

'I'd love that,' exclaimed Bobby. 'And I'm not joking. I'll definitely be taking you up on that offer!'

'The old-age pensioner's rap,' laughed Matt.

'The old-age pensioner's rap – like it,' said Bobby.

'I'm having that!'

'Be my guest,' said Matt.

'That's just it, Neil,' said Kitty. 'That's the whole point of these try-out gigs – to run some new stuff!'

At that point Matt looked down at his set list and felt a little concerned. New stuff? He had a couple of new bits, but they weren't fully formed routines.

Alex was up next. She was even more inexperienced than Matt and Neil and it kind of showed. She was good at the impressions for sure – her Adele, her Amelia Wong, Haley Wallaby, and of course her Theresa March were all spot on – but the gags weren't great and she looked nervous. After an initial few laughs the audience, sensing her lack of confidence, started to get restless. One or two of them took their phones out and checked their emails, others started chatting. Towards the end of her set there was a steady drift of punters to the bar.

Sadly Alex's response was to break one of the cardinal rules of stand-up comedy – she sped up. Matt looked over at Kitty who was mouthing the words 'Slow down!' at her, but poor Alex clearly couldn't see anything beyond the spotlight. She managed to do ten minutes of material in about two.

There was a smattering of polite applause as she signed off, hung up the mic and left the tiny stage. Barry went back on and announced the break and what was left of the crowd got up and headed to the bar or the toilets.

'Well done!' said Kitty as Alex walked up to them but she didn't stop to chat – she carried on walking.

Matt looked at Kitty and they both turned to follow her.

When they caught up with her in the hotel forecourt, Matt could tell she'd been crying.

'Hey, don't worry,' he said putting his arm round her.

'I was terrible,' spluttered Alex, turning to Matt and crying on his shoulder.

'Look at the positives, Alex ...' said Kitty. 'You got through it, you got some good laughs early on – you just need to work on some of the gags and maybe a bit on the timing. What did I tell you about speeding up?'

'You told me I shouldn't speed up, but I couldn't help it. They were all just staring at me,' sobbed Alex.

'Exactly! As soon as the crowd see you're panicking they start to panic too . . .'

'Kit's right,' said Matt. 'They can smell fear a mile off!'

'It really wasn't as bad as you think,' said Kitty. 'I taped it on my phone and when you listen to it through—'

'I never want to listen to it! In fact I never want to do another stand-up gig as long as I live!'

Matt looked at Kitty and they exchanged a knowing smile.

'Been there, done that,' said Matt reaching into his pocket and handing her a hanky. 'At this very venue, wasn't it, Kit?'

'It was, Matt, yes . . .' nodded Kitty.

'I died utterly and completely, and you know when it was?'

'No . . .' said Alex.

'The night before *The T Factor* gig!' He grinned. Kitty nodded. It was only a few weeks ago but it seemed like months. Alex pulled her head away from Matt's jacket and looked up at him.

'Really?' she said. 'You're not just saying that?'

'God's honest truth.'

Alex had a couple more sniffles, then her face broke into a half smile. 'So there's hope then?' she said, turning her big blue eyes to Matt.

'Oh yes, there's hope,' said Matt. She blew her nose on Matt's hanky and handed it back to him.

'Er, you can keep that,' he said with a chuckle.

'Honestly, Alex, it really wasn't that bad!' said Kitty.

'I s'pose you're right,' said Alex, brightening. 'I mean I got a good laugh on the Adele impression . . .'

'Exactly.'

'And the Theresa March . . .'

'Look, I'll email you the recording and we'll talk about it tomorrow. It was a good start.'

'The impressions were good,' said Matt. 'You maybe just need to work on your gags a bit.'

'That's just it,' said Alex. 'I can't write jokes like you can.'

'Well, maybe that's something Matt can help you with?' said Bobby, catching up with them and giving Matt a wink.

Matt shuffled awkwardly on the spot.

'Sorry about your jacket,' said Alex changing the subject.

Matt looked down at his lapel which was wet with a mixture of tears and snot.

'That's fine,' he said. 'It needed a clean, anyway!' Alex laughed and put on the voice of the woman from the TV show where they clean a house from top to bottom.

'Never mind, luvvie,' she said. 'Little bit of lemon juice on that will bring it up lovely!'

Matt and Kitty burst out laughing. 'You should put that in the act!' they exclaimed in unison.

'You think so?' said Alex.

'Yes! That's spot on!' said Matt. He was impressed – Alex had real talent. If she could control her nerves she could be great.

'Five minutes, ladies and gentlemen,' boomed a distant voice from the bar.

'Uh-oh. I'd better get my head together,' said Matt, remembering that he was on next. 'I'll talk to you later, Alex.'

Back in the bar the audience were still retaking their seats.

'Fancy a drink, Matt?' said Bobby, waving a fiver.

'I'm fine thanks, Bobby. I don't want to take on too much fluid . . .' said Matt.

'Absolutely, you don't want to have to deal with the call of nature while you're on stage. I'll get you one for when you come off,' said Bobby.

'I won't do long, Matt,' said Barry, leaning in between the two comics. 'I'll just settle 'em down.'

'I'll leave you to it,' said Bobby, giving him a paternal pat on the back. 'Have a good one!'

Barry wandered up on to the stage and made a few announcements about upcoming events at the hotel and various special offers, and gradually the audience filtered back and took their seats. Then came the moment they'd all been waiting for.

'Ladies and gentlemen, you've seen him on the telly and what's good enough for *The T Factor* is good enough for the Cavendish Hotel! Please welcome Matt Millz!'

There was a huge cheer and a round of applause as Matt walked on. He stood behind the mic for a couple of seconds just taking it all in – it was quite astonishing. A lady in the front row put her hand up to shake his hand and as he took it she pulled him in for a kiss.

'Hi, Mum,' he said straightening his tie. 'I thought I told you to wait in the car?' There was a big laugh. Matt looked around and could see the audience all sat back, confident in his powers.

'It's great to be back in Frittledean!' he bellowed. 'Frittledean – such a small town it's twinned with itself!' Another big laugh. 'Such a small town that when they painted the white lines down the middle of the high street they had to widen the road first!'

Another big laugh – these were all gags Matt had used before about another small town – he'd simply changed the name.

'Rumour has it that a light bulb blew in the post office three years ago and it made the front page of the *Frittledean Gazette*!' Another big laugh, building on the two before.

With the audience primed, Matt launched into the main body of his *T Factor* set.

'Yes, you probably saw me on *The T Factor* the other week . . .' he said. There was a huge cheer at the mention of the show's name – everyone was really rooting for him, proud of what was in their eyes a local boy made good.

'Yes, Simon Bewell, ladies and gentlemen, the only person in show business who has his hair dry-cleaned!'

There was a laugh after the gag, but a rather muted one – nothing like the one he'd got when he'd told it for the first time on *The T Factor*. Matt was momentarily thrown but pressed on.

'I know you're looking at me and thinking, blimey! He's young! It's true, I'm so young if I'm having a drink I still like to have a rusk with it!' On *The T Factor* that gag had not only got a massive laugh it had got a round of applause too – but tonight there was just a nervous titter from the lady down the front who'd stolen a kiss.

And so it went on. As Matt plugged away at his 'bulletproof' *T Factor* set, the laughs got steadily smaller and the crowd steadily more restless.

Matt couldn't understand it – these had been real zingers at the Apollo!

Then he heard something that made it all too clear why they weren't laughing.

'Heard it!' a voice shouted from the back of the room. There was a general murmur of approval from the rest of the crowd.

Quick as a flash Matt shot back with one of his heckle put-down lines.

'I was the same after my first pint!' he said.

That got a few laughs but also a few groans.

'You're not listening, mate,' the heckler retorted. 'You need to get some new gags – we've heard 'em all!' A large number of the audience nodded in agreement.

'I'm sorry, mate, I don't speak idiot,' Matt shot back, but the audience could tell he was rattled.

Trouble was, he wasn't sure that 'Heard it!' was strictly a heckle. It was in simple terms a statement of fact, and the audience knew it. Matt attempting to make a fool out of the heckler wasn't going to wash. Everyone could see who the real fool was, it was Matt.

He could see a figure approaching the heckler and whispering in his ear – it was Bobby. The heckler pushed him away, shaking his head and wagging his finger at the old comic. He then cupped both hands to his mouth and shouted it for a third time. 'Heard it, mate!' And this time he twisted the verbal knife. 'You're a flash in the pan!'

Without thinking Matt made his second mistake – he got angry.

'OK, well, if you think you can do better,' he growled, 'maybe you should come up here and have a go!'

He looked over at Bobby who was shaking his head. He then looked back at the crowd. To his utter horror the heckler was picking his way through the seats to the stage. Matt hadn't expected for one moment that the heckler would take him up on his offer.

'Go on, Dave!' jeered the heckler's girlfriend. 'You show him!' There was a smattering of half-hearted applause and the crowd looked at each other. Suddenly the gig had taken an unexpected turn!

Dave climbed up on to the stage and strolled nonchalantly towards Matt then held out his hand for the microphone. Matt looked at Bobby again who was shaking his head even more violently. Even at this late stage Matt could have told Dave to go and sit down but something in him allowed the grim scenario to play out.

Matt frowned, handed the mic to the bloke, took a couple of steps back, folded his arms and leant against the back wall.

'Bock! Bock!' Dave tapped the microphone to make sure it was on, then cleared his throat. 'Ahem!'

The audience was all concentrating on Dave, the room was as quiet as a library that had just been closed down due to government cutbacks, intrigued as to how this story was going to end.

'OK, here's one for you . . .' said Dave.

Matt shook his head and rolled his eyes. 'Who starts a joke like that?' he thought to himself. 'This won't take long.' This Dave was going to demonstrate just how hard the comedian's job was.

'OK! This bloke goes to the doctor's and says, "Doctor I keep thinking people are ignoring me," and the doctor says, "Next!".'

Suddenly, to everyone's surprise, there was a

massive laugh – so big was the laugh that even Dave looked surprised. He beamed a big broad smile, then turned triumphantly to Matt and nodded. Matt couldn't believe it. That doctor joke was older than he was! Before he could react, Dave was warming up for his next one.

'Knock! Knock!' barked Dave.

'Who's there?' replied the audience as one.

'Cash!' said Dave.

'Cash who?' came the response.

'No thanks, I've got a nut allergy!' said Dave.

Dave got his second big laugh, this time accompanied by a cheer.

'Go, Dave!' shouted his girlfriend, standing and waving.

This wasn't in the rule book! What was Matt supposed to do now? He was standing like a lemon on the stage while Dave was having the gig of his life! He looked over at Bobby and pulled a face as if to say, 'What do I do now?' Bobby did a sideways movement with his thumb and mouthed, 'Get off!'

Get off? Give up the stage? That really wasn't something Matt wanted to do. He'd been desperate for stage-time for weeks and finally he was back where he felt he belonged. Yet the gig was slipping through his fingers like a pig covered in margarine!

'No,' he thought, knitting his brow into a frown. 'I am Matt Millz! I can turn this around!'

Then Matt did something he'd never thought he'd find himself doing in a million years. He walked up behind Dave and tickled him under his arms. Dave immediately stopped mid-joke and let out a laugh.

So Matt tickled him again, then moved his hands down and tickled him on his tummy. Dave doubled over in uncontrolled laughter. The audience started laughing too. Matt did it again even harder. This time Dave sank to his knees and rolled on to his back. Matt leant down and went in for the kill, tickling Dave until he could take it no more.

'Stop!' cried Dave, his eyes streaming and his body convulsing in spasms of laughter.

After a few more tickles, Matt relented and

watched as Dave crawled off the stage on all fours and back to his seat. Then Matt picked up the microphone, looked at the audience for as long as he dared, then raised the microphone to his lips.

'See, Dave? I *can* make you laugh!'

The audience gave a huge roar, the biggest laugh of the night, followed by a round of applause. Matt remembered the old adage 'If it's going badly get off. If it's going well get off!' He knew he wouldn't be able to top that.

'I'm Matt Millz – that's all from me. Goodnight!'

he said returning the mic to the stand. He then walked head down through the crowd, past the bar and towards the exit.

The first person he came upon was Bobby.

'I don't know how you managed that, son,' said Bobby handing him a pint of diet Coke. Matt took a couple of long deep slugs of the drink and looked at Bobby.

'You knew didn't you?' said Matt, anger bubbling up.

'What's that?' said Bobby, shifting uneasily.

'You knew I was going to have a bad gig! That look you gave me in the car when I told you I was relying on my tried-and-tested stuff! You knew I was going to tank!'

Bobby looked at his feet and took a deep breath, then fixed Matt squarely in the eye.

'You can't do old gear, son,' he said shaking his head dolefully. 'Sorry, mate. You can maybe get away with one or two but it's not like a singer, where the audience want to hear the golden oldies over and over again. A joke has to be a surprise doesn't it? We both know that. Maybe when you've been around for a while you might develop what you might call "classic routines" – like Monty Python and their parrot sketch – but those are few and far between, and you certainly can't get away with it when you've only got a few gigs under your belt.'

'Why didn't you tell me?'

'How could I? What would you have done? It's not like you had a whole other set you could have turned to. I'm sorry, I thought you knew. It's another one of the golden rules of comedy – turnover. We all have to generate new stuff, and that's the hard bit. The other thing you were up against back there was expectation . . .'

'Expectation?' said Matt.

'Yes. You see when you first went on stage at the Apollo for the talent thingy, no one expected you to be funny. You looked like a clueless kid – no offence . . .'

'None taken!' said Matt, a little put out.

'So when you *were* funny that was a surprise. The audience in the theatre and at home felt they were discovering something new together. They were excited – there's nothing as exciting as seeing something new is there?'

'I s'pose not, no . . .' said Matt.

'The surprise added to their enjoyment.'

'And now?'

'Ah well, now they remember that feeling and they're expecting it as soon as you walk on. Oh, they'll give you a couple of minutes for free . . .'

'For free . . .?'

'You know – you probably noticed that they sat up and were smiling, they wanted to laugh. But if you don't give them what they want after those first few minutes – well, you saw it. If you don't live up to their *expectation* they're disappointed – or worse, angry.'

'Wow, this is a weird way to earn a living,' said Matt shaking his head. 'Just when you think you've got the hang of it . . .'

'It's the weirdest job of all and believe me, you never get the hang of it,' said Bobby. 'It's the best job in the world one day and the worst the next – and you know what? It never changes! One minute you're a nobody and you can't get a gig, the next you're a surprise and everyone wants you, and then you're a has-been like me and you can't get a gig again . . . Ha ha! I've been doing it for over fifty years and it still surprises me.'

'Yeah but when it works . . .' said Matt wistfully.

'Ah, when it works it's fabulous! You feel like a god! Like you could do anything – which is why we keep coming back for more! When it doesn't work you feel like a complete failure! The trick is to treat the two feelings the same. Ride 'em. Look on it as a game and whatever you do don't forget to enjoy it – good or bad. If you can keep your sense of fun you're half way there!'

'Sorry if I spoiled your show, mate.' It was Dave the heckler.

'That's OK Dave,' said Matt, shaking him by the

hand. 'I made a couple of big mistakes . . .'

'Yeah, but I shoulda kept me gob shut. Debbie was egging me on . . .'

'No hard feelings,' said Matt.

Dave waved his iPhone. 'Any chance of a selfie?'

'You've got a nerve,' said Bobby.

'No probs,' said Matt and smiled as Dave put his arm round him and leant in for a photo.

'Cheers, Matt. And better luck next time!'

'How you feeling?' said Kitty, joining them tentatively with a concerned look on her face.

'Not great, but I learnt a lesson.'

'We both did,' said Kitty.

'Where's Alex?' said Matt.

'Oh, she had to get back – her dad came to pick her up. I think she could be really good. She's got the technical skill – she just needs that killer instinct,' said Kitty.

'What, like me?' laughed Matt, draining his pint and sucking the last few drops of Coke off the ice cubes.

'How'd it go? Knock 'em dead as usual?' It was Ian who'd come to give them both a lift home.

'Bit of a sore point,' said Matt.

'I'll email you the recording and see you in the DMC at first break,' said Kitty as Ian pulled up outside her house to drop her off.

'Hmm, I'm not sure that's a show I want to hear,' said Matt.

'File it under experience,' said Kitty getting out of the car and starting to walk to her front gate.

'Oh, one more thing . . .' said Matt, winding down the window and calling after her.

Kitty Hope looked round expectantly.

'Yes?'

'Could I have Alex's number?'

'Alex's . . .? What for?'

'Um . . . I thought maybe I could help her hone her routine . . .' said Matt.

'Never heard it called that before,' chipped in Ian from the front seat with a grin.

Kitty produced her phone and scrolled through her list of contacts, then hesitated.

'I tell you what. I'll give her your number. How about that?' she said, tucking the phone back into her pocket.

'Um, fine,' said Matt. 'Yeah, fine! See you tomorrow!'

As the car wound its way through the streets of Staplefirst, Matt felt dejected. It was like he'd thrown away all the good work and publicity he'd managed to get from *The T Factor* audition. As they approached the house he glanced out of the window and spotted a figure in an anorak kicking a tin can down the road. It was Gary, the bloke that had been hanging out at the end of his path for the last three weeks.

'Er, Ian?' said Matt. 'You can let me out here if you like. I just want to have a word with Gary.' The car pulled up and Matt got out.

'Hi, Gary,' he said slapping him on the back and greeting him like an old friend.

'Huh?' grunted Gary, pulling his hoody to one side and looking at Matt. 'Oh, it's you.'

'Yeah! I've just come from a gig as a matter of fact ...' boasted Matt. 'Yeah, just a little comedy club. Didn't go too well, but that's the game – win some lose some. So, you want a selfie or an autograph?' he asked.

'Er, no, you're OK. I've gotta get home,' said Gary.

'Oh,' said Matt.

'Yeah, and to be honest I'm probably not gonna hang around your place any more coz, well, sort of done that now – if that's OK?'

'Yeah, yeah, that's fine,' said Matt unexpectedly disappointed. 'No problem, Gary ... whatever ... um ... keep in touch!'

'Yeah ... well, maybe.'

Gary pulled up his hood and continued down the road with his game of tin-can football.

Matt felt a lump in his throat as he walked back to his house. It seemed that not even his number one fan was interested any more.

He didn't get much sleep that night. The whole Frittledean gig kept replaying over and over in his head and each time he came up with another way in which he could have played it and made it work. Just as he was about to doze off, a thought entered his head that made his eyes snap open and sit up. That gig had been bad, yes, but if he hadn't taken Kitty's advice, it could have happened in front of millions on *Stand-up at the Apollo*.

16

The Bugle Calls

The next day Matt woke up with a feeling of purpose. He had just about got away with the gig the night before, but he was determined to never let himself be caught without any new material ever again.

As he approached the school gates he heard a voice from behind him.

'Oi! Millsy! Take a look at this!' He spun round to see a kid from the year above doing a wheelie on his BMX and clutching what looked like a rolled-up newspaper. He wheelied up to Matt and whacked him over the head with it.

'Hey! There's no need for that!' shouted Matt. 'And

yeah, I have seen a wheelie before you know . . .'

'Not that – this!' said the boy and he slung the rolled-up newspaper at Matt's feet. 'Looks like you're in trouble, mate!' he said and cycled off towards the school.

Matt bent down and picked the newspaper up. He unrolled it – it was a copy of that week's *Kent Bugle* ('All the News Fit to Print About Kent!'). It had been opened on the 'Arts and Review' page and the hairs on the back of Matt's neck immediately stood to attention at what he saw.

Taking up almost half the page was a grainy black and white photograph taken at the Cavendish gig the night before. It showed Dave the heckler at the microphone and Matt in the background leaning against the wall looking decidedly worried. The headline shouted 'Matt Takes a Back Seat as Comeback Show Flops!' Matt stopped dead in his tracks and his face turned a bright red as he read on.

MATT TAKES A BACK SEAT
AS COMEBACK SHOW FLOPS!

by our Arts Critic in the second row, Gina Heggarty

Local star Matt Millz has certainly had a good few of weeks. The Staplefirst boy who wowed the judges and won the hearts of the nation on ITV's hit *T Factor* talent show has had hundreds of column inches written about him. You can hardly turn the TV on without seeing the lad on some show or other talking about his experience in the big time. But now the hot air has stopped, the question is, 'Is Matt Millz anything more than a five-minute wonder?' Well, the answer, judging from last night's hapless performance at the Cavendish Hotel, Frittledean, is a resounding NO. Anyone hoping to see the confident, funny, fresh-faced comic they'd seen on the telly would have been sorely disappointed.

BODY-POPPING HIGHLIGHT

The show kicked off well with Anglebrook-based body-popper and rapper Neil Trottman. His moves were tight and his lyrics were for the most part sharp, although a couple of the songs felt like works in progress. Neil's short set was probably the highlight of the night as the evening rapidly nosedived after he left the stage.

PROMISING MIMIC

Next up was new impressionist Alex Williams who, although delivering some technically accurate voices of some of our top ladies from Adele to Theresa March, was let down by predictable and lacklustre material and rather outstayed her welcome. However she shows promise and could be a name to watch for the future.

AS SEEN AND HEARD ON TV

Which brings us to the low point of the evening – Matt Millz. The home crowd, who were all there to see the twelve-year-old wunderkind, gave him a rousing welcome which he then proceeded to throw away by churning out all the gags he'd done on his telly debut! Master Millz needs to learn that an audience doesn't leave the comfort of their front room to watch a repeat, and the Frittledean crowd didn't wait long to let the lame-duck comic know of their disapproval.

Pretty quickly he was heckled by audience member Dave Thompson, who hails from Cowdenhurst. Showing his inexperience, Millz then invited Mr Thompson up on stage. Unfortunately for Mr Millz, the 32-year-old mechanic proved much funnier than the headline star everyone had paid to see. It's quite an indictment of a comedy night when the audience proves to be funnier than the comic!

So does Matt Millz have a bright future ahead of him in show business? The verdict of this critic is very much 'Go back to school'.

Matt's phone buzzed through a text. 'Lame duck?' it said with an emoji of a yellow rubber duck. Then a second text buzzed through – 'I'm just a phone call

away.' They were both from Dickie Hart at Excalibur Management. Matt shuddered and put the phone back in his pocket.

'I'm staring into the abyss here,' he murmured.

'Ouch!' came a voice from behind him. It was Rob. He too was clutching a copy of the *Kent Bugle*, open at Gina Heggarty's scathing review. In fact, looking round him, pretty much everyone seemed to be poring over a copy.

'That's it,' said Matt in a daze. 'The game's up . . . it's over!'

'There were some positives . . .' said Rob, putting his arm round Matt's shoulder to comfort him.

'Oh yeah? Where? "Lame duck" it says. "Not as funny as the audience" . . . "Low point of the evening" it says . . . "Like watching a repeat" . . .'

'Well . . .' Rob hesitated, scanning the article yet again. 'Here, look, it says you got a rousing welcome . . .'

'Huh!' said Matt shaking his head and putting his hand through his hair in desperation. At that point his phone rang. It was Kitty.

'Don't read the *Bugle*!' she barked down the phone.

'Too late,' said Matt. 'I'm finished! It's over!'

'Now don't be ridiculous! It was one bad gig and actually it doesn't mention the fact that you managed to turn it around at the end, so you're by no means finished! That showed real guts, Matt. Besides, I've read a lot of Gina Heggarty's reviews and she's a nasty piece of work – particularly when it comes to comedy. She's got no sense of humour whatsoever. There's no way she could have preferred that Dave character's hackneyed old gags to yours. It shows a complete lack of understanding. She's just trying to make a name for herself on the back of yours! She's jealous. Simple as that. Critics are the lowest of the low. Take this as a lesson for the future – never read your own reviews.'

'I don't mind reading the good ones,' said Matt.

'If you believe the good ones then you have to believe the bad ones too,' she said.

'I suppose you've got a point.'

'Forget it! Put it out of your mind! Otherwise it will eat away at you and destroy your confidence, which is one of the comic's most powerful tools.'

'Yeah, OK, I hear you,' said Matt.

But he couldn't forget it. For the rest of the day it played on his mind. All the negative phrases from the review kept exploding in his brain like tiny bombs.

In maths he'd hear a tiny voice inside him saying, 'Lame duck!' or 'Go back to school'. Queuing for a sausage roll in Greggs at morning break with Rob, he was sure he heard someone behind him whisper, 'Audience funnier than the comic!'

It was torture.

'Bit lame,' said Ahmed as the three boys sat on the steps outside the science block at lunch.

'What's that?!' snapped Matt, spinning to face him.

'Just sayin' *Stand-up at the Apollo* last week was a bit lame,' said Ahmed, surprised at Matt's aggressive response to what was a fairly harmless comment.

'I suppose you think that's clever do you?!' growled Matt, giving him a shove in the chest.

'Hey! What's up, bruv?!' said Ahmed confused. 'No need to get heavy. I was just sayin' that—'

'I know what you were saying,' said Matt, giving Ahmed another, bigger shove that left him spreadeagled on the steps. Matt moved in and pinned him down with his left hand then raised his right hand in a fist over Ahmed's face.

'Take it back!' shouted Matt, his face red, his eyes wide and wild.

'Hey! Hang on, Matt! What are you . . .' protested Rob.

'What you talkin' about?' gasped Ahmed trying

to wriggle free.

'You know what I'm talking about. The review in the *Bugle*,' hissed Matt. 'Lame duck they called me!'

'I ain't seen no review,' pleaded Ahmed. 'The *Bugle* is not on my list of top reads!'

'Eh?' said Matt.

'I DON'T KNOW WHAT YOU'RE TALKING ABOUT!' shouted Ahmed, managing to slip free of Matt's grip and get up on his feet.

'What's going on here?' came a gruff voice from behind them. They turned to see Mr Gillingham looking very angry indeed.

'Thank god you're here,' said Ahmed running to Mr Gillingham and hiding behind him.

'Explain yourself, Matt,' glared Mr G.

'Er ... sorry ...' said Matt, suddenly feeling extremely foolish. 'It was a misunderstanding. I thought ...'

'He thought I was teasing him about some review in some paper but I wasn't. I just wasn't!' protested Ahmed.

'OK, Ahmed, I think you can go – after Matt's apologised.'

'I'm sorry, Ahmed. Really I am,' said Matt. His anger had turned to acute, crippling embarrassment.

'Yeah, OK, no probs, but hey, maybe you need some chill time.'

'Yes, thank you, Ahmed, that will be all from you on the subject,' said Mr G.

'Just trying to help, sir,' said Ahmed, grabbing his bag and loping off.

'I'll catch you later,' said Rob following suit.

'Take a seat, Matt,' said Mr G indicating the step. The two of them sat down.

'I read that review . . .'

'Hmm. Then you know that I'm a lame duck.'

'I've had a lot worse than that,' said Mr G gently.

'You, sir?'

'Yes,' continued Mr G. 'I had a brief fling with show business myself, when I was a student. Me and a couple of mates wrote a little comedy review and took it up to the Edinburgh Festival . . .'

'The Edinburgh Festival? I've heard of that . . .'

'Oh, you must go. I'm sure you will – it's brilliant. Thousands of shows every day from stand-up comics, to opera, to street theatre, to circus acts and beyond. Well, we took a show up there, and do you know what the critic of the big paper up there wrote about it?'

Matt shook his head.

'He wrote just five words – "This show is a dud!" Ha!' Mr Gillingham let out a laugh. 'This show's a dud! Imagine that. All that work . . . I mean don't get me wrong, we were devastated at the time but now I look back on it and think, maybe he was right! That doesn't excuse his bluntness, but what you have to understand is everyone has an opinion. As soon as you put your head above the parapet someone is going to take a pot shot. You're not a lame duck, you know that much I hope, but that gig the other night wasn't your best – you know that too – but don't take it out on poor Ahmed.'

Matt looked at his shoes awkwardly.

'You know what?' said Mr G, warming to his theme. 'We learn a lot more from our failures than we do from our successes. Ask anyone who ever achieved anything. That review did me a favour – it stopped me from writing another show. I wasn't cut out for that life. On the other hand I love teaching, so . . .'

'What about your pals who wrote the show with you?' said Matt.

'One went into engineering and now designs jet engines, and the other is Benedict Camber-Sprout,' said Mr G with a rather smug smile.

'What?!' said Matt, sitting up straight. 'You went to uni with Benedict Camber-Sprout?'

'I did indeed – but keep it to yourself. Ben's a bit shy.'

'He's a brilliant actor! I've seen all his films – *Sheer Heart*, *The Limitation Game*, *Doctor Stranglehold* . . .'

'*Hamlet*?' chipped in Mr G.

'Not so much,' laughed Matt.

'Everyone who ever did anything extraordinary

got criticised for it somewhere along the line, so ignore it. In fact, here's a bit of homework for you. I want you to collect as many quotes about critics as you can and bring them to me tomorrow. OK?'

'Yes, sir, sorry, sir, it won't happen again,' said Matt, cheering up a bit.

'It had better not. Now you'd better track down Ahmed and patch it up with him properly.'

'Yes, sir, on my way.'

That night when he got home Matt went straight to his laptop and started searching for quotes about critics and was stunned at just how many of them he found in a couple of clicks. He wrote them down on a large piece of poster-sized paper and stuck it on his bedroom wall above his bed, and when he'd done that he felt a lot better.

LIST OF QUOTES ABOUT CRITICS

'They laughed when I told them I was going to become a comedian. Well they're not laughing now!' – Bob Monkhouse

'There is one way to handle the ignorant and malicious critic. Ignore him.' – Anon

'Strike the dog dead, it's but a critic!' – Goethe, German poet

'Those who have free seats at a play hiss first.' – Chinese proverb

'Even the lion has to defend himself against flies.' – German proverb

'Brilliant people talk about ideas. Average people talk about things. Small people talk about other people.' – Anon

'Do what you feel in your heart

to be right. You'll be criticised anyway.' – Anon

'He who throws dirt always loses ground.' – Anon

'The public is the only critic whose opinion is worth anything at all.' – Mark Twain, American novelist

'A bad review is even less important than whether it is raining in Patagonia.' – Iris Murdoch, novelist

'It is from the womb of art that criticism was born.' – Charles Baudelaire, French author

'Those who can, do. Those who can't, criticise.' – Anon

'Don't mind criticism. If it is untrue, disregard; If unfair, keep from irritation; if it is ignorant, smile; If it is justified it is not criticism, learn from it.' – Anon

'Before you criticise a man, walk a mile in his shoes. That way, when you do criticise him, you'll be a mile away and have his shoes.' — Billy Connolly, comedian

17

Return to Sossinghurst

The car heater was turned up to max as Ian drove Matt, Kitty, Alex and Bobby down the same country lane that they'd got stuck in just a few weeks earlier.

'Remember the purpose of tonight is for you to try out some new stuff,' said Kitty giving an encouraging nod.

'Understood,' said Matt, running through his list of new stuff. He was still worried.

That morning he'd gone through his old stuff and filleted out any gags that he'd tried before but which had worked and hadn't been used in his *T Factor* set. There were more than he'd expected in fact. Plus

he had some other stuff that he'd been working on, and some new stuff he hadn't but would try out if the gig was going well. He'd even brought along the old Harry Styles doll just in case he was forced to resurrect his 'How to cook your sister's Harry Styles doll' routine that had gone so well at 'Anglebrook's Got Talent'.

'Not like last time is it, Matt?' said Ian as they wound their way up towards Sossinghurst. 'Thank god. I'm still haggling with the other bloke's insurance over the dent in my rear bumper. What they don't understand is it's a whole unit. It's made of fibreglass, designed to crush on impact so you can't just knock out a dent . . .'

As Ian droned on about the pros and cons of the design of the new Astra bumper over the old one, Matt suddenly started to worry. Ian was right, last time they'd made this trip the road had been completely blocked with cars. They hadn't passed a single car for ages.

'I know we're trying to keep a low profile,' said Matt, 'but this is weird isn't it? It's like a ghost town!'

'It'll be fine!' said Kitty. 'Besides, we only need a few people to make it worthwhile.'

'I guess . . .' said Matt looking over his shoulder at Alex who smiled thinly and shrugged her shoulders.

'This is my big comeback too you know, Kit!' said Bobby. 'Still, it's a nice evening for a trip into the country. I wish I'd brought my book of British birds – I could have had a great time!'

'It will be fine . . . don't worry, Matt,' said Kitty, ignoring Bobby.

But as they pulled into the car park of the Rose and Crown, even Kitty started to get concerned – it was empty.

'Plenty of parking space then!' said Ian, pulling up.

'Hmm . . .' said Kitty scrunching her face into a frown. 'I'd better go on ahead and find out what's going on.'

But before she could finish her sentence Matt was up, out of the car and striding towards the venue with a look of grim determination.

Not only were there no cars in the car park, there was no one in the pub either, and not a single poster or flier advertising the gig.

'Where is everyone?' said Matt. 'The gig's due to start in half an hour.'

'Oh hello, Matt! You're much smaller in real life than you were on that telly thing – you know, with that bloke and the other one!' said Jess the ruddy-faced landlady.

'Yeah, I know. TV makes you look bigger for some reason, but what about tonight's gig?' said Matt brusquely.

'I've had to cancel it I'm afraid, Matt – no one's turned up!' said Jess, shaking her head.

'No one?' said Matt looking round at the empty room with a mic on a stand positioned forlornly on its own on a low stage at the far end. To Matt it just seemed to be begging him to get up there and do a set, but he knew that while you can do a gig to a few people – you can't do it to no one at all.

'Well, no offence, Matt, you're not the name you once were,' said Jess. 'I mean that telly thing with, you know that bloke and whatnot, that was a while ago . . .'

'Not the name I once was?' Matt exclaimed. 'It's been one month! Four weeks ago I was being mobbed outside my house! Four weeks ago I couldn't go out without having to sign ten autographs and posing for selfies every few yards. Four weeks!' He was struggling to keep a lid on his frustration.

'That's showbiz I guess,' shrugged the landlady.

Matt whirled round to face Kitty who was walking through the door behind him.

'What's going on?' she said.

'Gig's cancelled, no one's turned up!' said Matt.

'No one at all?' said Kitty in wonder.

'I'm not surprised. There's nothing to tell people there's even a gig happening! Where are Rob's posters?' said Matt, his disappointment starting to turn to anger.

'Your manager told us to keep it a secret!' said Jess.

'Well, not a complete secret!' said Matt.

'I said you should email all your regulars and keep it low profile – not a secret!' said Kitty shaking her head.

'I did that!' protested Jess. 'But as you can see, it's dead as a doornail! Actually there's even fewer people here than on a normal night which is kinda weird.'

'Dead's the word all right!' said Matt.

Then his frustration tipped over into anger, an anger that he just couldn't keep bottled up any longer. All the frustrations of the last few weeks suddenly became too much to bear. He turned to Kitty and let rip.

'Cancelled!' he yelled. 'Cancelled! It's such a low-profile gig that no one even knew about it! What is it with you, huh? Either the gig's cancelled because there's too many people or it's cancelled because there aren't enough people! I just wanna do a gig! Is that so hard to understand? I'm supposed to be a comedian! But what kind of comedian never does a live show? I'm like a cowboy without a horse. Like a DJ without any tracks, like a flaming footballer without a match or any boots or ball! I'm right back where I started and it's all because of YOU! You . . . you . . . amateur!'

Neil and Alex winced at Matt's vicious attack, but Kitty wasn't having any of it. She stepped forward and stood her ground.

'How dare you use that word with me!' she said pulling herself up to her full height (three feet six). 'I organised this gig in good faith, down to the letter! I told Jess and her assistant to send the information out to their mailing list! I got regular updates on numbers and yesterday I was told it was heading for a sell-out! Something's happened, someone's sabotaged it – it's the only explanation!'

'Their mailing list! Ha!' shouted Matt. 'Look at it!

It's a clapped-out old pub in the middle of a field – the only crowd they're likely to get is a couple of sheep and a donkey!'

'Hang on a sec!' said Jess bridling at Matt's choice of words.

'That's not fair,' countered Kitty. 'It may be off the beaten track but it's well run and they have regular entertainment here with good crowds. I know, I came along to one of their nights last week and it was packed!'

'Thanks, luv!' said Jess with a told-you-so nod.

'How convenient!' shouted Matt. 'What you're saying is "You shoulda been here last week"? Yeah, well I don't have the benefit of time travel. All I'm looking at is an empty pub and another wasted journey!'

'I saw the figures – yesterday it was heading for a sell-out! I will get to the bottom of it, Matt, but please don't take out your frustration on me!'

'Hey, come on, you two!' said Bobby, stepping in between them. 'I know you're disappointed, Matt, but it's not worth falling out over surely? There'll be other gigs—'

'WHEN?' shouted Matt turning to face Bobby, his face red and his eyes wild with rage.

'When? Where are these so-called other gigs, Bobby? That reviewer from the *Bugle* was right – I'm a flash in the pan! I'm not a stand-up comic! I'm a schoolboy who was on a talent show once!'

With that he stormed out of the pub. Ian leant his head out of the window of the Astra.

'What's going on, Matt? Is it going ahead?' he said.

'NO!' snapped Matt.

'Right, well, you'd better get in then . . .'

But Matt kept walking.

'Where are you going?' said Ian, calling after him.

'For a very long walk!' shouted Matt without so much as looking back. He walked out of the car park, across the road and kept walking.

He walked across a couple of fields, through a ditch which deposited a large amount of stinking mud on his trousers, then it started raining. His stage suit became sodden and mud-stained and the quiff he was so pleased with fell down over his eyes and became plastered to his face. In amongst the rain were salty tears – not of sadness but of anger and frustration.

Why was it taking so long for him to become what he wanted to be – a stand-up. He had talent didn't he? The crowd at the Apollo bore testament to that and yet at every turn his plans were thwarted. Surely no comedian in history had had to put up with so many obstacles thrown in his path.

Then his thoughts turned to Kitty. He really liked her and respected her for supporting him from the start, for spotting something in him that others hadn't, for encouraging him and, yes, educating him in the history of comedy, but surely she was out of her depth? The fact was she'd never managed a single comedian before him, and the proof was there for all to see – he was in a worse position now than he had been one month ago. His head start had been thrown away. He felt in his pocket and produced the Harry Styles doll that had started it all for him – the routine he'd done with Rob at the school talent show. That

seemed an awfully long time ago now. He took the doll and pitched it high. It went looping through the air and landed in a tree, staring back at him like some sort of demented Christmas fairy.

Just then he felt a buzz from his inside pocket which meant he'd got a text. He fished out his phone.

'If that's Kitty Hope she can whistle,' he muttered swiping the screen with his finger. The text wasn't from Kitty. It was from Dickie Hart of Excalibur Management.

'Oh dear, looks like the bubble has burst. Call me before it's too late.'

Matt weighed the phone in his hand for a couple of moments. He sighed heavily, then dialled the number.

'Sorry, Kitty ...' he said aloud, 'this is just business.'

18
Professional Help

'I wondered how long it would take for you to wake up and smell the roses,' a gruff voice said at the other end of the phone.

'How'd you know?' said Matt.

'I know everything,' said Dickie.

'You were right, Mr Hart, Kitty's out of her depth. I need help, and fast. If that offer of management is still open I'd like to take you up on it.'

'Hmm, I like that . . .' said Dickie, savouring the moment. 'Say that again.'

'If that offer of management is still open, I'd like to take you up on it . . .'

'Not that bit!' he snapped. 'The bit about me being right. Yeah, I'm still interested. You'd better come over to the office and we can sort out the paperwork.'

'Thanks, Mr Hart, I really appreciate this,' said Matt with a sigh of relief. It was like a weight lifting from his shoulders. 'It'll take me a while. I'll need to look at train times ...'

'Nah, don't bother with all that, I'll send a car for you.'

Matt had come off the phone both relieved and excited. As he'd made his way back home across the fields his mind raced – this could be just the boost that he needed. Yes, Dickie wasn't the most likeable person he'd ever met – in fact if he was honest he felt there was something 'wrong' about him, something a bit shady. But no one could argue with his track record – surely that spoke for itself? After all, as Kitty herself had said, it was called show business not show friendship.

It was early the following morning by the time he'd finished his soul searching session and arrived home. He changed out of his wet things and lay on his bed staring at his phone. He knew what he had to do, and it sent a chill down his spine just thinking about it. He needed to let Kitty know his decision, and he knew she was going to be gutted. He selected her name from his list of contacts and was just about to call her when he hesitated.

'No, better if I do it face to face,' he thought. He started texting.

'Hi Kitty, we need to talk, r u around? Matt x'

As he was about to press send, the doorbell went. Standing on the step was Alf, the driver who'd taken him and the gang to the O2.

'Mr Hart has requested your presence, sir,' he said with a benign smile.

'Blimey that was quick!'

'Yes well, Mr Hart has an amazing ability to predict certain circumstances. Do you have an overnight bag, sir?'

'Overnight? Why ...?'

'Well, Mr Hart said that there is urgent work to be

done, which will require an overnight stay.'

'But where? I don't have anywhere to stay in London. Besides, I've got school!' said Matt frowning.

'Oh, I'm sure Mr Hart will take care of all that for you.'

Matt nipped upstairs and threw a few things into a suitcase.

'Where are you off to?' said Ian as he passed him in the hallway. 'You're not leaving home without telling your mother are you?'

'No, Ian, I'm not leaving home, it's actually worse than that. I'm leaving Kitty,' said Matt. That feeling of shame he'd felt earlier kicked back in with a vengeance.

'Leaving? You mean . . .?'

'Yeah, I'm meeting Dickie Hart. I'm being taken on by Excalibur Management!'

'Nice one,' said Ian offering Matt a high five. Matt wasn't in the mood to celebrate.

'I'm sure you're doing the right thing, Matt – they've got offices in London, and well, you've seen the car he drives around in. I mean, don't get me wrong, Kitty did do a good job for a while but she's got you as far as she can get you.'

'Yeah well, after the shambles at Sossinghurst last night I don't think I have any choice. Besides if I change my mind I can always leave them can't I?' Matt sounded like he was trying to convince himself as much as Ian.

'Exactly,' said Ian, nodding enthusiastically.

'So anyway, he wants me to go up for some meetings, and sign his contract . . .' said Matt pulling up the handle of his suitcase and wheeling it towards the front door.

'Hang on,' said Ian, a concerned look on his face. 'A contract? I don't think you should be signing anything without an adult present!'

'Hmm, I hadn't thought of that,' said Matt scratching his chin. 'I don't suppose . . .?'

'Wait there!' said Ian and he disappeared into his bedroom. There was the sound of drawers being opened and closed, then a thud and finally the ZZZZZip! of a suitcase, and Ian appeared at the door in his coat and trundling his battered old luggage behind him.

'Ready?' he said.

Matt once again sunk into the sofa-like leather seat of Alf's limo and watched as the little houses and gardens of his suburban home gave way to fields, woods and farmhouses, then another town and then the main motorway into London. 'The Mighty M20' as Ian called it.

His mind drifted to Kitty and how she'd be feeling right now, how upset she'd be when she found out, how disappointed Neil and Rob and even Ahmed would feel at what they could only perceive as his betrayal of Team Millz. In his mind's eye he saw the look of disapproval on Bobby's face as he heard the news.

Then there was Alex. He and she had been getting on really well ever since they'd met at the ill-fated Frittledean gig. He really liked her. How was she going to feel now he'd turned his back on Kitty and the gang? There was no reason why they couldn't all still remain friends though was there? Surely once they'd all got over the initial shock ... They'd understand that he stood a better chance of making it as a comic with a big London agent, wouldn't they? Then he remembered Russel Perkins' unhappiness at the O2 after-show party. His mind was in a churning turmoil of self-doubt and insecurity. Was he doing the right thing? What was he getting himself into?

An hour and a half later the limo wound its way haltingly up London's Piccadilly eventually pulling up outside a fancy-looking restaurant with the word 'Austin's' above the door.

'Here you are, gentlemen!' said the chauffeur, opening the door for Matt and Ian and handing them their suitcases. 'Mr Hart is running a little late but the maître d' will show you to his usual table.'

Matt stood on the pavement feeling bewildered and a long way from home.

'Oy! Move it would you?! You're blockin' the path!' snapped a voice from behind him, and someone clunked Matt in the back with his manbag with such force that it knocked him to the pavement. Matt shook his head, looked up and immediately recognised the culprit. It was Dickie Hart.

'Oh! It's you, Matt!' said Dickie, realising his mistake. 'Sorry, I thought you was . . . er . . . that's to say . . . SO you got here all right then?'

'Hello, Mr Hart! I must say that I'm really pleased that you're considering taking young Matt on to Excalibur's books . . .' said Ian.

'Oh yeah, and who are you when you're at home?' said Dickie Hart looking him up and down like he was a something the dog had retrieved from the bin.

'Ian! Ian Woodwood! Matt's stepdad? We met before, remember? You were interested in my old punk band, Dead Toys?' said Ian, his hand shooting out for a handshake.

'Hmm! This is private business, so . . .!' said Dickie ignoring Ian's gesture of friendship.

Ian took a step back, not quite sure how to react.

'Ian is my stepdad, Mr Hart,' Matt piped up.

'Exactly,' said Ian, recovering his composure and slightly annoyed. 'He's a minor and if there's a contract to be signed, then he needs an adult to advise him.'

Dickie hesitated and narrowed his eyes as if he was considering his next move in a game of Jenga. Then his face cracked into a huge smile.

'Of course! Nice to see you again, Ian,' he said. 'I hope you'll be joining us for lunch! Shall we . . .?'

With that Dickie grabbed Ian's suitcase, marched up the steps and led them through the huge doors of the restaurant.

Before being converted into a restaurant, Austin's had once been a car showroom, when Britain's car industry had been at its peak, back in the nineteen sixties. Where once were cars and auto paraphernalia, now sat London's great and good at tables covered in starched white tablecloths, set with cutlery and glassware that glittered, throwing spangled light back up at the high ceilings which were now hung with huge crystal chandeliers.

'Welcome, Monsieur 'Art!' said the maître d' in a thick French accent, helping Dickie off with his coat. 'We 'ave your usual table, in ze middle where everyone can see you!'

'Thank you, Maurice!' said Dickie, pressing a crumpled fiver into the maître d's hand. 'Ah, *merci*!' said the maître d', almost bent double in slightly desperate appreciation.

As they picked their way between the tables, the noise of the diners' chatter was deafening, gossiping about the latest twists and turns in showbiz, who had done what to whom, who was on the up and who was on the slide. Matt cast his eye around and saw a number of familiar faces – TV executive Avril Yentl chatted animatedly to long-established nature presenter Sir David Applebough; legendary star of the small screen Dame Joan Curlings sat holding the hand of a man half her age who was toying with a prawn; ex-boy-band star Dane Wanton was on another table deep in conversation with some men in suits. Then Matt heard his name being called. He looked over to see Amelia Wong waving at him. He waved back.

Ian dug Matt in the ribs with his elbow. 'This is a bit of all right!' he said.

'All right, Davinia?' said Dickie as he passed the table of the top TV presenter Davinia McLoud offering her his hand. The presenter batted him away dismissively and pulled a face at the other people on her table. They passed another table with five very serious, very affluent-looking businessmen who were engaged in dismembering a pile of lobsters. As they saw Dickie, their faces took on an angry countenance.

'Before you say anything, fellas ...' said Dickie to the men, 'the money will be with you first thing Monday!'

'It had better be,' growled one of the businessmen. 'Otherwise it's ...' He made a rather threatening gesture with the lobster tongs. Dickie gave a nervous laugh and pressed on into the room.

'Who were they?' asked Matt, catching up with Dickie at their table.

'Eh? Oh, they're what you might call business associates – nothing to worry about. I told you this day would come didn't I, Matt?' said Dickie, settling into a chair and opening the huge menu.

'How did the girl take it, Kitty wassername?' he said, grinning. He seemed to be relishing the misery he'd helped cause.

'I haven't told her yet,' said Matt with a wince.

'Well, she needs to grow some. It's a big boys' game. If you can't stand the heat, get out of the frying pan,' he said

'You mean kitchen, I think,' said Matt.

'Eh?' said Dickie scanning the menu.

'You said if you can't stand the heat get out of the frying pan, but if you get out of the frying pan you end up in the fire!'

'I don't know what you're talking about, but if you want something fried I'm sure I could have a word with the chef . . .'

'Does your young friend need any help wiz ze menu at all, Monsieur 'Art?' It was Maurice the maître d' again.

'He was talking about having something fried . . .' said Dickie.

Matt scanned the menu – it was an assortment of strange foreign-sounding words. What was confit of duck when it was at home? What was a cassoulet? Or coq au vin?

'I'll have the usual please, Maurice,' said Dickie folding the menu and handing it back.

'And I'll have the same,' said Matt and Ian clearly hedging their bets.

'Three fish and chips,' said Maurice jotting it down on his little pad. 'Splendido!'

'Thanks for seeing me, Mr Hart,' said Matt.

'No problem, but I don't like to talk business before I've had me lunch.'

They sat there pretty much in silence until the food came. It seemed Dickie Hart wasn't famed for his small talk.

When the food did turn up, Matt was rather surprised at the portion size. It was tiny. The fish wasn't a big slab of cod in a fat crispy overcoat of batter like he was used to from the chippy at home – it was three slivers dipped in breadcrumbs and, instead of being served on a plate, it was on what looked like a roof tile, and it had a sort of musty smell to it.

'What's this?' asked Matt in wonder.

'Goujons of monkfish cooked in truffle oil, *monsieur*!' said Maurice.

'Er ... right, and I think we ordered the fish and chips?'

'*Oui!*' sang Maurice. '*Les frites!*' and plonked down a small flowerpot with about ten extremely thin french fries in it.

'*Bon appétit!*' he said, then clicked his heels and trotted off to attend to another customer before Matt could utter the words 'tomato ketchup'.

There was the clink of a knife and fork from

Dickie's side of the table, a succession of snuffling noises, followed by a very loud burp and Dickie had finished his meal before Matt had so much as speared a single goujon.

'Very passable that,' he said leaning back in his chair and undoing the top button of his trousers. 'Right! To business then!' he said bending down to his manbag and producing a pile of printed papers about an inch thick and putting them on the table in front of Matt.

'What's that?' said Ian with a chuckle. 'The instruction manual for a Zanussi washing machine?'

'It's a contract, Ian. A five-year contract that I'd like you both to sign, just to formalise our relationship. It's fairly standard, nothing unusual . . .'

'Fair enough. I suppose I'd better have a little look through it though . . .' said Ian reaching for the bundle of papers.

Dickie moved his hand away.

'Like I say, there's nothing unusual or out of the ordinary in it.'

'Still,' said Ian, 'best I take a look . . .'

'What's up?' sneered Dickie. 'Don't you trust me, Mr Woodwinch?'

'Er ... well, it's not that exactly, and it's Woodwood, but I mean five years is a long time – Matt'll be nearly eighteen by the time he gets out of it!'

'That's just it, Ian, he won't want to get out of it! You shouldn't really look on it as a contract, more as our five-year commitment to you, Matt,' said Dickie handing Matt a pen. 'Here, son, just sign on the dotted and we can start planning our future together. I'll put your name in lights!' Dickie added – and suddenly the charm was back. it seemed to come and go like a viper's tongue. Matt gingerly took the pen and his hand hovered over the contract.

'What do you think, Ian?' said Matt turning to his stepdad.

'Um ... well, it was a very nice lunch, what there was of it ... and ... I mean Mr Hart here is very successful ...' Dickie nodded a thank you. 'Just one question, Mr Hart ...'

'Please, call me Dickie ...'

'Dickie, if for some reason things don't work out between you and Matt ...'

'If that was the case, Ian, of course I wouldn't want to hold a young lad like Matt to a contract that he wasn't happy with. No, if Matt's not happy then I'll tear the whole thing up, you have my word!'

'Well, that's good enough for me,' said Ian. 'It sounds like a really good deal.'

Matt took a deep breath and carefully signed on the dotted line. He then handed the contract to Ian who followed suit.

'Hello, Matt! What are you doing with this reprobate?' Matt looked up to see *T Factor* judge Simon Bewell.

'Hi, Simon!' said Matt, jumping to his feet and shaking Simon's hand.

'All right, Simon?' said Dickie Hart with a smug smile. 'Have a glass of bubbly with us – we're celebrating, aren't we, Matt?'

Matt nodded awkwardly. 'I guess ...' he said. He'd got what he'd wanted, he'd signed with the big London agent, so why was he feeling uneasy?

As Simon spied the contract his face fell.

'I hope that's not what I think it is.'

'It is!' said Dickie, beckoning to the waiter to bring him an extra glass. 'Yes! Matt has made the very wise decision to join us at Excalibur Management!' he said, carefully placing the signed contract into a large manilla envelope.

'But I thought you had management, Matt?' said Simon. 'I thought your friend Kitty was looking after you?'

'Er . . . she is . . . I mean she was . . .' stuttered Matt. It reminded him that he hadn't actually let Kitty know yet.

'Just a schoolgirl, Simon. Completely out of her depth, I'm afraid. She was throwing Matt's career down the toilet, so I felt it my duty to step in and chuck him a rubber ring,' said Dickie, about to pour Simon a glass of champagne.

Simon put his hand over the glass. 'Not for me thanks, Dickie,' he said coolly.

'Do I detect a little bit of jealousy, Simon? Too bad! You can't win 'em all, can you?' said Dickie with a laugh that made Matt feel a little bit sick. 'Well, if you won't toast our success, Simon . . . as nice as it is to see you, if you'll excuse me I've got a spot of business.' He licked a few residual breadcrumbs from his top lip and stood up.

'Of course, you go ahead, but I wouldn't mind

a quick word with your client here. Er ... with your permission of course,' said Simon. Despite the politeness, their exchange seemed decidedly forced.

'Not at all. Not at all. But remember, he's mine now, so don't go getting any ideas!' Dickie raised his finger and wagged it at Simon in mock warning, then he tucked his chair under the table and waved to a grubby-looking man across the room. He'd only walked about ten paces towards him when he turned back. He grabbed the contract off the table and put it in his manbag.

'Can't be too careful!' He grinned. 'There are a surprising number of dishonest persons about. I'll only be a couple of minutes, Matt, then we can get down to the nitty-gritty.' Matt shrugged and Dickie loped off in the direction of the grubby man.

'I've had dealings with Dickie Hart,' said Simon, lowering his voice. 'So just be careful, Matt, you've got my number if you need it.'

Matt nodded and thanked him for his advice.

'That was weird,' said Ian as they watched Simon

meander back to his table. 'Which reminds me, I must ask Dickie about the band. He said he'd listen to our demo tapes and maybe help us get a record deal.'

'Hmm, has he actually heard any of the Dead Toys catalogue?' said Matt sceptically.

Before long Dickie was back at their table, smelling strongly of alcohol and looking slightly the worse for wear.

'Right, Matt, as it's so late, I've booked you into the Jacobs Hotel two doors down.'

'Great! I've heard of it – there was a documentary about it on Channel 4 last year. Some of the rooms cost upwards of two thousand pounds a night!' said Ian rubbing his hands together at the prospect of a night in a top London hotel.

'Not you, mate, just him,' said Dickie pointing at Matt. 'I think Matt really needs to do this on his own don't you?'

'Er, not necessarily . . .' said Ian

'Yeah, he does, so you'd best get home. Tomorrow

Matt, I'll get you to my tailor and measure you up for some new suits, then my stylist will see you and see if she can't do something with your hair, then we really need to fix those teeth . . .'

Matt closed his mouth self-consciously. What was wrong with his teeth?

'Oh! Right! Sorry, yes of course,' said Ian, getting up to leave. 'One thing before I go – where should I send the demo tracks?'

'Eh?'

'The songs me and the band have put together – Dead Toys? When you popped round the house you mentioned you might be able to help us get signed, remember?'

'Did I?' said Dickie. 'Oh well. My advice is stick to what you know – estate agenting isn't it?'

'Er . . . yes . . . well. I mean it's a stopgap. It's music I really . . .' said Ian looking crestfallen and suddenly vulnerable.

'Yeah, stick to showing people round flats. I think you were going, Mr Windward, weren't you?'

'Er ... yes, yes, if ... you're fine with that, Matt, are you?'

'Er, I suppose so ... if Mr Hart thinks that's the right thing to do.'

'Fine. Well your mum and me are just on the end of a phone, so ... right then. I'll be off,' stuttered Ian. He gave Matt a hug and headed for the cloakroom to redeem his coat. He was back a couple of minutes later.

'Dickie? I think there's some sort of mistake – the girl in the cloakroom wants five quid off me before she'll give me back my coat!'

'And ...?' said Dickie.

'Oh, I see,' said Ian. 'Right, cheerio then,' and off he went.

19

New Suits and Teeth

Matt sat in room number 101 of the Jacobs Hotel (one of the 'Leading Hotels of the World' according to the brochure that had been placed on his bed) and looked out of his window. The view was of a brick wall with a pipe sticking out of it that intermittently puffed out what looked like steam. The steam then condensed as it hit the cool outside air giving rise to a steady drip from the end of the pipe on to the flat roof below.

He turned from the window to survey his 'five-star' room.

Mounted on the wall was a Corby trouser press.

Corby was a place wasn't it? he wondered. He took out his phone and googled it – sure enough, it was a town in Northamptonshire. A town where presumably, thought Matt, the entire population walked around with perfectly pressed trousers. He was just about to reach for his little black book to jot the idea down when his mobile phone buzzed through a text. His heart sank. It was from Kitty asking him to meet her the next day at the DMC.

He selected her text message and pressed the little blue phone symbol. As he did so a photo came up on the screen of him and Kitty that he'd taken that first time they'd visited the Hammersmith Apollo together, the time they'd been unceremoniously booted out. In the background above their heads was the blue plaque that had been erected to honour her late grandfather, the impresario Bernie Hopestein. Matt took a deep breath as he heard her answer.

'Kit, it's Matt. I'm afraid I've got some bad news . . .' His voice tailed off.

'I already know . . .' she said, her voice shaking with emotion.

'Eh? . . .?'

'You've signed with Dickie Hart at Excalibur!'

'But how . . .?'

'It's on the web – the news is everywhere!'

'Ah,' said Matt. He certainly hadn't planned this. Dickie Hart must have planted the story as soon as they'd finished their lunch.

'Oh, Matt, how could you?'

'I'm sorry, Kit, I just think Excalibur can open doors for me . . .' he protested.

'Not that! If you want a different style of management that's up to you. No, what's upset me the most is having to find out the way I did. I just look like such a fool,' She let out a sob then the line went quiet.

'Kitty? Are you still there?'

After a few moments she came back on the line – she seemed to have regained her composure.

'Anyway, I hope it all works out for you. I'll see

you around school so there's no point in us falling out. I understand your reasons even if I don't agree with them. I just hope you don't live to regret it . . .'

'Me too,' said Matt. 'I've signed up for five years, so . . .'

'FIVE YEARS!' exclaimed Kitty. 'Whatever for? Most agents just operate on a handshake!'

'Yeah well, not Excalibur! Five years is the minimum they'll take me on for, so . . .'

'When you say signed up, you didn't . . . you didn't sign a contract, Matt, did you?'

''Fraid so,' said Matt, trying to make light of his situation.

'Well, look, it's none of my business now, but promise me you'll be careful, and I'm always here if you need me.'

'Thanks, Kitty, I really appreciate it, and I'm sorry . . .' said Matt.

As he hung up he had only one thought – what on earth had he done?

20

New Beginnings

'Hello, Matt, sit down. Sleep all right?'

Matt shrugged. He'd spent a day and a half being ferried from one appointment to the next. Today he'd gone first to a very upmarket tailors in Saville Row, then to a dentist in Harley Street who had painted some sort of bleach on his teeth to whiten them up, then to a hairdresser in Chelsea who'd spent an hour and a half fiddling with his hair until it looked like a bird's nest – and it was still only lunch time. They were back at Dickie's usual table at Austin's.

'Yeah, it's not a bad little hotel that. Anyway, enough of the small talk, the meter's running let's get down to business. Your suit will be ready this afternoon ...'

'That was quick!' said Matt tucking into an odd-looking stew and finding out what cassoulet meant.

'Like I say, everything's possible. You're with the pros now. You'll have your photos done in the new suit as soon it turns up. Any questions so far?'

Matt thought for a moment, but Dickie didn't wait for an answer.

'So, holiday's over. We need to get you out there and working,' said Dickie, as a waiter placed a cup of coffee and a large frankfurter and mashed potato in front of him. 'You don't mind if I eat while I'm talking, Matt, do you? It just saves time,' said Dickie, taking a big bite out of the frankfurter.

'No, no ... That's great news!' said Matt sitting up.

'What is?' said Dickie spraying tiny lumps of sausage meat on to the tablecloth in front of him.

'About you getting me working,' said Matt. This was music to his ears. At last he was going to be doing what he'd been dreaming of for weeks – gigging.

'Yeah, right ...' said Dickie looking slightly confused as to why anyone would look forward to work. 'Now, first off, I've cancelled that poxy gig you had booked in at the school—'

'The Children in Need gig?' said Matt, concerned. 'But that's been in my diary for a while. The school are depending on me. Surely it wouldn't do any harm – I mean, it'll be a friendly crowd and it's a great cause!'

'Nah! Waste of time! You ain't doin' it,' snapped Dickie. 'Amateur hour. You're with the pros now and I don't care how good the cause is, no one gets you for free from now on. Hotel bills and new suits don't pay for themselves!'

'Hmm, about that . . .' said Matt.

'What?' burped Dickie.

'Who is paying for the suit and the hotel and . . .?'

'Don't worry about all that, Matt,' said Dickie, waving his hands dismissively. 'It's being taken care of. You worry about coming up with the funnies and I'll worry about the business. So I'm pulling the charity gig – actually I've already pulled it, agreed?'

'I suppose so ... but ...'

'No buts, just forget about it. Concentrate on payin' gigs. I've had an offer from *I'm A Celebrity Get Me Outta This Tree* – interested?'

Matt knew of the show but wasn't a fan – it was a reality show set in a forest. A number of celebrities had to live in trees for as long as they could, surviving off stuff that was either in the tree already – like nuts or fruit – or by completing tasks and winning supplies which usually meant eating bugs and generally humiliating themselves.

'So far they've got Rylan Clark, one of the Sugababes and that bloke that won that show on the island, you know where they have to survive off bugs and that ...?'

'Er ... that's *I'm A Celebrity Get Me Outta This Tree* isn't it?' said Matt.

'Er ... it's similar, only they don't live in a tree, they live on an island ...'

'Well, to be honest it's not the sort of thing ...'

'Anyway, I've said yes – just waiting on how much they're gonna pay you. Great for your profile – an appearance on that alone will win you six months of paid work and if you win it, well, the sky's the limit.'

'Yeah but I'm a comedian . . .'

'Whatever!' said Dickie ticking it off his list. 'We'll talk about it later. Now, you'll like this one – I've had a lot of interest for corporates—'

'Corporates . . .?' said Matt. 'What . . .?'

'You know, office dos, that sorta thing. You turn up and mingle with the hoi polloi, then go on and do as long as you can before they lose interest.'

'Well, hopefully they wouldn't lose interest until I'd finished my set . . .'

'Yeah, right and what's that out the window? Oh, it's a pig riding a unicycle and juggling with satsumas,' said Dickie sarcastically. 'No one ever goes down well at these dos. Most of the punters aren't interested in listening to comedy – they're just waiting for the disco so they can get off with Doris from accounts.'

'So why would I want to do one then?' said Matt,

starting to get a little bit exasperated.

'They're good payers. The people booking them realise celebs don't want to do them and so they have to pay them over the odds. Some of my clients, that's all they do – corporates. Pays the bills, plus has the added attraction that no one knows you're doing them.'

'Again,' said Matt with a frown, 'if no one knows about them, how's that going to further my career?'

'Huh!' said Dickie annoyed. 'For someone who's only ever done one gig you've got a lot to say! Now how'd you feel about adverts . . .?'

And so it went on.

Dickie outlined a whole series of moneymaking ventures that seemed to Matt to have nothing to do with comedy. There was a fly spray commercial for TV, a photo campaign for spot cream, a voice-over for a teen dating website . . . As the list went on Matt became more and more dispirited. It seemed Dickie had plenty of well-paid projects to keep Matt busy – it was just that not one of them seemed to involve stand-up comedy.

'Er, sorry to stop you mid-flow, Dickie . . .' interjected Matt.

'Eh?' said Dickie, looking up from his precious list. 'Yeah, what?'

'Er . . . don't get me wrong. All that's great, what you've got planned – some of which I need to think about . . . Um, but I am, or should I say my main interest, is in stand-up comedy, so what I'm really keen to do is some gigs. So I'm wondering if somewhere on your list you've got me down to do any . . . you know, some of the clubs in London?'

'Stand-up?' said Dickie .

'Yeah, you know like, maybe some ten-minute spots to try out some new gags, building to some paid twenties?' said Matt hopefully.

'Oh! Yes! I have got you a nice stand-up gig – I almost forgot! You're gonna love this. It's ten minutes and it's really well paid.'

'Great!' said Matt – it sounded too good to be true. 'Whereabouts?'

'You know it. In fact you've actually played it before . . .' said Dickie.

Matt was confused. He'd only done four gigs in his whole life, three if you didn't count the school talent show.

'Not the Cavendish?' he asked trying to work out what Dickie was on about.

'Not the Cavendish, whatever that is . . .' said Dickie.

'Surely not the Rose and Crown, Sossinghurst!' said Matt.

'Of course it isn't some poxy pub in the middle of nowhere!' replied Dickie.

'Well,' said Matt, still confused, 'the only other gig I've done is the Apollo so . . .'

'Exactly!' said Dickie with an oh-so-pleased-with-himself look on his face. 'I've only got you booked on the top stand-up show on TV! *Stand-up at the Apollo*! Ha ha!' He punched the air in triumph and then held it up to Matt for a high five – but Matt didn't offer his hand in return. He sat back, feeling like he'd been kicked in the stomach.

'The Apollo . . . but . . . but Kitty said I wasn't ready for the Apollo . . .' he said.

'Kitty says this, Kitty says that! If I hear that name one more time I'll . . . I'll . . .' snapped Dickie. 'When I start taking the advice of a schoolgirl I'll know I'm really in trouble. Forget her, Matt, put her out of your mind. That was the advice of an amateur and now you're with the professionals!'

Matt shuddered – that word 'amateur' again. It was the word Matt had used to describe Kitty. If only she knew what he was up to now.

'Yeah, you're on with my boy Russ as a matter of fact – Russel Perkins. Yeah, I finally got them to take him. Nice wedge on it too, so we all get our snouts in the trough!'

Dickie Hart stopped talking for a second and took a good long look at his client who had gone as white as a sheet.

'What's up with you?' he said.

'I . . . I . . . I dunno . . .' stuttered Matt. 'I mean, I've always wanted to do that show, but I . . . I need to do a lot of work to get match fit for it don't I?'

'Oh, you'll be fine,' said Dickie, batting Matt's concerns away like they were a couple of paper planes. 'Besides, I've already booked you in so . . .' he said absent-mindedly.

'You've what?!' said Matt.

'Relax! I've booked you in, but don't worry, you'll have plenty of time to get yourself straight for it.'

'Wow!' said Matt starting to come round to the idea. If he had enough time to work up some new material then surely it was a good idea wasn't it? Dickie had a point – *Stand-up at the Apollo* was the show Matt had most wanted to do when he'd started out. He'd never missed an episode. Surely, provided he had enough time to work on some new material, it could be a really big break – in a way a kind of relaunch.

'When did you have in mind then?' said Matt taking out his phone and looking at his diary.

'Tomorrow!' said Dickie.

'What?! B-B-B-B-B-but I've got no new material!' said Matt.

'What do you need new stuff for? Just do the stuff you did on *The T Factor* – that had them rolling in the aisles! Bish bash bosh! Job's a goodun'! You get paid! And more importantly so do I!' said Dickie with a smirk.

'But you don't understand,' protested Matt. 'They'll have heard all my jokes before – no one will laugh!'

'Pah! I wouldn't worry about that! Besides, if no one laughs they can dub them on in the edit! Job's a goodun'! Right, that's enough chat for one day,' said Dickie, getting up to leave. He put his hand deep into his trouser pocket and produced a roll of fifty-pound notes, more money than Matt had ever seen in his whole life. He peeled off a couple and threw them on to the table.

'There'll be a car to pick you up tomorrow afternoon at three. I suggest you get workin' on that act of yours! Cheery bye!' And with that he was gone.

That evening Matt sat in his hotel room looking at his set list. His gums were still sore from where that dentist had tried to whiten his teeth. He looked in the mirror. 'The only reason my teeth look whiter is that my gums are bright red,' he thought to himself. What was happening to him? He looked over at his two new suits hanging on the back of the door. There was no doubt that they were beautiful, but it wasn't the kind of new material he was looking for.

He needed new jokes and stage-time to run them in, and he knew that between now and 3 p.m. the next day when the car was due to pick him up, he wasn't going to get either.

He flicked through his notebook. Sure, there were some really strong ideas for gags and routines but without trying them out in front of a crowd, how could he possibly know which ones would fly and which would drop like stones? He looked around the room. It was much nicer than his room at home, but it wasn't his room and he had no one to share it with. He was bored witless. There was absolutely nothing to do. There were only so many times you could press your trousers in a Corby trouser press, and a limit to the amount of Highland shortcake biscuits a twelve-year-old boy could consume. He picked up his phone and scrolled down his list of contacts. The person he really wanted to talk to was Kitty Hope but of course that wasn't possible.

Next on his list was Rob Brown. He clicked on his number and walked over to the hotel room window with the phone to his ear. There was a click as Rob picked up.

'Hello? Matt?!' Rob was shouting over what sounded like a Nicki Minaj number. Matt could hear shouting and laughter in the background.

'Oh, hi, Rob!' said Matt, incredibly pleased to hear his old friend's voice. 'What are you up to? Sounds like you're at a party or something?'

'Eh?!' shouted Rob. 'Sorry, Matt, I can't hear you, I'm at Ahmed's birthday-do – are you gonna be turning up? He said he emailed you the invite?'

A wave of homesickness swept over Matt. He'd got Ahmed's invite but with all that had gone on over the last few days he hadn't got round to replying, the date had fallen out of the bottom of his inbox and he'd forgotten all about it.

'Sorry, Rob, I can't. I'm stuck up in London.'

'EH? You what?! Hang on I'll go outside . . .' Rob broke off and then Matt could hear footsteps and a door being opened and closed. The music became muffled.

'You still there?' said Rob.

'Yeah, yeah ... still here, worst luck,' said Matt biting his lip.

'That's better! I can hear you now. Sorry I haven't called but I've been working on the poster for the big Children in Need gig – and you'll be pleased to hear that your picture is very much centre stage ...'

'Ah. OK ... cheers!' said Matt feeling a pang of guilt. He didn't have the heart to tell Rob that Dickie had pulled him from the gig.

'So anyway, how's it going? How's life in the big city?' Rob continued.

'Er ... it's OK ...' said Matt. 'You know, I've had some new suits made and photos done and that ...'

'You don't sound too sure?' said Rob. Matt couldn't hide his true feelings from Rob – he knew him too well.

'How's it working out under the new management?' said Rob.

'Well, if I'm honest, it's not really,' said Matt.

'No? How come?'

'That Dickie Hart bloke has only gone and booked me in to play *Stand-up at the Apollo*!'

'That's fantastic news, Matt! Wait till I tell Ahmed! Any chance of tickets? What's the date? I could get my mum to drive us up . . .'

'That's just it, it's tomorrow!'

'Tomorrow? Jeez! You don't hang about. Let me think. I'm supposed to be going to drama club but I can probably get out of it. Hang on, let me just check with Ahmed . . .'

'NO!' said Matt forcefully.

'No? What . . .?' said Rob, suddenly chastened.

'I don't want you to come,' said Matt.

'Why ever not? I'd love to . . .'

'Because I'm gonna die,' said Matt bleakly.

'No you won't! You're Matt Millz, what are you talking about? Besides, you said that last time you played the Apollo and what happened? You ripped the roof off!'

'It's different this time,' said Matt ruefully. 'I was ready for it then, or as ready for it as I was ever gonna be. The fact is I haven't done a good gig since then – I'm still stuck with the same material. Kitty was right, I'm just not ready. No, I'm gonna die and there's nothing I can do about it.'

'You're exaggerating,' said Rob trying to cheer him up. He seemed completely wrong-footed by his friend's tone and was seriously starting to worry about him. 'Do you want to talk to Kitty? She's just in the other room, I could get her if you like?'

There was no one right now that Matt wanted to speak to more than Kitty Hope but he knew he mustn't, that it just wasn't fair after the way he'd treated her.

'No, no, it's OK. You're right, Rob, I'm probably overdoing it, it's just nerves. It'll probably be fine.'

'Yeah! Exactly, that's more like it! Well, if you change your mind about us coming along . . .'

'Maybe another time . . .' said Matt.

'Yeah, cool. Alex's just walking by – do you want a word?'

Alex? Suddenly the image of those big blue eyes

flashed into Matt's mind.

'Yeah OK,' he said, clearing his throat and self-consciously adjusting his fringe with his free hand.

'Hello?' came a girl's voice. 'Matt?'

'Alex?' said Matt, feeling suddenly a little shy and awkward. 'How's it going?'

'Hi, Matt! Yeah good, I think. We've got another go at the Sossinghurst gig, so hopefully it'll go better than last time.'

'We never had that writing session, did we?' he said.

'Ah well, you're incredibly busy. How's things your end? Rob said you were in London or something?'

'Yes, I am. Pretty cool, but kind of boring too if I'm honest,' said Matt.

'I'm sure you're being modest. I'm really pleased things are going well for you.'

'Thanks, Alex. Anyway, I'll be back in a couple of days – I have to be. I can't miss any more school!'

'Oh, you're not missing much!' she said. 'While you're away I've been helping Rob out with your school magazine joke page. It's not as funny as when you do it, but I've enjoyed it.'

'Oh,' said Matt. The mention of the joke page brought all sorts of happy memories flooding back. Him and Rob had always had such fun making up jokes about the teachers and seeing what they could get away with. Matt could hear them starting to sing 'Happy Birthday' in the background.

'You'd better go . . .' he said.

'OK then. Looking forward to seeing you again though,' she said.

'Yeah, me too.'

'She's great, Matt!' said Rob, coming back on the phone. 'Anyway, when you back?'

'Not really sure, Rob. Dickie hasn't told me yet. I'm hoping at the weekend . . .'

'Well, let me know and we'll hang out. OK?'

'Yeah, thanks, mate, you've cheered me up,' said Matt forcing a smile as he stared out of the window at the dripping pipe.

'Oh, hang on, I can see Ahmed's mum and she's

got a cake and it looks like a big chocolate one, so I'll catch you later. Good luck tomorrow!'

'Thanks, Rob.'

'Text me how it went!'

'Will do,' said Matt and he pressed the little red phone icon and the screen went dark.

Matt sighed and returned to his set list, which now just looked like a jumble of stray words, crossings out and arrows. It was no use – he threw his trusty black book on to the bed and decided he needed a bit of fresh air to clear his head.

He took the lift down to the lobby and lingered at the window. Looking along Piccadilly he could see a mass of bright lights. Then it dawned on him what lay at the end of Piccadilly – Leicester Square – and for the first time that day his face broke into a smile.

21

Comedy Central

It was about ten o'clock as Matt stepped out of the revolving door of the Jacobs Hotel and into the cool night air of Piccadilly. He turned right and headed up towards the bright lights he'd spotted from the lobby window. He was amazed at just how busy it was. It seemed that no one ever went to bed in this town! He walked up past Piccadilly Circus with its famous winged statue of Eros, the god of love with the bow and arrow. Matt had someone in mind that he'd like to fire an arrow at right now and his initials were DH.

He looked up to the left as he came to Leicester

Square and could see a string of Chinese restaurants and a huge oriental arch which screamed 'Welcome to Chinatown'. Matt's interest, however, lay to the right, at the corner where Piccadilly petered out, just by the Prince Edward Theatre. A huge hoarding advertised the hit musical 'I Can't Sing!' Ignoring this, he turned right down Oxenden Street and just a few yards on the right lay the object of his interest – The Comedy Store.

A burly minder stood outside looking . . . well . . . thoroughly burly. His hair in braids, his gaze fixed on the middle distance, he looked like he could pick Matt up with just one of his hands. Matt approached and looked up at him.

'Ahem!' he coughed clearing his throat. The minder didn't move a muscle.

'Er . . . hello?!' said Matt hopefully.

The minder slowly lowered his gaze until he was looking directly into Matt's eyes. Suddenly his frown broke into a huge smile that revealed several gold teeth.

'Matt Millz!' he said, sticking a hand out in welcome. 'I'm Mark but everyone calls me Big Mark – dunno why! Welcome to The Comedy Store!'

Matt shook his hand. 'Wow!' he said. 'You know who I am!'

'Of course I do! I know just about every comic in Britain – and ninety-nine per cent of them have come through this door! Are you doing a spot?'

'I wish,' said Matt shaking his head.

'Well, the first show's almost done but you're welcome to stand at the back,' he said. 'Follow me, I'll get you in.'

He opened the door and Matt followed him down the stairs into the yellowy-orange light. At the bottom of the stairs were a pair of black double doors with porthole-like windows through which Matt caught his first glimpse of the stage. Framed as it was by the windows, it appeared to Matt like twin circular jewels.

'Ah, good, we're on a break ...' said Big Mark peering through one of the portholes.

'There you go, Matt, enjoy the show!' said the bouncer and Matt stepped through the doors and stood at the back of a huge horseshoe of tiered seating that reminded him from his history lessons of a Roman amphitheatre. At the centre was a relatively small – perhaps five metres wide – slightly raised stage. The entire room was painted black apart from the laughing-mouth logo of The Comedy Store that hung behind the stage.

On the wall were grainy black and white photos of past glories. Comedy Store alumni like Charlie Baker, Alexei Sayle, Arnold Brown, Lee Hurst, Eddie Izzard, Dominic Holland, Jo Brand – it struck Matt as rather old-fashioned that they were mainly men. The air was thick and fuggy from the lights and the crowd, it smelt of beer and sweat and ladies' perfume and generally of people determined to have a good time.

'Please take your seats, the show will start in five minutes,' came a voice over the PA.

Some of the audience were still in their seats, but

most were up at the bar or wandering back, clutching drinks. There were no seats free, so Matt found a piece of wall to lean against and waited for the show to commence.

Pretty soon the lights dimmed, the music started to get louder, building to a crescendo, and the audience started applauding and stamping their feet in anticipation. For Matt it was utterly thrilling. Then through a door at the back of the stage bounded the compere.

'Welcome back to part two,' he said grabbing the microphone. 'Did you have a good break?'

'Yeeaaaah!' the audience replied as one. He'd been on for less than a minute and already had them eating out of his hand.

'I'm glad you had a good break,' said the compere, 'because I'm afraid I had a bit of bad news . . .'

'Ahhhh!' said a handful from the crowd. The compere grinned wryly – they knew he didn't really have any bad news, they knew that they were being pulled into a set-up for a gag but they were more than happy to go along for the ride.

'Yes, thanks, I appreciate your sympathy. I went to the doctor's today and complained that I'd been to three other doctors and none of them agreed with his diagnosis. My doctor said, "Wait till the post mortem – they'll see I'm right!" That's not good, right?'

The audience rocked back in laughter, then a man in a beer-stained suit appeared with a big tray of drinks and wandered down one of the rows to his seat, handing out foaming pints of beer to his friends as he went. The MC spotted him immediately. 'Hey! Where's mine?' he said to a huge laugh. The guy with the drinks shrugged and tried to get to his seat that bit quicker.

'Don't just ignore me! Where's my drink?' said the compere. He was determined not to let him off the hook – Matt understood the psychology perfectly. He needed to establish who was in control of the room and deter anyone else from even thinking about wandering around while the other acts were doing their stuff. The guy shrugged again and looked at a loss as to what to say. The audience meanwhile were loving every moment of his embarrassment and were even more thrilled that none of it was directed at them.

'Go and get me a drink!' said the compere sternly. The late guy hesitated for a moment then turned and headed back to the bar – to a huge round of applause from the crowd. The compere laughed too and shook his head and pressed on with the rest of his act. 'Hey, I went to a gypsy fortune teller the other day, yes, and the fortune teller said, "Pay me twenty quid and I'll tell you your future – you can ask three questions." I said, "About what?" She said, "About anything." I said, "Isn't twenty quid a bit steep?" and she said, "That's two … and what is your last question?" Another big laugh.

And so it went on. Matt was watching the audience as much as the compere, watching as their faces lit up in laughter, how they exchanged a knowing look when the compere mentioned something that resonated with them. Although Matt was enjoying the compere's act, it was the ad libs that really made this comic stand out – he had lightning quick reflexes, nothing seemed to floor him, and that in essence was, Matt decided, the thrill of watching a live performance. Anything could happen! On any one night the audience were getting a one-off performance just for them and it was thrilling.

After a few minutes, just as the compere seemed to be winding up and preparing the crowd for the first act, the guy with the drinks appeared at the side of the stage with a pint for him.

'At last!' said the compere, then he took the pint, put it to his lips and drained it in one go. He let out a satisfied burp, then handed the empty glass back to the hapless latecomer.

'Nah, mate, that was lager. I fancied a gin and tonic!'

The room went crazy with laughter. The guy just stood there holding the empty glass, wanting the ground to open up and swallow him, then the compere let him off the hook.

'That'll teach you to be late to my gig! Now go and sit down before I have another go!'

A look of relief flooded across the guy and he made his way back to his seat, his friends all slapping him on the back and giving him lip as he went.

'He'll never hear the last of that,' thought Matt to himself with a chuckle.

'Right,' said the compere, signalling a change in pace. 'Every now and then at The Comedy Store we get some very special people dropping by to try out a few gags and we're very lucky to have such a special guest tonight . . .'

A murmur of excitement went through the crowd as they speculated as to who the 'special guest' might be.

'Ladies and gentlemen, you are very lucky indeed. It is my great honour to introduce the star of *Stand-up at the Apollo* – the one and only Eddie Odillo!'

With that the door at the back of the stage burst open and there was Matt's all-time comedy hero. The audience went wild as Eddie shook the compere's hand and took the mic. Then he stood centre stage and peered at the audience with a very serious look on his face, staring at them until the applause finally died down. There was an awkward silence as the audience wondered what on earth was wrong with him. Was he ill? Was he drunk? Was he 'on' something?

Just as that confusion was about to turn to concern he pulled an incredibly funny face. 'Hey heeeeeey!' he boomed into the mic. The tension he'd created in those few short moments was suddenly released in the form of a massive laugh. Matt laughed too and shook his head in wonder. How did he do that? How had he known exactly how long to wait before pulling that face? How did he know that that particular face was going to be so funny? Had he tried various faces before settling on that one? This guy was a master of the craft!

Matt looked at the crowd again. They'd been laughing hard at the compere's antics but the reaction Eddie was getting was on a completely different scale. People were literally doubled up, the veins in their necks bulged, their faces were red and swollen, their eyes wet with tears – if a stranger walked in now and didn't know it was a comedy gig they might think they were looking at a room full of asthmatics.

'However funny I am,' thought Matt, 'I'll never be as funny as this . . .' He felt a sudden deep ache in the pit of his stomach as he remembered that tomorrow he'd be facing an audience of his own.

'He's going to be a tough act to follow,' whispered a voice from behind him. Matt looked round to see a small dapper man of about seventy in clothes he'd seen advertised in the Sunday supplements as Country Casuals. He had grey hair and deep laughter lines around his gently smiling eyes.

'Ron Wardle,' he said shaking Matt's hand. 'I run the store. You're Matt aren't you?'

'Wow! You're a legend!' said Matt, shaking the little man's hand a little too enthusiastically. Ron winced. 'Aargh! Mind my arthritis!'

'Oops, sorry!' said Matt, releasing his grip.

'I caught your spot on *The T Factor* on YouTube the other day, Matt – some of the acts were looking at it in the dressing room. You show promise. Think you're ready to play The Store yet?'

'I'd love to at some point,' said Matt, mindful of biting off more than he could chew again.

'What have you been doing between then and now?' said Ron.

'Sadly not a lot. There's not much of a comedy scene in Kent, where I live.'

'Kent! Lovely part of the world! My mum's got a place down in Folkestone. You need to get plenty of gigs under your belt – stage-time, that's the key. I've seen 'em all come through here of course. Young Eddie up there – he wasn't at all funny when he started. I remember the first time he came to us, he was just a bit older than you – just a spotty kid, with buck teeth and big ears. The audience hated him! He died on his proverbial! Ha! But I could see he had something. I told him to go away and come back in a year. He came back twelve months later and stormed it. The thing to remember, Matt, is it's a marathon not a sprint . . .'

There was that phrase again, thought Matt, the one Kitty and Bobby had used. A marathon, not a sprint.

'Take your time, work hard, you'll get there. Ah! Talk of the devil!' said Ron looking over Matt's shoulder. Matt turned to see Eddie Odillo making his way towards them.

'Mr Millz! We meet again!' said Eddie clapping his arms around Matt and greeting him like a long-lost friend. 'You on next?'

'We can't afford him!' joked Ron.

'Hi, Eddie,' said Matt blushing and suddenly becoming extremely self-conscious. 'No, no, I was in the area and I've always wanted to see this place so . . . you were great up there! Are you working up new stuff for a tour or . . .?'

'A bit of that, but mainly just brushing up my stuff for tomorrow night's Apollo show.'

'I'll see you there then,' said Matt sheepishly.

'You're doing the Apollo and you haven't even played here yet?' said Ron incredulously, exchanging a knowing look with Eddie.

'Bad idea right?' said Matt.

'Not necessarily,' said Eddie, trying to stay upbeat. 'But it's a big show. I mean ... yeah ... well, you've already played the Apollo so that's an advantage.'

'My agent booked it ...'

'That girl, right? Katy ... er ...'

'Kitty? No, she doesn't look after me any more,' said Matt staring forlornly at his shoes.

'Wow, that was a quick turnaround ...' said Eddie, raising his eyebrows.

'No, I'm with Excalibur,' said Matt.

'NOOOOOOOO!' said Eddie holding up his two index fingers in a cross and sinking to his knees like in a horror film. 'Not Excalibur!'

For some reason Ron found this incredibly funny.

'Ha! That explains everything!' he said. 'I wish you'd come to me first, Matt. That Dickie Hart is

trouble. He's hobbled more careers than he's made.'

'Hey, they're not all bad, Ron. He's doing well for Russel. How many nights did he do at the O2? Something like two weeks wasn't it?' said Eddie.

'I heard he papered it and Russ lost money, a small fortune in fact.' said Ron.

'Papered? What's that?' said Matt.

'It's when they can't sell enough tickets so they give them away free. Sometimes they dress it up as prizes for competitions, other times they just stand outside and hand 'em out,' said Ron.

'Doesn't make for a good show,' said Eddie. 'If you

haven't paid for your ticket you're probably not a fan.'

'That explains a lot,' said Matt. 'I went to that show . . .'

'Of course! Did you pay?'

'Ha! No!'

'Neither did I!' laughed Eddie

'You're right,' said Matt, nodding. 'It wasn't great either, and Russel seemed really pee-d off after it.'

'Ha! He probably just got the bill!'

'The bill? I don't understand. Why would Russ lose money? Surely filling the venue is the promoter's job?'

'It certainly should be,' said Ron. 'But that's not how Excalibur work. They make the acts take the financial risk. It's outrageous!'

'Ah well, it works out great if you're a sell-out – but if you're not, you can lose your shirt. The O2 is a big old place to fill,' added Eddie.

'You didn't seem to have any problem,' gushed Matt.

'You're too kind, good sir!' said Eddie bowing low,

like he was an actor in a French farce.

'Eddie!' came a girl's voice from behind him. 'Can I get a selfie?' The early show at The Comedy Store had finished without Matt even realising it, so engrossed was he in his chat with these two comedy giants. The girl and her friend were level with Eddie and had a hand on each of his shoulders and were trying to kiss him.

'Easy, girls! Steady on now!' said Eddie rolling his eyes at Matt. The girls were clearly the worse for wear. 'Don't crumple the suit please!'

The girls were holding their smartphones up but in their inebriated state were having difficulty getting them to work. As Eddie waited patiently he turned to Matt.

'Anyway, Matt, don't worry about tomorrow. Just be as funny as you were on *The T Factor* and you'll be fine. Now if you'll excuse me I must attend to my adoring public.' He then took the smartphone from one of the girls' hand, pulled a face at the camera and took the selfie she was after. By the time he'd done that, a small queue had formed behind them.

'Nice man . . .' muttered Ron. 'You're welcome to stay for the late show, Matt.'

'Late show? It's half past eleven, that's late enough for me,' said Matt. 'Really good to meet you, Mr Wardle, but I'd better get back. Bit of a day of it tomorrow!'

'Indeed. Any time, Matt. Oh and let me know if I can help,' said Ron giving Matt one of his business cards.

The next morning Matt wished he'd stayed for the late show. There had certainly been no point in going to bed – he hadn't slept a wink all night.

FUNCTIONS OF A COMPERE

Settles the audience down, warms them up, gets them laughing. Draws any hostile fire and deals with it. Doesn't do so long as to tire out the audience. Is able to judge exactly when to bring on the acts. For instance if someone goes fantastically well the compere may need to settle the audience down otherwise it makes it harder for the next act to follow them. Similarly if an act bombs, the compere will have to go back on and whip the audience back up to give the next comic a chance.

Often under appreciated, audiences sometimes don't think of the compere or MC as a comic at all – sometimes he or she is even mistaken for the manager of the club! It's a highly skilled job that requires particular talents. As well as being able to make an audience laugh, they need to be able to improvise and it's as much audience wrangling as entertaining.

22

Return to the Scene of the Crime

'I can't do it, Mr Hart, I can't go on! I'll die! I've got no new jokes! I just haven't had time – what with all these meetings and press and stuff. They'll have heard them all!'

It was ten past three in the afternoon and the car had arrived at Matt's hotel to take him and his manager to the Apollo for the evening's recording.

'It'll be fine!' said Dickie through gritted teeth. 'They can dub the laughs on later!'

'No! It won't be fine, I'll tank on national TV and that'll be it! It'll be over! I can't! Look at me, I'm a bag of nerves!'

'Then borrow some,' said Dickie Hart with a growl.

'Eh? What's that? Borrow what?' said Matt, hardly believing his ears.

'Nick some gags off someone else!' barked Dickie Hart, grabbing Matt roughly by the lapels of his jacket and pinning him up against the wall of the hotel room. 'Look, I don't really care how you get them ... just get them, and get on that stage and be funny!'

'Well I couldn't do that,' said Matt, suddenly calm again. In an instant all his misgivings about Dickie and his agency had been confirmed. Stealing jokes? That was against everything Matt and Eddie and anyone who earned a living out of comedy stood for.

'Can't or won't?' sneered Dickie, leaning his face in so close to Matt's that any closer and technically they'd be married!

'OK I won't!' said Matt. 'I won't steal another comic's material, OK? It's against my ...' but his voice tailed off.

'Against your what?' snapped Dickie. Matt could smell the nauseating pine aftershave that seemed to exude from every pore of the agent's body.

'. . . principles.' said Matt, his voice sounding thin and weak, like the whine of a puppy. The lack of sleep and his emotions suddenly drained all the energy out of his body.

'Principles? Pah!' said Dickie with utter disdain. 'You can't afford to have principles, sonny Jim!'

He then released his grip and Matt slumped slowly down the wall until he was sitting on the floor with his legs stretched out in front of him.

'It's against my principles, Mr Hart,' said Dickie mimicking Matt and waving his hands around like a toddler having a tantrum. 'Let's get one thing straight, here and now! You *are* doing that show! You've got no choice! You owe me, big time! Now pull yourself together and get in that car!'

Matt quietly stood up and as if in a trance picked up his suit bag and walked out of the hotel room, followed by Dickie. They took the lift to the ground floor, crossed the foyer and went through the revolving doors to Alf and the waiting limousine.

He didn't exchange a single word with Dickie for the entire thirty-minute journey to Hammersmith.

23

That Pie's for You

Matt shuddered as the limo pulled up outside the Apollo. When once he'd been excited to see the huge hoarding advertising the *Stand-up at the Apollo* show, now it just made him feel sick to his stomach. He and Dickie were ushered through the stage door by a girl with a clipboard and shown to a dressing room. He hung his suit bag on the back of the door, still in a sort of haze, like he was sleepwalking – as if the grim inevitability of his imminent failure was almost too much for his waking self to bear.

'Right then, Matt!' said the girl with the clipboard breezily, having gone through various timings and rules about the use of mobile phones. 'If you need anything just let me know!'

Matt nodded, not having taken in a single word, and sat down at the dressing table.

'Good lad . . .' said Dickie, trying his best to sound sympathetic. It clearly wasn't an emotion that came easily to him. 'Russel P's on the show too, and he wants to have a word with me . . . I'll leave you to it. The car's booked and will take you back to the 'otel afterwards. I'll give you a ring later, yeah?'

Matt didn't answer, just sat there staring into space.

'Right well . . .' said Dickie, backing towards the dressing-room door, not really knowing how to react. '. . . Knock 'em dead!'

The door clicked shut behind him and Matt was all alone. Again.

He turned and looked at his reflection in the dressing-room mirror. He looked haunted. He had dark rings around his eyes from lack of sleep, his hair was lank and greasy and he had what looked like the beginnings of a cold sore on his top lip. He sighed, then retrieved his set list from his sports bag, unfolded it and flattened it out on the table in front of him. As he looked down it the weird detached feeling gave way to despair. Here were jokes that a few weeks ago he couldn't wait to share with an audience but which now just seemed old and out of date.

Kitty's words came back to him like a bolt out of the blue: 'Confidence is one of the comic's most powerful tools!'

His confidence was rock bottom. What on earth was he going to do?

Just then there was a knock at the door. Matt rose to his feet reluctantly and answered it to reveal what looked like a big bunch of flowers on legs.

'Mr Millz?' came a voice from behind the flowers that Matt vaguely recognised.

'Yes?' said Matt more than a little confused.

'Flowers for you!' Then a face appeared through the flowers, a face that Matt was more than relieved to see. It belonged to Bobby Bath.

'Bobby!' exclaimed Matt, forgetting his troubles for a moment and giving the old comic and the flowers a big hug.

'Matt, I hope you don't mind but I happened to be passing and I know Wilf on front of house from the old days, so he let me pop back here to wish you luck! How's it going? You got all your gags ready?'

'Oh, Bobby, am I glad to see you!' said Matt, pulling Bobby into the dressing room and shutting the door behind him. 'No, no I haven't got all my gags sorted – well, I have but they're the same ones as I did last time I was here. They'll have heard every single one before! I've not had a chance to test-drive any new stuff! They're gonna rip me to shreds!'

'Hang on, hang on ...' said Bobby, putting the flowers in the sink and sitting down in a threadbare red-velvet armchair, the one other chair in the tiny room. 'Now just take a minute. I'm sure things aren't as bad as you think – although I must say I was surprised when Rob told me you were doing the

Apollo show. I mean that's really hanging out with the big boys. Eddie wossername hosts it doesn't he?'

'Eddie Odillo, yes. I bumped into him last night and he couldn't believe it either! Dickie booked me on to it – it was all his idea!'

'Eddie Odillo, that's right – funny man, even to an old fogey like me. I'm sure if your new agent booked you on to the show then he must feel you're ready for it. Why else would he do it?'

'Money!' said Matt. 'It's all he seems to be interested in!'

'Is that right?' said Bobby crossly. It was the first time Matt had seen Bobby looking anything other than cheerful.

'Listen, Matt, I'll tell you what Bruce Forsyth once told me—'

'You worked with Bruce . . .?' exclaimed Matt. He was a big fan of one of the few men who could claim to be an all-round entertainer.

'I did, in 1986, lovely bloke. Summer season. One night after the show we both went on to the pier for a pie and chips. Well, Bruce had to wear a hat and a scarf pulled up right under his nose – he couldn't go anywhere back then without being mobbed, and that chin of his was a dead giveaway,' chuckled Bobby. 'Anyway, we were sat on the pier, looking out over the beautiful waters of Eastbourne – not exactly Barbados, but it has its own charm! Anyway, Bruce wolfs down his dinner but I'm struggling to finish my pie. Then Bruce turns to me and says, "What's up?" I told him I couldn't finish the pie and I hate to waste good food. And he says – and I'll never forget this – he says, "That pie is for you, you're not for that pie!" Wise words.'

As Bobby finished his story, he nodded and sat back in the armchair with a self-satisfied look on his face.

'Eh?' said Matt. He'd been hoping for a bit of advice on how to deal with his old set list and all he'd got from Bobby was advice on pies! 'What are you talking about?'

'Oh! Yeah, sorry . . .' said Bobby. 'What I meant

was, your agent is like that pie ...'

'Wha—?' said Matt shaking his head, still none the wiser. 'Let me get this straight, you're saying Dickie Hart is like a pie?'

BRUCE FORSYTH (1928 – 2017) FACT FILE

TV presenter, actor, comedian, singer, dancer – one of the few truly all-round entertainers. Holds world record for longest television career for a male entertainer (over 75 years.)

Style – Didn't tell jokes as such, brilliant off-the cuff/improv.

Shows – Sunday Night at the London Palladium, The Generation Game, Play Your Cards Right, Strictly Come Dancing.

Influences – Stand-up comic

Max Miller (1894 – 1963), singer/
dancer Sammy Davis Jr.
   Catchphrases – Nice to see you,
to see you nice / Didn't they do
well!

'Exactly,' said Bobby, sitting forward. 'Your agent is supposed to be there for you – you're not supposed to be there for your agent. You employ him, he doesn't employ you. Get it?'

Finally the penny dropped.

'Yeah, you're right,' said Matt nodding his head, 'but I don't see how that's going to help me right now. Dickie's booked me on to this show so I'll just have to do it.' Suddenly the awful realisation of what was about to happen to him came back in a massive wave and he lost it completely.

'Oh god, Bobby, I'm just so scared! I mean I always get nervous but it's usually a sort of excitement nerves, not like proper fear! My mind's a jumble,

I can't think straight, what am I going to do? I just don't feel funny!'

'Then you mustn't go on, Matt, simple as that ...' said Bobby calmly, a look of quiet determination settling in his eyes.

'But you didn't hear Dickie Hart – I've got no choice!'

'That's where he's wrong – you do have a choice. This is show business, son. There are no emergencies, the stakes aren't life and death – it's just silly stuff, fluff, here one minute, gone the next. Believe me, if you go on that stage tonight you'll regret it for as long as you live.'

'But how can I get out of it?' asked Matt.

'I've got an idea,' said Bobby, tapping the side of his nose with his index finger.

'An idea ...?

'Now listen very closely ...'

24

One Good Turn

'So you see, there's no way he can go on ...' said Bobby to the producer and virtually the entire production team of *Stand-up at the Apollo* who were crowded into Matt's dressing room ten minutes later.

'I see ...' said the producer, soberly looking at Matt who was lying, panting in the armchair. 'I had no idea he had asthma.'

'Yes well, it's not normally a problem,' said Bobby, 'but there's a lot of dust in these old theatres you see, which must have set it off and as you can see he's in no fit state so—'

'But that leaves us an act short!' interjected the

stage manager. 'And he's due on in ...' she looked at her watch, '... exactly seven minutes.'

'Well, you'll have to get someone else or get Eddie to fill or pick that bit up next week and edit it in or something ...' said Bobby knowledgeably.

'I'm afraid that's out of the question,' said the producer. 'This is the last show in the series. We can't afford to reconvene the whole thing – it would cost the production a fortune and we're already over budget having had to fork out for Russel Perkins! Besides it's being broadcast later tonight!' The production team all nodded in agreement.

'What about your warm-up man?' said Bobby. 'Couldn't you promote him to one of the acts?'

'Hmm, that's an idea!' said the producer, brightening.

'I sent him home,' said the stage manager. 'Ray's wife had a baby last week and with just one act to go I didn't think we'd need him.'

'Well, that's that then,' said the producer. 'With one act short the whole show is unusable. Dickie

Hart's going to kill me when I tell him that!'

Matt forced out a cough and all eyes turned to him. He'd been silent through the exchange so far, but now he sat up and, feigning a hoarse, wheezy voice he said, 'Bobby!' and pointed at Bobby.

'What's that?' said the producer, starting to get irritated now.

'Bobby's a comic, he could do it,' wheezed Matt.

'What is the boy talking about?' said the producer.

'We really need to go and tell the audience that there won't be a third act, Jenny,' said the stage manager tapping her watch.

'What's he talking about, Bobby?' said the producer.

Bobby looked at Matt and rolled his eyes as if to say, 'This wasn't part of the plan.' Matt smiled back at him and gave him an encouraging nod.

'Well, I mean, yes, technically I suppose I am but . . .'

'Technically?' said the producer, raising an eyebrow. 'Either you're a comedian or you're not . . .?'

'Yes well, I am – I was ... no ... well, that's to say ... I am ... but ...'

'You are what?' snapped the producer. 'Spit it out! I've got three and a half thousand people sat out there who think Matt here is going to be entertaining them!'

Suddenly, as if to remind them all, there was a distant roar and the corridor echoed with applause.

'That means Russel's just come off,' said the stage manager. 'What shall I tell Eddie, Jen?'

'Tell him to fill,' said the producer.

'Right,' said the stage manager pushing through the crowd of people to the dressing-room door and hurrying down the corridor towards the stage.

'Now we haven't got all day! Are you a comedian or not!?' barked the producer.

'YES! Yes! OK! I am a comedian! A stand-up. I'm Bobby Bath.'

The producer took a step back, narrowed her eyes and looked Bobby up and down. Suddenly her face changed from one of concern to that of complete surprise.

'Bobby ... Bobby Bath! Yes! It *is* you! But you were ...'

'*Opportunity Knocks* winner 1974, headlined the Royal Variety Show in front of Her Majesty the Queen, star of *Bobby Bath's Bath Time* 1975 to 1976, host of *Bobby Bath's Swing Time* 1977 to ... well, 1977, and I haven't been on TV for over forty years!' said Bobby with a weary sigh.

There was a brief silence as this information sunk in to the assembled group. Then the producer's face lit up like Blackpool illuminations.

'How quickly can you be ready?' she said.

'Eh?' said Bobby with a frown.

'How quickly can you be ready to go on and take Matt's place as closing act on *Stand-up at the Apollo*?'

'Now hang on a minute,' said Bobby. 'I'll never be ready. I mean this isn't my crowd. They've never heard of me. Most of that audience weren't even born when I was a somebody!'

'Well, now's your chance to show them that you still are! You're our only hope!' said the producer.

'Miriam, get Dan to write a fresh intro for Bobby here – mention all his past glories, but don't overdo it, we don't want to build up any false expectations. Then get it loaded into the autocue for Eddie. Bobby, you've got four minutes to get your act together! Congratulations, you're closing the last in the series of *Stand-up at the Apollo*!'

'But . . .!' spluttered Bobby.

The producer didn't wait for Bobby's reply because she didn't want to hear it. She turned towards the door and the gaggle of people followed her out like ducklings. Bobby was left looking at the empty doorway, eyes bulging, his mouth wide open in shock. This hadn't been in his plan at all. He heard a snigger from behind him and looked down to see Matt, who was laughing.

'You said it, Bobby, there're no emergencies in show business!'

25

Bath Time Again

For Bobby Bath, four minutes had never gone so fast. No sooner had he been told that he was the new closing act than he was being marched towards the stage by Miriam the runner.

'You're booked for ten minutes, Bobby . . .' she said.

'No, luv, you're wrong there . . .' said Bobby. 'I'm not booked at all.'

'We'll give you a red light at nine minutes, so that's when you should start wrapping it up.'

They'd reached the back of the stage now – Bobby, Miriam and Matt – who was struggling to keep up his wheezing, although no one seemed particularly interested in him any more.

Matt could see the warm glow of the stage as they entered the wings, and could hear Eddie chatting to the audience. He could sense the excitement of a full house who have had a great night and who are just waiting for the icing on the cake – their closing act.

'What do I do?' said Bobby turning to Matt. It was the first time Matt had ever seen Bobby flustered.

'I'm used to doing a whole show. I haven't practised a tight ten!'

Eddie Odillo had started Bobby's intro. Matt shrugged helplessly. He hadn't thought of that when he'd put Bobby forward.

'Ladies and gentlemen, there's been a change of plan,' he said. 'I'm afraid that due to illness, Matt Millz will not be appearing tonight . . .'

There was loud groan from the audience. 'I'd offer to give you your money back,' joked Eddie, quick as lightning, 'but since you all got in for nothing . . .' There was a big laugh. 'I'm sure you'll join me in wishing Matt a very speedy recovery.'

Matt felt a bit guilty at the ensuing polite but apparently heartfelt round of applause.

'Hopefully we'll get him on the show another time. But we have a little surprise for you ...' A murmur spread through the crowd as if they were trying to guess who their surprise might be.

'Jack Whitehall,' someone shouted out from the back of the stalls.

'It's not Jack, no ...' said Eddie.

'Jimmy Carr,' shouted another.

'We haven't got that sort of money!' Eddie flashed straight back. 'No, we have for you a stand-up comedy star who once entertained none other than Her Majesty the Queen ...'

Matt looked over at Bobby who looked absolutely terrified, and suddenly had an idea.

'Bobby? How long was your Royal Variety set?'

'Eh?' said Bobby. He was staring from the wings at Eddie, transfixed.

'Your Royal Variety set, back in the day! How long was it?'

'Well . . . er, they were very strict. We were told no longer than ten minutes,' said Bobby snapping back to the here and now.

'Well, do that then,' said Matt.

'Eh? Do my . . .?' said Bobby with a look of surprise.

'Do your Royal Variety set!'

'My Royal . . .?'

'Yes! You're always telling me how it was the best gig of your life! Now prove it!'

'But that's forty-odd years old!'

'What is it you keep telling me?' said Matt. 'Oh yes, I remember – funny's funny!'

'Yeah but . . .!' protested Bobby, but the time for thinking was over. Eddie was announcing him on.

'Ladies and gentlemen, please welcome Bobby Bath!' A huge round of applause shook the building, a sound that immediately took Matt back to the last time he'd stood in that very spot as he waited to go on for *The T Factor*.

A look of determination settled on Bobby's face. 'No, Matt,' he said through gritted teeth, staring firmly at the mic stand. 'I'm not doing a forty-year-old set. I'm a comedian, I'm going to give them the new stuff!'

With that he fixed a big smile on his face and set off towards the centre of the stage. As he emerged into the spotlight the applause stopped almost as quickly as it had started and was replaced by a murmur that rippled from the front of the auditorium up to the back of the stalls then up into the dress circle and beyond – as if the audience were all asking the same question: 'Who is this old bloke, and what is he doing on our favourite show?'

Eddie shook Bobby's hand as he passed him and moved his hand up and down to the audience, trying to encourage them to keep the applause going. By the time Bobby reached the microphone even the murmuring had died down – you could have heard a pin drop.

Eddie joined Matt at the side of the stage and whispered. 'Wow! I loved that guy when I was a kid! I just hope he's still got it.'

Matt nodded. 'So do I.'

There was a click and a clunk as Bobby unhooked the microphone from the stand. Then he stood for what seemed like an age, squinting at the audience. Under the harsh spotlight he looked even older than his eighty-two years, the huge stage making him look smaller and kind of shrivelled.

'Come on, Bobby, you can do it . . .' said Matt under his breath – he was now feeling more nervous for Bobby than he had for himself. 'If you don't say something funny soon, I'm going to have a real asthma attack!'

Bobby cleared his throat to speak. The audience sat forward in anticipation.

'I know what you're thinking . . .' he said, looking first at the people in the stalls, then at those in the dress circle, then at those right up at the top in the gallery.

'You're thinking, who's this old git and what's he doing ruining our favourite show!'

The tension that Bobby had created was suddenly

exploded and there was a laugh. Not a massive laugh, not even a big laugh, but a laugh nonetheless. 'Well, what you have to remember is this skin was originally made for a much bigger bloke!'

Another laugh.

'This is what a mouse would look like if it had as much skin as a cat.'

Another laugh, bigger than the two before.

'Basically I need to have my body circumcised!'

A really big laugh now. They were building with each gag.

'Fortunately I'm so old I've forgotten what I used to look like. My face is so wrinkled my phone thinks it's a fingerprint.'

Another laugh. The audience were beginning to relax and enjoy what Bobby had to offer. Then the spell was broken by a lone voice from high up in the gods.

'Go home, old man!'

'Ouch!' thought Matt. Eddie looked down at him and winced.

'I would go home . . .' shot back Bobby, 'but I can't remember where I live!'

Bang! There was the massive laugh that Matt knew Bobby had been waiting for. 'Besides,' he continued, not allowing any gap for the heckler to reply, 'my daughter sold it to pay for my facelift!'

Pow! Another huge laugh. He was really starting to hit his stride now. 'Yeah, I know what you're thinking, how come I haven't been on TV for over forty years? Well, my agent died! Cause of death, depression – yeah, he was watching one of my shows at the time!'

Suddenly something strange happened to Bobby. He seemed to grow, his back straightened, he was moving more nimbly, it was if he was getting younger before Matt's eyes!

'I'm so ill, the other day the Grim Reaper knocked on my door, took one look at me and said, "Sorry, I didn't realise I'd already been round!" It's like someone took a photo of my face and faxed it back to me! Let me explain that last gag for anyone still in nappies – a fax was a piece of paper that came through your phone. You're thinking, "Now the old guy's really lost it!". But listen, I've worked with some of the comedy greats – Morecambe and Wise, Tommy Cooper, Les Dawson, Frankie Howerd ... Yeah, get the message, people, if you work with Bobby Bath, you die! A little tip – before you work with me, Eddie ...' He looked over at Eddie standing in the wings. 'Make a will, put your affairs in order! I'm so deaf now it makes no difference to me if you're laughing or booing! My eyesight's so bad, the other day I did my whole act to an old school photograph. I've got a cataract – it's not a big deal, I just keep thinking I'm being handed a doughnut!'

And the laughs kept coming, and coming and coming. Wave after wave of that special sound and none were laughing harder than Matt and Eddie.

Just when Matt thought it couldn't get any better, Bobby took it to another level when he launched into a sort of rap.

'Put your hands together and start to clap

As I lay down my Pensioner's Rap!' sang Bobby to a huge cheer.

Sure enough the audience started to clap out a regular beat.

'I can't work a phone, I don't use a computer

But I've got sat nav on my mobility scooter!

I still play football but it's not the same

I scored a goal when it bounced off me zimmer frame!'

It was getting huge laughs – and was made even funnier by Bobby's attempts at body-popping.

'Body-popping?' he ad libbed. 'I think I just popped me back out!'

Suddenly Matt remembered a conversation at the Frittledean gig when Bobby had asked Neil to help him come up with a rap. This was it!

'This is magic,' whispered Eddie turning to Matt, his eyes wide in wonder. Matt nodded. Bobby was jumping around like a man half his age.

*

'I may be falling apart but I won't ever
    stop
Though the pain in my hip really makes
    me hop
I said a hip-a-hop a hippety hop
I may be falling apart but I won't ever
    stop!
Put your hands in the air like you're
    losing your hair
I need a chair lift to get up the stairs
I got false teeth and a hearing aid

It's been twenty-five years since I last got
     paid!
There's another little thing that I'd like to
     mention
It ain't much fun on an old age pension!'

Bobby stepped back and held his arms wide to signal the end of his act.

'Thanks for listening. You made a happy man feel very old – no wait a minute! The other way round! I'm Bobby Bath – and no I don't want a doughnut! Goodnight!'

Well, the roar that followed was completely off the scale. The audience jumped to their feet and whooped and cheered. Bobby bowed low and blew a kiss to a lady in the front row, he waved to the people up in the gallery and winked, and then with a huge smile on his face, marched towards Matt. As he passed Eddie coming the other way, Eddie shook his hand and leant in briefly to chat to him. Matt strained to hear what he was saying above the din but could only make out the word 'legend'.

Bobby continued walking and mouthed, 'I did it!' Then something very strange happened. All the blood seemed to drain from Bobby's face, he clutched his chest with his left hand and as he took the last few steps to the wings, his knees went from under him and he pitched forward. Matt managed to get under him to catch him and gently lower him to the ground. He was like a sack of potatoes.

'Bobby?' Matt said lifting the old comic's head. 'Hey, stop kidding around ...' Bobby's skin was cold and clammy and Matt knew straight away that something was very wrong indeed.

In the background he could hear Eddie eliciting another round of applause for his old friend.

'Bobby?' Matt said, more urgently now. Bobby's eyes rolled back into the top of his head. He didn't appear to be breathing.

The stage manager rushed in, took one look at him and yelled at the top of her voice, 'Somebody call an ambulance!'

26
Total Eclipse

Matt hadn't been allowed to travel with Bobby in the ambulance, and not really knowing what to do he'd phoned his mum. She'd told him to get the next train home and was waiting for him with a sandwich when he got there. As she gave him a hug he burst into tears. The whole day had been so emotional. First the drama and worry of backing out of the Apollo show, then Bobby standing in for him and storming it, and then collapsing in his arms.

'Any news?' he said with a sniff.

'I phoned the hospital. They say Bobby had a heart attack, quite a big one I'm afraid.'

'But he's going to be all right?' said Matt.

'All they said is that the next forty-eight hours are critical.'

'We saw the show,' said Ian, his eyes red from crying too. 'Bobby was brilliant.'

'Yeah,' said Matt, 'the best!'

'Now eat your sandwich and have a bath. Try not to worry too much about him, he's in the best place . . .' said Matt's mum. 'We'll phone the hospital again in the morning.'

Matt made short work of the sandwich – he realised he hadn't eaten anything since breakfast. He put in a call to Rob to fill him in on the situation and asked him to call Kitty and tell her too. Poor Kitty, she'd been right about Excalibur Management and Dickie Hart all along, but at this point Matt didn't have the headspace to worry about his so-called career. His ups and downs in the world of showbiz seemed incredibly trivial compared to what poor Bobby was going through.

He had a quick bath and went to bed but although

he was physically exhausted he couldn't sleep. All he could think about was Bobby lying somewhere alone in a hospital bed. He blamed himself. If he hadn't ducked out of the gig, Bobby wouldn't have had all that stress and would still be fighting fit. When he finally did get to sleep he had a hideous nightmare – he was in the wings at the Apollo and Bobby kept collapsing onstage in front of the audience but Matt was unable to go to help him.

He woke with a start and looked at his phone – there were about twenty texts, all saying how brilliant Bobby had been on the Apollo show. The last one was from Rob. It read simply, 'Turn the TV on NOW and check out the news.'

Matt, still in his pyjamas, rushed downstairs to the kitchen, grabbed the remote and flicked on the TV. There was a reporter outside a London hospital. Underneath was the headline 'Star's Comeback Ends In Tragedy'.

'Oh my god!' said Matt. 'Please don't tell me

he didn't make it!' He turned up the volume and listened to what the reporter had to say.

'Veteran comic Bobby Bath's TV comeback was watched by over seven million people last night . . .' Then a short sequence of Bobby from the night before onstage at the Apollo flashed up. '. . . the comic, who was a big star back in the seventies, made an unexpected comeback after *T Factor* whizz kid Matt Millz pulled out at short notice . . .' the report went on. 'However just moments after he came off stage he collapsed with a suspected heart attack and is currently in a critical condition behind me here in Charing Cross hospital.'

Matt's phone rang – it was Rob.

'You watching it?' said his old friend.

'Yup,' said Matt, trying to keep a lid on his emotions.

'We've got to get down there, Matt,' said Rob. 'It might be our last chance to see him.'

Matt glanced at his watch. Trains from Staplefirst went at ten past the hour – the next one was in twenty-five minutes. 'I'll see you at the station,' he said and hung up. He threw on his clothes, grabbed a Kit-Kat from the larder, scribbled a note for his mum and Ian, and headed out of the front door.

Rob was waiting for him at the station when he got there. They did something they didn't usually do – they hugged each other.

'I've missed you, mate,' said Matt, choking back a tear.

'Yeah, it's been weird without you,' said Rob, equally overcome.

Matt filled Rob in on what had happened with Dickie Hart and the circumstances surrounding Bobby's comeback.

'So it's all kind of my fault,' he said.

'Well, they said on the news it could have come at any time, so ... Anyway, it's happened now,' said Rob trying to make Matt feel better.

The train pulled in, they pressed the flashing, bleeping button on the door and they got on.

'Look, there's an empty four seats,' said Rob as

they walked down the train, but as they got level there seemed to be someone sitting in one of them. The occupant was so small she couldn't be seen from behind. 'Kitty!' said Matt, sitting down opposite Kitty Hope.

'Great minds!' said Rob.

Her eyes were red from crying. 'I just hope he's OK,' she said, producing a hanky and dabbing the tears from her eyes.

'Listen, Kitty, I'm really sorry,' said Matt.

'What for?'

'For . . .' stuttered Matt, '. . . for everything!'

He then proceeded to explain once again exactly what had happened the previous night at the Apollo – about how Dickie Hart had manipulated him into accepting the gig, how he and Bobby had hatched the plan to pretend that Matt was ill so he could get out of it, and how, fatefully, he'd set Bobby up to take his place. He went through how funny Bobby had been onstage and how he'd collapsed in his arms.

'So I blame myself,' he said, finishing up. 'And I'm really sorry that I ever doubted you as a manager.'

Kitty nodded slowly as she took in what he'd said. She turned to look out of the window at the fields racing by. Matt looked at Rob, Rob looked at Matt and raised his eyebrows. After a few moments she turned back and spoke.

'Two things,' she said, her old businesslike manner returning. 'We both know Bobby and he lived – lives – for his comedy. Watching him on that stage on TV last night was one of the proudest moments of my life – second only to seeing you there on your *T Factor* audition. I could see that Bobby was loving it, so no, don't blame yourself, Matt. You should take credit for putting Bobby back where he belongs – top of the bill! As for the other thing, your … fling … with Excalibur Management – I appreciate your apology. I knew how it would probably end, that's why I was so upset when you got involved with them. Like I said to you at the time, Dickie Hart is a bad egg – he's in it for all the wrong reasons. It's just a shame you had to find out the hard way. *But* . . .' she said, pausing briefly for effect, 'I still believe in you and think you've got the makings of another Bobby Bath!'

'Thanks,' said Matt awkwardly. 'I don't suppose . . .'

'Don't suppose what?' said Kitty.

'Oh, it doesn't matter . . .' said Matt, turning away.

'Jeez!' said an exasperated Rob. 'He wants to know whether you'll be his manager again.' Kitty turned to the window once again.

'Of course I would,' she said quietly.

'Eh?' said Matt – he wasn't sure he'd heard her correctly.

'I'd be happy to take you back, you big idiot,' she said.

'Yaay!' cried Matt and he gave her a kiss. 'I promise I won't let you down!'

'Again!' chipped in Rob.

'Again!' said Matt.

'Yes all right,' said Kitty, flustered, her face going a bright red. 'On one condition.'

'Anything, name your price,' said Matt.

'That you do do the Anglebrook Children in Need show tonight.'

'I'd be happy to. I've still got a problem with my material though.'

'Just turn up and tell them about your adventures over the last few weeks. They'll be happy with that.'

'Deal,' said Matt shaking Kitty's hand.

'Hang on, what about the contract I signed . . .?' said Matt. But they had no time to finish the conversation as the train had stopped at the next station – the doors swooshed open and in walked a figure they all knew.

'You lot going where I think you're going?' said Ahmed. 'Well, I couldn't miss seeing the Bobster could I?' he grinned.

27

Touch and Go

Charing Cross hospital is nowhere near Charing Cross station. It is in fact about half a mile from the Hammersmith Apollo. As Matt and the gang approached it, Matt's heart sank – there was a large gaggle of reporters and a number of camera crews camped outside, just as there'd been outside his house following his *T Factor* appearance.

'You'd better pull your hood up,' said Kitty. 'They're not going to leave you alone – you're part of this story.' Matt nodded and did as he was told. He shoved his hands in his pockets and kept his head down. The others fell in around him to form a human shield. He'd just made it past them and up the steps to the main door when someone called his name. 'Matt!'

Matt hesitated, only for a nanosecond, but that was long enough to confirm his identity to the paps. They rushed forward as a pack. Matt started running but tripped and went tumbling to the floor. As the pack of photographers closed in for the kill, Kitty stepped in front of them with her arms outstretched.

'STOP!' she shouted, and to a man they froze. 'You should be ashamed of yourselves!' she continued. A couple of paps lowered their cameras and shifted

awkwardly on the spot. 'Respect my client's feelings and kindly desist from hounding him in this way,' she said, and as Matt picked himself up off the ground and limped through the hospital doors she just stood there glaring at them, daring them to take another photo. Not one of them did.

'Thank you,' she said. 'Matt will be issuing a statement shortly.' With that she turned and marched through the doors and after her friends.

'Thanks, Kit,' said Matt admiringly. 'You were magnificent!'

'Too right, Kitty,' said Ahmed nodding. 'You could be prime minister the way you did that!'

A little old lady approached them. She looked vaguely familiar to Matt.

'You're Matt, aren't you?' she said in a northern accent. 'Are you here for Bobby?'

'That's right, um … how …?' said Matt a little perplexed. He'd got used to being recognised by strangers but this lady wasn't his usual demographic.

'I'm Winnie, Bobby's sister,' she said. 'Bobby's

always talking about you.'

'Winnie! Of course,' said Matt, hugging her close. 'You look a lot like him.'

'It's a shame to be meeting under these circumstances,' said Winnie.

'How is he, Winnie?' said Kitty stepping forward.

'Kitty!' she said and gave the girl a hug. 'Well, what can I say? He's not out of the woods yet. The doctors say he needs to rest – but I'm sure it'll give him a boost to see your young faces! I was just off to get him a paper. He's in the CCU up on the third floor. Don't talk to anyone who's not wearing a name badge though – the place is crawling with journalists.'

'Yes, we'd noticed,' said Matt.

They said their goodbyes and headed towards the lift.

The nurse on reception at the CCU told them they could only go in two at a time, so Matt and Kitty went first. Matt felt nervous, worried at what he'd find. What if he wasn't like the old Bobby? What if he'd suffered some sort of permanent damage?

'I hate hospitals,' he confided to Kit as they both rubbed the antiseptic gel into their hands before going in.

'No one likes them,' she said pushing the door open and entering Bobby's room. At the top of the bed there was a monitor that had a green trace on it and made a bleeping noise that Matt recognised from the TV as an ECG machine or heart monitor. There was another machine that was connected to a syringe which led to a tube. He followed the tube down to the bed where it was connected to Bobby's right arm. Bobby had his eyes shut and was breathing shallowly through his mouth. Matt felt a lump in his throat and could hardly speak.

'Bobby?' whispered Kitty stepping forward and gently taking the old comic's hand. Bobby grunted and turned his head, then slowly opened his eyes.

'Sarah? Is that you?' His eyes appeared to be focussing on something in the distance. 'I'm coming, luv ...' he said weakly and then he let out a long breath, closed his eyes and slumped back on to the bed.

'Bobby!' cried Matt, with tears in his eyes. 'Quick, Kit, call the nurse. He's died!'

'Ha ha! Fooled you!' said Bobby opening one eye. 'Ha ha! Hitler didn't manage to finish me off and there's plenty of life left in this old comic! Mind you it wouldn't be the first time I'd died and probably not the last! Ha ha! You should have seen your face, Matt! Priceless!'

'You ... you ...' said Matt, relieved but still very emotional. 'You ...'

'Comedian?' said Bobby.

'Yeah, you comedian,' said Matt.

'I showed 'em, eh?' said Bobby sitting up.

'You certainly did,' said Kitty smiling with relief.

'I knocked 'em dead! Unfortunately I nearly knocked myself dead in the process!' Bobby laughed.

'The nurse said you were to get some rest, Bobby,' said Kitty. 'We just wanted to pop in to say hello and check you were OK.'

'Yeah,' said Matt. 'Rob and Ahmed are outside.'

'Great!' said Bobby. 'I'm in all the papers you know! I've just sent my sister out to get them. I don't know what happened to me. I was fine one minute, taking the applause, then I remember seeing you in the wings, Matt, and then I just blacked out . . .'

'You had a heart attack, Mr . . . Bath?' said a woman's voice from behind them. It was the doctor.

'No thanks, I had one this morning!' said Bobby. 'Actually I didn't but I could do with one!'

The doctor adjusted one of the drips and looked through the charts at the end of Bobby's bed.

'Are you comfortable?' said the doctor.

'I make a living . . .' joked Bobby.

'You know what I mean,' she said, rolling her eyes. 'Any pain?'

'No, I just feel a bit washed out that's all, doc.'

'That's to be expected,' said the doctor turning to leave. 'Like this young lady says, get some rest and I'll be round again to see you later.'

'Oh, doctor, before you go, I've been meaning to

ask – after I'm discharged from hospital will I be able to play the trombone?' said Bobby.

'Er . . . yes, I see no reason why not. Why do you ask?'

'Well, they must be great tablets you're giving me because I couldn't play the trombone before I came into hospital! Ha ha! Oh, doc, you walked into that one, you really did!'

She shook her head. 'Get some rest, that's an order,' she said and went out of the room, passing Bobby's sister coming the other way clutching a bundle of newpapers.

'There's your papers, Bobby – front page too! You haven't been front-page news since you won *Opportunity Knocks*!' said Winnie.

'I've had lots of phone calls, Bobby, there's lots of interest – all the shows want you,' said Kitty.

'Great! He he!' said Bobby, rubbing his hands with glee. 'I'm back! Ha ha!'

'But we'll talk about that another time. Matt? If you're going to get back in time to do the Children in Need show we'd better go.'

'Hmm, I'm not sure I want to leave Bobby,' said Matt

'You go, son,' said Bobby. 'I'll be fine – the show must go on, remember!'

'Well, if you're sure . . .'

Bobby nodded. Matt took Bobby's hand and gave it a squeeze. 'Make sure you get some rest and I'll phone you in the morning to let you know how it went.'

'No, phone me when you come off,' said Bobby. 'I want to hear the excitement in your voice. You'll smash it, Matt, I know you will . . .'

'Mr Bath?' said a nurse.

'No thanks, luv, I had one this morning,' said Bobby with a weak smile. The exertions of the last few minutes had taken their toll on his energy levels and for the first time in a while Bobby looked all of his eighty-two years.

'Did he do the gag where he pretended to die?' asked

Rob as they walked back to Hammersmith tube station.

'You too, eh?' Matt laughed. He was still worried about his sick friend, but felt a lot better for having seen him.

He felt his phone vibrating and fished it out of his pocket.

He took one look at it and a shiver went down his spine. 'Uh-oh!' he said, holding it up to show Kitty. Emblazoned on the screen was one word: EXCALIBUR.

'You'd better answer it, Matt,' she said. 'You're going to have to deal with them at some point. I don't think they're the type to just disappear.'

Matt took a deep breath and pressed the little green phone icon.

'Hi, Dickie,' he said as brightly as he could manage. 'I'm glad you've called, I've been meaning to—' But before he could continue Dickie cut in.

'Listen, you little guttersnipe! No one treats Dickie Hart like that . . .!' There was then a string of unrepeatable four-letter words. 'You'd better get yourself to the Excalibur offices pronto or you're not gonna know what's hit you!'

'But I—' said Matt, but the line had gone dead. Matt slowly lowered the phone from his ear and looked at the blank screen.

'Looks like I'm in ten tons of doo-doo with Excalibur,' he sighed.

'Rather you than me,' said Rob.

'If you die . . .' said Ahmed, 'can I have your suit?'

Matt punched Ahmed playfully on the arm.

'Aargh!' joked Ahmed, clutching his arm. 'A mean left hook *and* a comedy genius!'

Matt wondered how on earth he would have got through the last twenty-four hours without his friends.

'What did he say?' asked Kitty.

'Says he wants to see me at Excalibur HQ now,' said Matt.

'Do they still have their headquarters in the base of a volcano or have they moved it?' joked Rob.

'Very funny. No, they're in the West End, off Leicester Square,' said Matt.

'Well, you'll have to go,' said Kitty. 'No use delaying it. You're obliged to inform them you're letting them go ...'

'Sacking them!' interjected Rob.

'And they're entitled to three months notice, but no more. Do you want me to come with you?'

Matt hesitated. He was dreading seeing Dickie Hart again and would have loved some moral support but he knew he'd put Kitty through enough trouble as it was.

'No,' he said. 'No, this is my mess and I've got to sort it out.'

'Well, if you're sure,' she said nodding. 'They'll lay it on pretty thick but provided you read the small print on the contract and there's nothing out of the ordinary you should be fine.'

'Ah,' said Matt, his heart sinking even further.

'Oh, Matt, you didn't?' she said with a real look of concern on her face.

'I'm afraid I did,' he said.

'Better make that twenty tons of doo-doo then!' said Rob.

'Have you got a copy of it, on an email or something?' asked Kitty. 'It's just that I could ask my great-uncle Buddy to have a look at it – what he doesn't know about contracts is not worth knowing . . .'

'Yes!' said Matt, scrolling through his inbox on his phone. 'Here it is. I'll forward it you, yeah? Honestly, Kit, anything you can do to help would be great. I've just got a very bad feeling about this . . .'

28

Always Read the Small Print

As Matt sat on the tube from Hammersmith to Leicester Square, he mentally rehearsed what he was going to say to Dickie Hart when he saw him.

'Hi, Dickie. Listen, I'd like to thank you for all you've done for me over the last few days, but I've decided that it's not for me ...' No, he needed to make it sound like it wasn't anything Dickie had done. 'Dickie, I'm really sorry, I know that Excalibur are a brilliant organisation but I don't think I'm ready for this level of top management yet, so I'm afraid I won't ... be ... er ... needing? No, not needing, requiring? No that wasn't right either ... this wasn't easy. A little voice inside him wanted to just tell the truth: 'You're an awful bloke with bad aftershave who only cares about money, and for that reason you're fired!' Ha! He chuckled to himself. That would be like trying to put a fire out using petrol – BANG!

About twenty minutes later Matt was walking up to the frosted-glass frontage of Excalibur HQ. He looked up at the huge building towering above him. He felt a dull ache in the pit of his stomach. This wasn't butterflies, he thought, this was two ferrets wrestling!

He pressed the button on the entryphone and while he stood waiting for an answer he studied the names etched in the glass. It was a list of all the various pies that Dickie Hart had his fingers in. There was Excalibur Management, Excalibur Promotions, Excalibur Television, Excalibur PR, Excalibur Motion Pictures, Excalibur Voice-overs, Excalibur Cars, and rather oddly, Excalibur Plumbing Services.

'Yes?' came a bored, disembodied voice.

'Er ... Matt Millz. To see Mr Hart please,' said Matt leaning in close, his breath steaming up the polished steel of the entryphone.

There was a click, then a buzzer sounded, indicating that the door had been unlocked.

Matt hesitated. 'Oh well,' he muttered to himself. 'Here we go!'

He pushed open the glass door and walked inside.

There was a young lad on reception with a haircut that looked like he'd been dragged through a car wash backwards. He appeared to be watching something on his laptop. Matt walked up to the desk and waited. The lad didn't even look up. Matt waited a little longer. Still there was no response from the kid on the front desk. 'What a lovely welcome,' he thought to himself.

'Ahem!' coughed Matt finally.

'Yeah?' said the kid, still engrossed in his laptop.

'Er ... I'm Matt Millz ...' he said nervously.

'And ...?' said the kid.

'Um, what do you mean "and"?' said Matt.

'I mean what do you want?' said the kid, finally looking up.

'Oh! I'm here to see Mr Hart,' said Matt.

'If you'd like to take a seat I'll be with you in a moment,' said the kid.

Suddenly the strains of the *EastEnders* theme tune rang out from the laptop and the kid's face broke into a broad grin.

'Nice one! Right,' he said, looking at Matt. 'What can I do for you?'

'I'm here to see Mr Hart . . .' said Matt.

'That's right, yeah,' said the kid and lifted the phone.

'Hello? Chenice? D'ya see *EastEnders*? Oh man, that Georgie, eh?' He chuckled, then caught sight of Matt glaring at him from across the room. 'Anyway, that's not why I phoned. I've got some geezer here reckons he's here to see Dickie . . . Sorry, what did you say your name was again?' he said, breaking off from the phone.

'Matt Millz,' said Matt through gritted teeth. How dumb could one person be?

'It's Matt Millz. Yeah . . . OK, I'll tell him. She says it's fine to go up. Level . . .'

But before he could finish, Matt had marched past him towards the lift.

To get to Dickie Hart's office you had to go up to the twelfth floor then down a long corridor which was lined with photos of all the great stars and TV shows that Excalibur had had a hand in making. Looking at the photographs, Matt realised that ninety per cent of the comics were no longer actually represented by them. The last but one was of course Russel Perkins standing onstage at the O2 Arena. Next to that was a big photo of Matt from his recent photo shoot. Matt looked at himself in his new suit – he looked so excited and pleased to be joining the big agency. How times had changed.

As he approached Dickie's office he could hear a commotion going on inside. Raised voices, a hand being whacked down on a desk. This didn't sound very promising. Matt strained to catch what was being said.

'Yes?' said the girl on the desk outside Dickie's office, busy filing her nails, who Matt assumed was Dickie's PA.

'I'm here to see Dickie,' said Matt. It seemed it might be easier to get an audience with the pope than a meeting with his agent!

'And you are . . .?' said the girl.

Matt rolled his eyes. This really was very trying.

'Matt Millz – the kid at the front desk just called you . . .'

'One moment,' she said nodding, then she picked up the phone. 'Mr Hart?'

Matt could hear some more muffled shouting through the door of his office.

'Yes, I'm really sorry to disturb you . . .' said Dickie's PA. 'Yes . . . really sorry . . . no . . . I promise it won't happen again, sir . . . no . . .' She broke off, covered the receiver with her hand and turned to Matt.

'Mr Hart says he'll be with you in a minute,' said the girl and went back to filing her nails.

Suddenly the door to Dickie's office burst open and Matt could hear what Dickie was saying loud and clear.

'. . . and if I ever catch you going behind my back again, I'll do you so much harm you won't be able to be funny,' he bellowed. 'Now get outta my sight!'

Matt peered into the doorway and wondered who on earth Dickie was talking to in such an insulting manner. A lacklustre figure emerged moments later, his head hung low. It was Russel Perkins. He looked at Matt and shook his head. 'Good luck,' he muttered dolefully as he passed him.

Matt took a big gulp, his heart was in his mouth. 'Maybe I don't need to do this today,' he thought to himself and turned to follow Russel P to the lift.

'Where do you think you're going?' boomed Dickie's voice from behind him. Matt stopped, turned and shuffled into Dickie's office.

'You . . . you w-w-w-wanted to see me, Dickie?' stuttered Matt nervously.

'Yeah, just a bit, Matt,' said Dickie from behind his

huge desk, leaning back in his chair. 'Take a seat . . .'

Matt sat down in the chair opposite Dickie, which was a good twenty centimetres lower.

'Cup of tea? Or a fizzy drink perhaps?'

'No thanks, Dickie, I'm fine.'

'Good,' said Dickie gently. Matt started to think that maybe this wasn't going to be so hard after all. Then without any warning Dickie leant across the desk and half screamed, half shouted at him.

'What the hell were you playing at the other night at the Apollo!?'

Matt nearly jumped out of his skin.

'I'm r-r-really sorry,' he stammered. 'It's just that I had no material left after I'd done *The T Factor*, and I knew that if I went out on to that stage I was going to die!'

'So you got some old codger to stand in for you?' roared Dickie.

'Yes,' said Matt. 'I mean no. I mean he's old but he was brilliant!'

'That's just the problem!' shouted Dickie, his face

bright red now. 'Russell Perkins was supposed to be the star of that show, not some old has-been! Look at all this coverage!' He held up a couple of newspapers, each with a photo of Bobby on the front. 'That should have been my boy, Russel. Do you realise how many tickets he's gotta sell? I've booked him in to do fifteen nights at the Royal Albert Hall and we can't give 'em away! He's gonna lose his shirt because of your selfishness!'

It took a moment for what Dickie had said to sink in.

'My selfishness?' muttered Matt, but Dickie was in full flow now and like a pig on a log flume he was stopping for no one.

'If I tell you to do something, you do it!' bellowed Dickie. '*Comprenez*? I'm your manager and you do what I say or you're out!'

'Ah, well about that …' said Matt realising this might be the moment to break his news.

'What about it?' said Dickie, sitting back in his chair.

'Well, I've been thinking and . . . I mean I feel that maybe I'm . . . that is to say we . . . um . . . I mean don't get me wrong . . . I think you do a brilliant job here at Excalibur management . . . and I mean just look at how successful Russell is . . . I'm just not sure . . .'

Dickie smiled and rocked back in his chair.

'I understand,' he said nodding wisely. 'You're young, you're new to this whole scene, it's only understandable that you have concerns about how things are run in the professional world . . .'

'Yes, Mr Hart, but it's a bit more serious than that. I'm just not sure it's for me, that's all.'

There was a brief pause during which a look of consternation slowly took over Dickie's face as he started to realise where the conversation might be heading.

'What's not for you?' said Dickie.

'Well . . .' said Matt. 'I'm thinking this is my problem not yours, but I think I might be better off with a smaller management agency . . .'

'We know what's best for you, Matt,' Dickie cut in with a knowing nod. 'And what's best for you is staying here under the protective umbrella of Excalibur Management, Excalibur Promotions, Excalibur Television, Excalibur PR, Excalibur Motion Pictures, Excalibur Cars and Excalibur Plumbing Services – I mean, actually you don't have to use the plumbing services, that's optional, but I'd strongly recommend that you do because—'

'That's just it, Dickie,' replied Matt. 'I don't think you do necessarily know what's best for me. That's why I don't want you to represent me any more.' Wow! He'd actually said it. Matt had actually told Dickie he was fired. At least, he thought he had.

'Sorry ...' said Dickie looking confused. 'I don't understand what you're trying to say.'

'Well ...' said Matt. 'It's not working out for me here. And so I want to leave.'

'It's all going to be fine,' smiled Dickie completely ignoring him and reaching for the calendar. 'Now we need to get some TV spots booked in for next month . . . How'd you feel about *Stuff the Week*?'

At that moment it was like someone had flicked a switch inside Matt's brain. Suddenly he just didn't care what Dickie thought any more, he wasn't scared of the shouting and the threats, he was tired of having to repeat himself over and over again and tired of beating about the bush.

'No, Dickie,' he said, standing up and leaning across the desk, directing his annoyance straight at the hapless agent. 'I don't want you to do that, because you're fired,' he said. 'Sacked. Dismissed. I'm giving you the elbow, the order of the boot. I don't want to be looked after by Excalibur Management any more. I quit!'

That wasn't how he'd planned it at all, but the words just tumbled out of his mouth in a splurge. Dickie looked nonplussed. Never had anyone's gob looked quite so smacked!

'I mean, that is to say – it's me, not you,' Matt added in a late attempt to soften the blow.

Matt sat back down and looked across at Dickie

who was at a complete loss as to how to react. Then something very odd happened. Dickie's lower lip started to tremble, tears started to well up in his eyes and he started to cry.

'It's just not fair,' he sobbed, falling forward, head in his hands on the desk. 'Why does everybody leave me!?'

'Awkward,' thought Matt, shifting uncomfortably in his chair. He reached into his pocket, fished out a hanky and offered it to Dickie, who took it, blew his nose loudly – Bbbrrrrraaaaarp! – then handed it back to him. Matt looked at the hanky and quietly dropped it in the bin in front of the desk.

'Listen, Dickie,' said Matt weakly. 'I'm really sorry, but I'm sure it's for the best.' He could see no real reason to hang around any longer and so he stood up and started backing towards the door.

Then the situation took a sudden turn.

'Where do you think you're going?' growled Dickie lifting his head from the desk, a look of what Matt could only describe as pure evil on his face.

'Um . . . sorry, I thought I'd made it clear that . . .'

'You thought you'd made it clear?' said Dickie. 'No, mate, you don't get out of it that easy. As a matter of fact, I've been meaning to give you something.' He tapped his keyboard and his printer sparked into life chugging out a couple of sides of printed A4. Dickie snatched them as they appeared in the out-tray and handed them to Matt with a flourish.

'Wh-what's this?' said Matt, scanning the sheets – there were two columns, one a list of items, the other of figures.

'That, my little friend, is your bill,' said Dickie with a self-satisfied look on his face. 'The bill for all the services that I've provided for you up until today!'

Matt looked down it – there were charges for paper clips, photocopying, stamps, a large one for 'Two suits', a hefty one for 'Accommodation', and an even bigger one for 'Executive cars'. There was a bill for two hundred quid for four tickets to see Russel Perkins at the O2! There was even one from Austin's for 'Fish and chips' – the very meal that had got Matt ensnared in Dickie Hart's web in the first place.

'The cars and hotels?' said Matt. 'I thought they were free.'

'Ha!' snorted Dickie. 'Didn't anyone ever tell you? There's no such thing as a free lunch! It was all in the small print.'

Matt ran his finger down the column of figures to the total at the bottom. It was over ten thousand pounds! There was no way he'd ever be able to afford to pay it back.

'I can't pay it, Dickie,' he said, his earlier anxiety flooding back only multiplied by a hundred. 'I'll never be able to . . .'

'That's where you're wrong,' snapped Dickie. 'You're gonna work it off! I'm booking you into every crummy club in the country and on to every two-bit TV show that'll have you! And all your fees will come straight to me until I've got my money.'

'But it'll take me years!'

'Exactly. And if you think you can just walk

away . . .' he said, reaching into his desk, 'remember this?'

With that he produced a manilla envelope. Matt instantly recognised it. It was the contract he'd signed just a few days earlier.

'Ah,' said Matt, feeling physically sick now.

'Ah indeed,' said Dickie getting to his feet. 'We have a contract. You signed with Excalibur for five years – and five years is what you are going to serve.' Matt shook his head in dismay. Dickie was talking about it like it was a prison sentence and right now that's exactly what it felt like – he'd be nearly eighteen by the time he'd be free of him.

'Five years,' said Dickie tapping the envelope with his index finger. 'And during that time you will do what I tell you!'

'No he won't,' came a voice from behind them.

29

Hope Springs Eternal

Matt whirled round to see an elderly man in a trench coat and a fedora hat standing in the doorway. He couldn't have been more than five feet two and his face bore a slight resemblance to someone he knew, but couldn't quite place.

'You will release him from that contract right now,' said the stranger in what Matt recognised as a broad New York accent.

Behind the American and more than a little out of breath was Dickie's PA, Chenice. 'I tried to stop him, Mr Hart, but he barged straight past me!'

'Too right I did, sister,' said the elderly gent in the hat.

'Who the freak are you?' snarled Dickie Hart.

'Oh, forgive me! How impolite!' grinned the old man, then he thrust his hand out to shake Dickie's. 'My name's Buddy, Buddy Hopestein!'

The penny dropped with a clang – that was it! The old man reminded Matt of Kitty. It was Kitty's great-uncle Buddy!

'Hang on ...' stuttered Dickie, his eyes wide in wonder and confusion. 'You mean ...? You're *the* actual Buddy Hopestein? The Buddy Hopestein

who runs Channel 12 in the States, and Hope Incorporated, the largest independent production company in the world?'

'You know another Buddy Hopestein?' said the old man.

'Brother of Bernie Hopestein, and great-uncle of Kitty Hope!' said Matt proudly.

Buddy turned to Matt. 'Correct! Hi, Matt. Kitty told me you were breaking a little bad news to our friend here, and having heard of his reputation I thought you might appreciate some help.'

'Well, you may be a big shot ...' said Dickie, regaining a little of his composure.

'The biggest,' smiled Buddy.

'But that doesn't alter the fact that I've got a contract, signed by this little whippersnapper, for exclusive management for five whole years, which leaves another four years and three hundred and sixty days to run.'

'The boy's twelve years old!' said Buddy.

'Thought of that,' said Dickie proudly shuffling

through the contract until he found what he was looking for. 'There, you see? Witnessed by his stepdad. It's legally binding.'

'No it's not,' said Buddy, undeterred. 'And I'll tell you why. Firstly, the contract between a comedian and his manager is a personal services one and therefore can be broken at any time, provided a notice period of no more than three months is served, although the comedian in this situation wouldn't expect to be actively managed by the said manager during the notice period, but yes the manager would be entitled to his usual percentage of their income. That's with a regular contract. However the problem with this contract ...' Buddy snatched the contract from Dickie's hands and thumbed through it. 'Ah yes, the problem with this contract is the clause where you stipulate that Matt is obliged to use your production company, your promotions company, your motion picture company, your limo company and your ...' Buddy looked surprised, '... your plumbing services! Really?'

'Ah well, I would waive the plumbing services bit,' said Dickie, 'but I do run a very efficient service – there's an initial call-out fee of —'

'SILENCE!' shouted Buddy, flourishing the contract in Dickie's face. 'Who negotiates Matt's fee with Excalibur Television?'

'Um, me,' said Dickie.

'And who do you negotiate it with at Excalibur Television?'

'Well, with me I suppose . . . but—'

'And who decides what Matt should get paid for gigs?'

'Well, Excalibur Management talks to Excalibur Promotions . . .' said Dickie.

'You mean you talk to yourself again? It seems to me you don't need a phone in this office – you need a mirror!' said Buddy triumphantly. Matt giggled – this was starting to get interesting. 'You're putting yourself first. It's a clear conflict of interests. There's not a court in the land that would uphold this contract, and for that reason . . .'

Buddy moved over to the window and before Dickie could stop him he'd flung it open and thrown Matt's contract out of it.

'NOOOoooo!' cried Dickie running to the window and watching as the wind took the papers and scattered them to all four corners of the West End.

Dickie turned and scowled at Buddy, who merely beamed back. Then Buddy twisted the knife even further.

'And your other acts may be interested to know this information because it applies to their contracts too. Now, if you'll excuse us, there's work to be done. I understand you have a gig to get to, Matt?'

'Er . . . yeah . . . I guess . . . I mean if that's OK . . .' he said, looking first at Dickie and then at Buddy.

'Yeah, it's OK,' said Buddy turning to leave.

'You'll be hearing from my lawyer,' snarled Dickie.

'I doubt that very much,' said Buddy, pushing past Chenice. Matt skipped down the corridor after him.

'Give me a hand with this . . .' said Buddy as they got level with Matt's photo in the corridor, and between them they levered it off the wall.

'Hmm, I feel a bit bad taking this,' said Matt.

'Well, don't, you paid for it!'

They marched on down the corridor, took the lift to the ground floor and walked past the scruffy kid on reception. It was just getting dark as they got outside. They were met by a man in a motorcycle helmet carrying a large bag.

'Twelve-inch Meat Feast, potato wedges and a litre

of Coke?' he said to Matt.

'Thanks,' said Matt taking the food. Matt looked at Buddy. Buddy looked back and nodded. 'Well, I paid for it!'

They both laughed.

'Thanks, Buddy, you saved my life back there,' he said, shaking the older man by the hand.

'Kitty showed me some of your stuff – you're a funny kid! We need funny guys where I come from, now more than ever! Kitty probably told you I'm over on business. She also told me you could do with some moral support. Talk of the devil!' he said looking past Matt. Matt turned to see Kitty coming round the corner to join them.

'How did you get on?' she said sheepishly.

'Come here,' said Matt and pulled her in for a big hug. 'I can't thank you enough. I was very nearly hung out to dry by that . . . that . . . idiot!'

'Idiot's too kind, kid,' snorted Buddy.

'If it hadn't been for Buddy here, I would have been working for Dickie Hart for the next five years!'

'The dangers of not studying a contract,' said Buddy. 'If you ever get asked to sign another one, get Kitty to send it over to me first.' As they spoke, a huge Rolls Royce Phantom pulled up next to them, a chauffeur got out and opened the passenger door.

'Now, I need to get to the airport. Can I give you kids a lift anywhere?' said Buddy.

'No thanks, Uncle Buddy,' she said giving him a big hug. 'Thanks so much for your help, but Matt's got a gig to get to.'

'Of course, yes. You know my brother would

be thrilled to know you're carrying on the family business, and I'm proud of you. Give me a call – you really should come over and see me in New York sometime, see how we do things over there. That goes for you too, Matt!'

'Thanks, Mr Hopestein, thanks for everything,' said Matt shaking his hand.

They watched as the chauffeur helped him climb into the Rolls then followed the car's tail lights as it gently purred up the road and out of sight.

Matt let out a sigh of relief – what a day! And it wasn't over yet. He looked at his watch.

'Hang on, Kit, what time's the show finish?'

'About half past seven, why?'

'Well, it's half five now!' he said tapping his watch. 'There's no way we'll be able to get a train and then get from the station to the school in an hour and a half!'

'Ah, that's where a friend of yours comes in,' said Kitty. As she said this a large stretch limo pulled up beside them. The front tinted window lowered soundlessly and there was the familiar face of Alf, Dickie Hart's chauffeur. 'Ready when you are, Matt, and this one's on me!' he said. 'But we'd better get a wiggle on.'

Matt looked at Kitty and grinned. 'You think of everything, don't you?' he said.

'I try,' she replied, opening the passenger door.

They both climbed in and the car sped off into the night.

'They're a bad bunch, sir,' said Alf, looking at Matt in his rear-view mirror. 'I'd say you were better off out of it. Although it pains me to say it, Mr Hart has always been a nasty piece of work, ever since he was a kid.'

'Since he was a kid?' said Matt, puzzled. 'How come you've known him that long?'

'I'm his dad, sir. Yes, I'm ashamed to say I'm his dad. Now, we'd better get you to your gig!'

The sleek black limo cut through London, then as they reached the outskirts the roads started to empty and Alf was able to put his foot down. 'Hold on in the back, we might be breaking a few speed limits!' he said.

'Feels like you're about to break the sound barrier,' laughed Matt as they sped up the mighty M20 and back towards Kent.

30

Knock 'Em Dead

'We've got five minutes to get you on that stage or Mr Gillingham will close the show with Neil!' panted Kitty as she rushed Matt across the playground to the assembly hall.

'How come?' said Matt.

'They don't know you're coming! I wasn't sure whether I'd be able to get you here on time and I didn't want to get everyone's hopes up.' They pushed through the double doors and into the backstage area.

'Hi, Matt Millz!' said a small girl dressed as a chicken when they whooshed past. As they got to the wings Matt was met by a couple of familiar faces.

'What time do you call this?' said Ahmed with a broad grin, slapping him on the back.

'How'd you get on with the big-shot agent?' said a concerned-looking Rob. Matt gave him the thumbs up.

'I'll tell you all about it later.' he said. Then he felt a gentle hand on his shoulder – it was Alex. 'Good to see you, Matt,' she said. Matt gave her hand a squeeze.

'Neil's only got a couple of minutes to go,' said Kitty, snapping Matt into the here and now.

He looked through the black drapes at the stage. Neil was in full flow, but he wasn't in his usual get-up. He was in a black tracksuit and Nike trainers, he'd had his hair plaited into tight braids, and he wasn't dancing, he was rapping – the crowd were loving it. 'He's got really good!' said Matt, turning to Kitty.

'I know,' she said proudly. 'I always believed in him, he just needed to believe in himself.'

Matt nodded and glanced at the list of stuff he'd written on his hand in the limo. It wasn't a set list as such – he hadn't had time to write any proper jokes. It was more just a loose collection of ideas, stuff about what he'd been up to – Ahmed's brush with Amelia Wong, Nelson the pigeon, Mr Tubbs' hilarious breakdown, his visit to The Comedy Store.

He felt a rush of nervous energy which he knew was down to adrenaline. It wasn't a scary feeling like he'd experienced last night at the Apollo, but one of excitement, like a sprinter waiting for the starter pistol, or a boxer waiting for the bell to ring for the first round. Neil finished up – no splits this time – and there was a huge round of applause from the crowd. Matt and the others joined in.

'Hey, Matt!' said Neil as he walked from the stage to the wings. 'You made it!'

'Yeah,' said Matt. 'Listen, that was awesome! How'd you get so good?'

'Practice I guess,' he shrugged. Suddenly he was back to the same shy boy that he had been a few weeks ago.

Mr Gillingham had picked up the mic. 'Well, I think you'll agree we've had a great time here tonight ...' he said. 'I'd like you to join me in thanking Mr Pavey for agreeing to it all ...'

'He's wrapping it up,' hissed Matt to Kitty.

'What?' she said with a frown. 'He hasn't seen you!' She started waving her arms, then jumping up and down but Mr Gillingham was at the front of the stage now, addressing the audience – she wasn't even in his field of vision.

'So all that remains is for me to say thanks to all those who ...' he continued. Suddenly there was an ear-piercing noise like an injured seagull. Matt looked round – it was Ahmed with his fingers in his mouth, whistling. Mr G hesitated, then turned his head to see where the noise had come from and finally caught sight of Matt and Kitty furiously waving at him. His face broke into a huge grin and he nodded to Matt. He then turned back to the audience.

'But before I do that ...' he said, 'I've got a very special surprise for you!'

A murmur went through the crowd as they tried to guess what was coming next.

'Will you please put your hands together for Anglebrook's most famous son – come on out, Matt!'

Matt took a couple of steps on to the stage – there was a stunned silence, then the whole room erupted. Kids were clapping, kids were cheering and stamping their feet. Matt felt a lump in his throat, and tears welled up in his eyes. He approached Mr Gillingham to take the microphone and shook him by the hand.

'Knock 'em dead!' said Mr G.

And that's exactly what he did!

That's all from him, for now anyway.

Goodnight!